Chasing Forever

PIPER RAYNE

Cover Design: Whiskey Ginger Goods

1st Line Editor: Joy Editing

2nd Line Editor: My Brother's Editor

Proofreader: My Brother's Editor

2nd Proofreader: Olivia Winston

About Chasing Forever

It was a fun Vegas getaway—until I woke up married to my ex-fiancé's brother.

After Watson brother #1 ditched me at the altar, I stopped believing in happily-ever-afters. So Ihave no clue how I ended up saying "I do" to Brooks—Watson brother #2—somewhere between tequila shots and bad decisions.

Okay, that may not be true.

Sheriff Watson has been a charming thorn in my side ever since his brother left our small ranch town in his rearview mirror. He's a little too steady, a little too sweet, and way too intuitive because he sees through my facade. But no matter how tempting he is, he's still a Watson.

I demand an annulment. He refuses, bargaining four real dates before he signs.

Fine. I'll sabotage each one and keep my heart safely locked away. It's easier this way because he has no idea the secret I'm keeping.

Of course, Brooks doesn't go down easy—he has enough faith for both of us. He tackles my fears at every turn, making me wonder what would happen if I went all in.

But trusting the wrong man once nearly ruined me—doing it again might finish the job.

PLAIN DAISY RANCH

CHASING
FOREVER

The Noughtons Family
Parents
Bruce and Daisy (deceased) Noughton
Children
Ben Noughton – Gillian Adams
(*The One I Left Behind*)
Jude Noughton – Sadie Wilkins
(*The One I Stood Beside*)
Emmett Noughton – Briar Adams
(*The One I Didn't See Coming*)

The Owens Family
Parents
Brad and Darla Owens
Children
Lottie Owens – Brooks Watson
(*Chasing Forever*)
Bennett Owens
(*Chasing Love*)
Romy Owens
(*Chasing Home*)

The Ellis Family
Parents
Wade and Bette Ellis
Children
Poppy Ellis
Jensen Ellis
Scarlett Ellis

To see more of the Plain Daisy Ranch
family tree visit our website:
https://piperrayne.com/noughton-family-tree

Chapter One

A protective arm drapes over my back, anchoring me to the plush bed as my legs slide effortlessly along the soft sheets. Heat radiates from the body beside me, luring me into its warmth. I turn and burrow into him without hesitation. As if he answers my unspoken need, his arms welcome me, and I melt into his side. Our legs tangle together, perfectly woven, as though we've done this a thousand times.

This isn't my reality, but damn if I'm going to try to wake myself up from such a beautiful, intoxicating dream.

His thigh shifts—strong, deliberate—pressing between the apex of my legs just enough to send a jolt of pleasure straight through me. I don't resist the urge to move, shamelessly grinding against him, taking what I need. A shiver of exhilaration coils in my core as his lips find my forehead, their touch featherlight.

It's been so long. Too long since I've let myself feel this—wanted, cherished, adored. Dare I say, loved. That elusive, unattainable feeling I've abandoned the hope of ever finding. And yet, here, wrapped in his arms, the dream feels so real.

Our bodies move in silent agreement, a slow exploration

1

of touch. My fingers trace the hard lines of his chest, mapping every inch of him, while his fingertips ghost along my spine, sending delicious shudders through me. No words are spoken, but the heat between us is a language all our own.

He nudges me onto my back, hovering above me, his solid frame grinding me into the mattress. His strong thighs part mine effortlessly, positioning himself between them, claiming the space as if he belongs there. As if he always has.

It's been so long. But god, it's never felt like this. No one has ever felt this right.

My hands roam across his broad shoulders, desperate to pull him closer. His lips brush mine, too fleeting, too teasing.

"Show me those beautiful brown eyes," he murmurs, his voice a hushed whisper, his breath mingling with mine.

That voice, there's a familiarity to it I can't place.

He chuckles, and his mouth captures mine again, but vanishes too soon. "Wakey, wakey."

That drawl. That unmistakable *Nebraskan* drawl.

My eyes snap open.

Panic jolts me upright, and my head slams into his. I press a hand to my forehead, wincing as splintering pain ricochets through my skull.

"Fuck!" he groans.

My heart pounds as I scan my surroundings, but nothing —nothing—about this space is familiar.

"What the hell are you doing?" My voice is hoarse and raw.

I scramble back against the headboard, pulling my knees to my chest, one hand still gripping my head as if that might piece some thoughts together as to why *Brooks Watson* was just lying on top of me.

Brooks flies off the bed, completely naked—and damn.

I blink.

Don't look. Don't look.

I look. Then I look a second time.

That's the body that's been hiding under his sheriff's uniform all these years? Sure, I've noticed the way his biceps stretched his sleeves, how his arms—tattooed and solid—commanded attention. But this? The sharp V-cut of his waist, the valley of abs, the corded muscles?

Brooks Watson is hot as hell.

For a second—just a second—or maybe two—I stare, unable to stop myself from admiring the view. Until reality slaps me in the face.

You're ogling Brooks Watson.

"What the hell happened last night?" I stretch my legs out in front of me, gaze darting around the room, looking for something, anything familiar. My attention lands on a sofa—then a coffee table. My stomach drops, and my pulse stutters. "Wait. My room doesn't have a sofa. Or a coffee table."

Brooks exhales sharply, tilting his head back, squeezing his eyes shut from the pain of my forehead hitting him. He's not listening to a word I say.

"You have a suite?" My voice rises, the pieces still not fitting together as to how I got here.

His head drops forward, jaw twitching. "That's your concern?"

"Excuse me? I have no idea where I am."

Brooks runs a hand over his face, then groans. "I think you broke my damn nose."

I blink at him. He's standing completely unbothered—naked—while I can barely string a thought together.

How is he so calm?

I squeeze my eyes shut, forcing myself to think, to retrace my steps, but only fragments of last night return. Nothing that would lead to the reason why I'm in this hotel room with him. Why he's *naked.*

"Brooks?"

He tilts his head in my direction with annoyance etched on his face, but still says nothing. The man is so irritating.

"Explain!" I gesture with my hand in the air as if to say, *Look at your naked body.*

He mimics my motion, running his hand back my way. I glance down to see that I'm naked as well. With a yelp, I grab the sheet, tugging it up and over me.

"You think I didn't already see you?"

I grip the sheet tighter and move to slide out of bed. "You did not."

I'm not sure why I'm arguing. It's obvious I'm naked under this sheet, but maybe if I pretend we didn't most likely sleep together last night, we'll both come down with amnesia.

"Lottie, can you please lower your voice?" He sits on the edge of the bed, still hanging out for everyone and anyone to see.

I search for my clothes, my knuckles white and aching from fisting the sheet so tight every time I bend down. "So, we got drunk and slept together." I shrug. "No big deal. No one has to know."

His eyebrows raise. "You think no one saw us leave together?"

He grabs his boxer briefs from the floor, finally covering himself. A small, very tiny part of myself is disappointed I don't remember last night because Brooks is working with some impressive machinery down there.

"Well, since you seem to remember, want to enlighten me?"

He stares at me long and hard. "I wish I could." I shake my head, and his eyes flare wider, staring at my hand. "Look at your left hand."

I blow out a breath and lift my hand.

A silver band sits snug around my left ring finger.

My gaze flies to his left hand, but he already has it raised, eyes narrowed. Sure enough, there's a matching band on his.

"You forced me to marry you?" A cold breeze flows over my body.

Brook's face holds no reaction, and I realize he's not looking at my face. His attention is on my breasts.

I glance down at the puddled sheet on the floor. "Seriously?" Bending, I grasp it and pull it back up.

"You can't blame me. You have an amazing body." When my mouth is too slack-jawed to respond, he continues, "Although I'm sure I didn't marry you because of it." He chuckles.

I don't.

"And FYI, I didn't *force* you to marry me. Thanks for letting me know exactly what you think of me. Who's to say you didn't ask me? Beg me?"

I balk and spot my panties hanging off the corner of the couch. I shuffle over and snatch them. "Doubtful."

"Want to see the video?"

His idea of a joke. So... him. I try to step into my panties while still covering myself with the sheet. Brooks is back on the edge of the bed, shirtless, and unapologetically watching me, that damn smirk prominent on his delicious lips.

"Did I lose a bet?" I ask.

"Do you think you'd wager a bet with me as the prize? Aww... that's sweet. I'm touched."

I scoff, then abandon the whole idea of trying to get dressed discreetly and opt for faster, dropping the sheet and stepping into my underwear.

"Why would being married to me be so bad anyway?"

I search the room and head to the side of the bed where my bra hangs from a lampshade. "Oh, I don't know, how about the fact that your brother is my ex-fiancé? Do I need another reason?"

He blows out a breath but says nothing.

I snap my bra in place, but in order to get to my dress, I have to cross past his almost naked body to reach the other side of the room. "It's probably not even a real marriage. I mean, where did we go, some sketchy chapel open twenty-four hours?"

"According to this, it's real," he murmurs, reaching over to the nightstand and holding up a piece of paper. "Congratulations, Mrs. Brooks Watson."

I step into my dress and slide my arms into the sleeves. "Easy fix. We'll just get an annulment back in Willowbrook."

He drops the paper on the mattress and stretches back on his hands, watching me struggle with the zipper. "Want my help?"

I tug again, but the zipper refuses to budge. "No."

"I'm probably the one who unzipped it..."

I stop and glare. "Don't remind me." I point at his nearly naked body. "And put on some pants." I circle my finger in the air at his sizable bulge.

"I bet that's not what you were saying last night." He grins.

I clench my jaw, reminding myself everyone makes mistakes. Although there's something about the Watson brothers that just short-circuits my brain. It's as if my talent for bad decisions levels up around them.

"Think about it. Me prying you up off your knees, you begging me to let you suck me off." His damn smirk widens. "I wonder if I gave up my opportunity for head in the hopes of sinking inside you and hearing you moan my name like you needed me more than air."

Our eyes meet, and I attempt to keep a cool demeanor as if I'm not racking my brain to remember that moment. To feel him fill me.

Thankfully, the zipper finally loosens, and I secure my

dress. Searching the room one more time, I beeline it over to my purse on the chair and slip into my shoes. "You say one word about this, Brooks, and you're dead." I put my hand on the doorknob, ready to leave this room.

"You can't run from this."

A knock sounds from the other side, and I jolt back.

Brooks laughs, and I inch up on my tiptoes, seeing my brother through the peephole. "It's Bennett," I whisper.

"Interesting." He raises those too-perfect eyebrows. "So, what's your next move, Lottie?"

I look around the room and decide my best bet is the closet. "Get rid of him and take off that ring."

I rush into the closet, hoping whatever Bennett wants is quick, so I can get the hell out of here and remember how and why I married Sheriff Brooks Watson.

Chapter Two

BROOKS

Bennett knocks a second time, and Lottie sticks her head out of the closet, pointing from me to the door.

"I'm not your dog," I mutter, making my way over.

I love this family. Always have. Hell, Lottie's cousin Ben is my best friend. But there are times—like this—when the interruptions that come with a big family wear thin.

With a sigh, I slide the ring off my finger and tuck it into the pocket of my slacks from last night. Then I unlock the door and crack it open.

Bennett's standing in the hotel hallway, already showered and dressed, looking as if he just stepped out of a damn *GQ* shoot—perfect dark hair, fresh clothes, and a to-go coffee cup in his hand.

"Shouldn't you be enjoying sleeping in and maybe ordering room service with some hot woman you picked up last night since you're not on daddy duty?" I ask.

He groans and strolls in, plopping down on the couch as though he's got nowhere better to be. "I tried and gave up, finally got showered and ready. The breakfast buffet is pretty good if you're interested."

I'm not.

What I *am* interested in is getting him the hell out before he realizes his big sister is hiding in my closet.

"Why don't I meet you down there?" I blurt out. "I just need to shower."

Please, man. Please take the hint.

But no—he sinks deeper into the couch. If he only knew he was sitting right where Lottie picked up her discarded thong ten minutes ago...

"What's on the agenda today before we head to the airport?" he asks, as though he's got all the time in the world. He tips his head back as if he's nursing a raging headache.

"I think a lunch or something."

We're here for his and Lottie's cousin's wedding. Emmett married Briar last night. Hey, look at that, Lottie and I are going to share a wedding anniversary with her cousin.

Bennett nods, totally oblivious. "I have no idea how you're standing," he mutters, taking another sip of coffee.

"What's that mean?" My forehead wrinkles.

"You and Lottie just kept asking for more shots." He sets his paper coffee cup on the side table then looks around, seeming to register his surroundings for the first time since he walked in here. "Why do you have a suite?"

The question of the morning apparently.

"They made a mistake on my reservation and gave me an upgrade," I say. Not a lie. Although if they hadn't, I might've tried to upgrade after... everything that happened last night. After Lottie and I apparently stumbled back from the chapel.

My gaze cuts back to the closet door.

I need to talk to her. I need five minutes. I need one goddamn second to figure out how to fix this before she bolts. Because she's going to.

"It's nice," Bennett says, picking up the takeout coffee cup and sipping again.

I nearly clench my hair in my hands and scream up toward the ceiling.

"What's up, man?" I ask, forcing my tone to be casual even though my brain is begging him to leave.

"Ah." His shoulders lift and fall as if he's carrying the weight of the world. "Emmett's busy."

I rock my head back, trying not to visibly twitch.

Emmett's newly married and no doubt eight inches into his bride this morning, probably knocking her up again.

But I get it.

Ever since Gillian returned to town and she and Ben got back together, my time with my best friend has diminished drastically. Then again, Ben had been gone for years playing professional football, so I was used to not needing him to help me solve my problems. And maybe because of how lost I felt when Ben left for Clemson after high school, though every muscle in my body is screaming to get Bennett out of here so I can talk to Lottie, I drop down into the chair across from him.

"What's up?"

A low growl rumbles from the closet.

Bennett frowns toward the noise. "Is someone here?"

"It's the air conditioner. Been making that noise all damn night."

He's too distracted to question it further, thank God. He just spins his coffee cup between his palms. "You know how many times I was hit on last night?"

"You come here to brag, Danson?" I smirk.

He shakes his head quickly. "No. But I went to my room last night alone." He exhales slowly. "I can't seem to pull the cord, you know?"

I don't know. I can't even imagine what he's been through. Losing the love of your life and the mother of your child has to change you. And now he's looking to me for advice? If he knew his sister was hiding in my closet because we drunkenly got married last night, he'd realize how terrible of a choice I am to come to with his problems.

"It's okay," I say, but it sounds hollow even to my own ears.

"It's been almost seven years."

"And you've never..." I ask, surprised.

He shakes his head but lifts his gaze to mine. "Once. At a convention. Walked a woman up to her room... but once it got down to it, I couldn't go through with it."

Holy shit. This is so much worse than I thought.

"I see you judging me." His mouth twists. "But it's not like I've had a ton of time. I've been raising a little girl. Being both her dad and her *mom*."

Bennett keeps talking, pouring his heart out—the fears, the loneliness, the weight of raising Wren all on his own. It guts me in a way I'm not ready to admit. I move to the mini fridge to grab a water, trying to appear casual so he doesn't catch the lump in my throat.

There's no way I could ever be a therapist. I'd be out of Kleenex on day one.

"I gotta use your bathroom," he says, pushing off the couch.

"You don't want to use yours?" I ask, immediately regretting it.

He stops, frowning at me. "I'm not taking a shit. I'm just taking a piss. Get dressed, and we'll head to breakfast."

I force a weak smile. "You said you already ate."

"They make these mini egg quiches that are addicting as hell."

The second the bathroom door shuts, I turn toward the closet.

The door cracks open, and Lottie has tears shining in her eyes and heartbreak etched across her face.

"I'm a horrible sister," she whispers.

I breathe her name, hoping she'll stay. But she's already tiptoeing toward the door.

"Stay. I'll get rid of him," I plead quietly.

She's shaking her head before I even finish the sentence. She turns back once, right at the door, and I swear my heart shatters a little at the pain written all over her face.

"We'll talk back in Willowbrook," she whispers, then slips out before I can stop her.

The door clicks shut, and she takes all the air from the room with her.

Bennett strolls out of the bathroom as though he didn't just bulldoze my world. "I thought you were getting dressed?"

"I have to shower first." I force a smile so brittle it could snap.

"Cool. Just come get me in my room."

I nod because what else can I do? "Give me twenty."

"Sounds good." He grabs his coffee, opens the door, but then pauses, his face turned down the hallway. "There you are, Lottie. Romy was looking for you."

The door swings shut before I can hear her reply.

I pull the ring out of my pocket, twirling it between my fingers and staring at the small band as though it holds all the answers.

I don't know how the hell I got Lottie Owens to marry me. But the bigger question—the one that's going to haunt me until I fix this—is how the hell I'm going to convince her that it wasn't just the alcohol that led us here.

That maybe, just maybe, this was the best mistake we ever made.

Chapter Three

LOTTIE

I'm almost to my room when a door opens down the hall.

"There you are, Lottie. Romy was looking for you."

Bennett. Jeez, Brooks couldn't have stalled him a little longer?

I turn and smack on a smile, hoping he doesn't see my red-rimmed eyes from hearing his confession to Brooks minutes ago. He doesn't need my pity. "Hey, B."

His gaze runs down my body. "Where are you coming from?" His long legs eat up the distance between us. Suddenly, the hallway feels about an inch wide.

"Oh, I... um..." I could easily admit defeat. I'm not even sure Bennett would react much to the news, but after Holden got me labeled as Willowbrook's jilted bride, I guess I'm a little like my brother in that I despise pity. "Do you really want to know?"

I hate the fact that the memory of Brooks's eyes when he took me in as he hovered above me this morning flickers through my mind. As if I'd just stepped out of a *Vogue* magazine photoshoot instead of looking like a disaster.

Bennett's forehead wrinkles, and he seems to take in my

rumpled dress, tangled hair, and smudged makeup. "You're right. I don't."

Man, he must really be distracted this morning. It's unlike him not to drill me. Although he's younger than me, he's taken on the role of the oldest for sure. I guess that's what happens when you get married first.

"Didn't think so." I force a smile that suggests I did hook up with someone. He doesn't need to know it was my new hubby, Brooks Watson. God help me. "I'm going to go shower."

"Come to my room when you're done. Brooks and I are going down to breakfast. They have these quiches you'll love."

He walks by me, and I wish now more than ever that when we checked in, the entire group of us weren't all on the same floor.

When he stops at his room a few doors down, I smile. "I think I'm going to wait for lunch. I need a long hot shower."

I wait for him to swipe his keycard, opening his door. "Thanks for not telling me the details. See you then."

He disappears inside, and I run my keycard over the lock, hoping that Romy is down at breakfast enjoying those amazing quiches Bennett can't stop going on and on about, but no such luck.

She springs off the bed, jumping into the small hallway opening. "Where have you been? You know you're supposed to text me a picture of the guy and where you're going." She waves her phone in the air. "I've called everyone."

Fantastic. Now the entire family knows I didn't come back to my room last night—and considering how foggy my memory is, I can only guess at the rumors already swirling.

"I tried to call Brooks too, and he didn't answer. One minute the two of you were going to the bar to get more drinks and then you never came back. You scared the shit out of me, although I assume you were with Brooks?" She waggles her eyebrows. "I'm right, aren't I?"

I drop my purse on the desk and keep my back to her, ashamed to let her see what I'm about to admit. "I can't really remember," I whisper.

She huffs, and I circle around to see that she's sitting on the edge of the bed. "Was it Brooks's face you woke up to this morning?"

The pit in my stomach churns.

How not discreet were we last night?

"Why would you ask that?" I stall, needing to gather whatever shreds of information I can.

"You two were all over each other. Huddled in secret conversations. Always going to the bar together. You were actually... getting along. It was weird." Her phone vibrates, and she swipes the screen open. "Hey, Sadie, she just got back. Sorry for bothering your baby-free time. See you at lunch." She hangs up.

"How many people did you call looking for me?" I slip out of my shoes and sit on my bed.

"Just the girls and Bennett." She shrugs and leans in eagerly. "So tell me where you were."

I could tell her. She's my sister, and she'd keep the secret for me. But just the thought of anyone knowing is embarrassing. I'd rather not be the new scandal to hit the gossip mill in town—been there, done that. Don't recommend. Then again, if she knows, she can help me dodge Brooks until we return home. "Fine. I was with Brooks."

She smacks her palm on the mattress and smiles wide. "I knew it."

"Look at you, you're Sherlock Holmes." I head toward the bathroom. "I'm going to take a shower."

She jumps in front of me. "Oh no, you're not. Details."

"Gross." Why would she want to know any details? I'd never want to know about her having sex.

"Not his dick size or anything. Like, how did it happen? Do you remember? Because you seemed pretty wasted."

I want to tell her his dick puts Holden's to shame. Hell, Brooks would never let Holden live it down if I told him he's so much bigger than his older brother. "I told you, I don't remember."

Her shoulders sink and her eyebrows lift. "Nothing?"

I shake my head. "Maybe my memory will come back in the shower." I edge around her, crank on the water, but when I turn back, she's leaning on the doorframe.

"So, like... this morning... did he remember?"

God, Romy's relentless. I should've said I hooked up with some random at the slots. But she knows as well as everyone else in my family that if I was with Brooks, he never would've left me by myself to wander drunk in Vegas. He might not be blood, but he's family in every way that matters.

"Fine, I'm going to tell you, but you can't tell anyone else, okay?"

Her eyebrows lift again. Romy does enjoy gossip. She's always in the know with the latest news about all the reality shows and celebrities. She holds out her hand with her pinkie extended. "Pinkie promise."

"I'm serious, Romy. I can't deal with it right now, and if everyone finds out, I'll just go back there again." My throat tightens.

She drops her hand to her side. "This is scaring me, what happened?"

I shake my head and blow out a breath. "If I tell you, will you let me shower and decompress from it all?"

She nods, putting her finger across her heart. "Cross my heart..."

"We can stop the childhood promises, just please don't betray my trust."

"Of course." Her lips straighten and concern lines her eyes.

The same concerned eyes everyone always looks at me with. Wondering whether Holden destroyed the Lottie they've always known. Will I ever return to the fun-loving, full-of-life girl who isn't hiding under that hard shell?

I inhale a deep breath and just spit it out. "It turns out while you weren't babysitting me last night, I married Brooks."

Her mouth opens, not even coming back that I'm the older sister, and she doesn't need to babysit me. Which I just threw in there to try to blame anyone else besides myself that I married Holden's brother, knowing in the end, it's all my fault.

After her shock, she clutches her hands in front of her heart. "That's so romantic."

"Spare me." I roll my eyes and nudge her out of the doorway, and finally I'm able to shut the door. "Now I'm going to shower."

"Lottie, you can't just drop that bomb and leave me here without any more information."

I open the door a sliver. "It's not fate or kismet. It was just good ol' alcohol and bad judgment. We're going to get an annulment."

I go to shut the door again, but Romy plasters her hand on it. "What if it wasn't?"

"Wasn't what?"

"I see the way he looks at you, and I know you do too. You guys play these weird games with each other."

I try to push the door shut again, but obviously she's been doing some hardcore strength-training classes. "We were drunk. Stop romanticizing it, Romy. It was a stupid mistake that no one will ever find out about. We're both taking this to our graves."

A smile teases her lips. "I think you're wrong."

"Because you believe there's such a thing as true love. That one day your white knight is going to gallop onto Plain Daisy Ranch and confess how he's searched every square mile of land to find you."

She giggles at the thought of it, and I seize the chance to finally slam the door shut and flick the lock.

Through the wood, her dreamy voice calls, "Just think about it, Lottie. The brother of the man who shattered your heart and your belief in love could be the one who pieces it back together. It's so perfect, it could be a book."

"Get your head out of the clouds, Romy, and come back to earth. It doesn't work like that."

I strip out of my dress and step under the hot spray of the shower, letting the water wash away the night, the memories, and most of all—Romy's happily-ever-after fantasies.

Because real life doesn't work that way.

It never has.

Chapter Four

BROOKS

I thought maybe Bennett might take a nap, and I could bail on breakfast with him. No such luck. My new BFF is stuck to me like glue today.

We've eaten breakfast—where he couldn't shut the hell up about those damn quiches. Then we walked the Strip and did some shopping, him buying Wren a souvenir—or five to make up for not going to Hoover Dam and taking pictures for her since he couldn't get a rental.

I tried to suggest that maybe he call Lottie to meet up with us, but he didn't take the bait, and now we're walking into the lunch that Emmett and Briar put together before we ride to the airport to fly back to Willowbrook.

Lottie hasn't messaged me, and it guts me when we walk into the restaurant and she's not there yet. There's so much I need to say to her. Things I should've said before last night.

"Nice disappearing act." Ben shoulders up to me as we all wait for the hostess to make sure our private room is ready. "What happened with you and Lottie last night?"

Ben's my best friend. I can trust him, but this situation is sticky, and there are some things I have to say to her first.

"Nothing."

He rocks back on his heels, eyeing me as if I'm going to crack. He probably knows we hooked up, which honestly, I don't even know if we did.

The fact that I could've finally touched Lottie, kissed her, and not remember? It's the cruelest kind of punishment.

"Okay."

"That's it?" I should let it go like he is, but that's never been my style. Sadly.

"I don't really want to hear any details when it comes to my cousin anyway."

He's either being a solid best friend by not calling me out, or he really thinks we went our separate ways last night.

"Then maybe we can talk about Danson's quiche obsession."

Ben laughs. "Shit, he's over there trying to convince Jenson to make them."

Sure enough, I glance at Ben's other cousin, and Bennett is talking and demonstrating with his hands the same way he did to me on the elevator ride down to breakfast this morning.

I laugh. "The highlight of his Vegas trip—mini quiches."

"Too bad he wasn't eating them off a woman." Ben shakes his head.

The circular doors move, and I eye them, stupid heart hammering, hoping it's Lottie. It's not. Just an older couple.

When I let my vision stray back to him, I find Ben staring at me. He shakes his head again. "Listen…"

"I don't want to hear it." I put up my hand to stop him from giving whatever advice he's decided to impart on me.

"I just don't want to see you get hurt."

"Why would I be hurt?" I stuff my hands into the pockets of my shorts and circle my neck to get rid of the kinks.

"Let's not play that game. You've wanted Lottie for as long

as I can remember, but she's not the same person after your brother. She's never going to give you an honest shot."

His truth is an arrow to my heart, but I can't blame him for trying to warn me.

He's not wrong. I saw Lottie for all she was before Holden ever even noticed her. But he had the guts to act when I didn't. He won by default—because I never fought for her.

"You don't have to worry about me. I'm a grown man now."

I refrain from telling him that drunk or not, Lottie cracked open a door last night—and I'm not letting her slam it shut without a fight.

I've tried the long game—coffees at her store, bad jokes, flirting, praying she'd look at me the way I looked at her. Not anymore. I'm done waiting. I'm done hoping. This time, I'm showing her I'm the man she's been looking for—whether she knows it yet or not. Whether she likes it or not.

Ben saying she's never going to be the same? Bullshit. And yeah, it makes me want to punch something. Him actually. But causing a scene won't win Lottie's heart either.

The circular doors spin again, and this time—it's her. Romy's beside her, but it's Lottie I see. Only ever her.

Ben pats my shoulder. "You're a lost cause."

She's in leggings and a sweatshirt, hair down but not really styled. No makeup. Still the most beautiful thing I've ever seen.

I step forward to approach Lottie, but the hostess picks this moment to tell us all that our private room is ready. And of course everyone funnels into line, and I end up with Bennett at my side, once more asking me what I think was in the quiches that made them so great. I'm about to offer the chef my firstborn for the recipe just to get him to shut the hell up.

We file into the room, everyone too busy talking about last

night or this morning to bother finding their chairs. There's a lot of whispering and sly looks thrown between Lottie and me. Which isn't surprising—the Noughton family doesn't allow a lot of secrets to stay secrets.

"Danson, did you tell Jude about those mouthwatering quiches?" I ask, dodging Bennett and leaving Jude in his wake as I weave my way to Lottie's side.

"I heard, and I don't care," Jude says, but I'm already locked on my way to her.

All the girls are huddled together and exhaustion lines Lottie's face. I'm sure they're all bombarding her with questions about last night and whether anything happened with us.

"Shit, is that Zander Shaw?" I lie, pointing out the window toward the terrace.

Romy bites instantly, dragging the girls toward the glass.

I'm not stupid. I know Lottie's probably told Romy to stay close and keep me away.

"Romy!" Lottie says through clenched teeth, but Romy's already at the window with all the other women, pulling their phones from their pockets as though they're about to spot the popular country singer.

Watson for the win.

Lottie's shoulders fall, and she eyes me as if she'd like nothing more than to see me put in a meat grinder—with her hand on the crank. "Cute."

"We need to talk." I'm not avoiding the issue. I've waited all day, and I'm not going to stay in the back seat any longer.

"Not here." Her gaze skirts around the room at all the wandering eyes and eavesdropping ears.

"Then you're riding with me to the airport." I grab the back of a chair and pull it out for her. "Have a seat."

She scoffs. "Um. No."

"Would you rather me announce to everyone that we're newlyweds?"

"I didn't think blackmail was your style." She crosses her arms.

She doesn't know how much I love it when she's stubborn and ferocious.

"All I want is to talk to you."

She steps up close, her gaze darting around the room, measuring threats, calculating escape, as she always does. A repercussion of my brother screwing her over. "We will talk, but give me until we get to Willowbrook. Then I'll meet you wherever you want, and we can make our plans for the annulment."

A hot flick of disappointment slashes through me. She's already plotting my exit.

"What if I don't want an annulment?"

She straightens and glares at me. Slowly, flames rise in her gorgeous brown eyes. "You can't be serious."

I shrug, and her eyes widen, turning into a blazing inferno. She's been a fighter her whole life. Holden snuffed out that fire. I watched her bow her head to him—and it killed me every damn time.

"I think there's a reason—"

Emmett and Briar walk into the room, and Emmett raises their joined hands in the air to everyone's claps and cheering. "Let's welcome another Noughton to the family."

There goes any talk about us for now.

We all move to take a seat, everyone buzzing with new energy. Romy gives me a pissed-off look—probably about my bullshit Zander Shaw stunt—but I don't care. Because Lottie's right here. Close enough to touch.

Everyone sits as Emmett and Briar stand at the head of the table.

"So that makes how many Noughtons now?" Emmett points around the table. "Ten, right?"

He skips over Lottie, and she tenses next to me. I feel her shoulders locking tight, her breathing stalling.

He knows. I have no idea how. No one else will probably understand that Lottie's now part of another family, my family, now that we're married, but Lottie and I sure as hell do.

"Eleven, you skipped Lottie," Romy says before snapping a bite off a celery stick from the Bloody Mary she no doubt grabbed after realizing her favorite country singer is not in the restaurant.

"Oh, did I forget you, Lottie?" Emmett asks, tilting his head and wearing that smug, knowing grin.

Lottie's face grows red as Briar slides into her chair, leaving Emmett to stand by himself. Everyone's questioning gaze turns to Lottie. The whole room tightens, leaning in without even meaning to.

Briar tugs on Emmett's sleeve, pulling him down into the chair beside her, but that damn playful grin sits bold on his face. Add on Briar peeking at Lottie, and I know those two know something.

I slide my hand to Lottie's forearm, even though I'm the one drowning. If this goes south right here, right now, I might lose any footing and any chance I have with her.

Whatever Emmett's plan was doesn't matter now because Lottie tosses her napkin on the empty plate, shoves her chair back, and stands. "Fine. You all want to know so bad because your lives are so goddamn boring? Well, Brooks and I got married last night. There. Are you all happy now?"

Her admission is reckless and messy.

And it's so damn Lottie.

I love her all the more for it.

Chapter Five

LOTTIE

The gasps that ring out around the table give me a small feeling of accomplishment, like I just won the Nobel Peace Prize, because I've managed to shock my family. With so many of us, it's nearly impossible to keep anything a secret. Emmett's triumphant smirk and his sweet wife Briar's empathetic expression tell me that both of them already knew. How, though, is beyond me.

"You were in the closet," Bennett accuses, his jaw slack.

I don't even want to think about the heartache I heard in my brother's voice while I hid in the closet in Brooks's room.

"Wait? What are we missing?" Sadie asks. Disappointment fills her voice that I didn't tell her, my best friend, about drunk-marrying the sheriff in Vegas.

Heat floods my face as I look at Emmett, my younger cousin, silently blaming him for my late-night poor life choices. Him, of all people getting married and finding love—it made that small seed of doubt inside me bloom into something reckless last night. That fear that I might never find someone—or worse, that I'll never be able to trust someone again. And somehow, the only thing I remember from early in the night is the simple way Brooks looked at me and made me believe, for a stupid second, that maybe I could. I can't believe I put myself in this position. I feel like a complete idiot.

"Why don't you answer?" I mutter to Emmett, since he seems to know everything, and I'm desperate to deflect.

Briar groans and glances at her new husband. Emmett's about to answer, but Briar puts her hand on his to stop him and straightens in her chair.

"We went to pick up our pictures—did you all see that screen with the newly married couples on the wall?" Briar doesn't wait for anyone to answer before she continues. "We saw the picture of you and Brooks walking out of the chapel, married, late last night."

Her forehead crinkles, and her lips press down. Sympathy. The one emotion I loathe more than pity when it's aimed directly at me.

"What are the chances?" Brooks mumbles.

"Pretty high since you went to the same chapel as us." Emmett's eyebrows lift.

He's not wrong, but choosing the same chapel wasn't even close to the dumbest thing we did last night.

"There you have it." I clap my hands together. "Now, I need to ask you all not to tell all our parents because Brooks and I would like to keep this between us until we can get it annulled."

Silence descends across the room.

Which is how I know I'm truly screwed.

Silence in my family is more unnatural than a snowstorm in July. As I scan their faces, they're all giving that same look— and it's pointed more at Brooks than at me. The one that says, *Sorry, man.*

Even Sadie's lips are tipped down as she concentrates on her lap.

My shoulders drop. "Oh my god, what?"

Sometimes I hate that I can't just allow them all to have their feelings and sit back down, eating the lunch Emmett and Briar have planned for us. Maybe I was never that way, but I feel as if I had a lot more patience for what people thought about me or the things I did before the asshole came into my life.

No one answers me.

"I'm going to go to the bathroom. Come with me, Lottie?" Sadie slides her chair out, placing her napkin on her seat.

And this is how you know my family is truly dumbstruck. Not one of them makes a joke like, *Does she have to hold up your dress?* They know exactly what's happening. Sadie, my calm, nurturing best friend, will guide me into the bathroom while they sit here and tell Brooks how sorry they are that he drunk-married the one person in the family who's emotionally broken, while Sadie tells me that it's okay I made a mistake, and she'll help me survive the aftermath.

With a growl of frustration, I turn to follow her, but Brooks's finger runs along the back part of my forearm, sending a jolt of goose bumps slithering up my skin.

What the hell was that?

I follow Sadie toward the bathroom, hearing the hushed conversations starting before I've even left the room.

"I'm not answering anything," Brooks says, and I stop dead in the doorway.

I circle back around to see him leaned back in his seat with his hands up in front of him.

"And respectfully, I know you're all her family, but this is between her and me."

As if he knows I'm still within earshot, his gaze lifts to mine, and my eyes sting with tears. All he does is give me a slight nod and a half smile.

Everyone knows Brooks Watson is a good guy. Hello, he's

the sheriff. I think sometimes I forget that just because he shares blood with the man who practically put me on a spit in the middle of town square, but he's not anything like his brother.

Sadie's hand grips mine, and she nudges me to follow her.

Shaking my head, I let her guide me toward the bathroom, and once we're inside, she spins me around. "I'm sorry. I should have been there for you last night."

"What?" I frown.

"It's just that since Daisy, Jude and I don't get a lot of alone time, but I was a shitty best friend to leave you knowing you were struggling with Emmett getting married."

I shake my head as if the thoughts will connect to help me understand what she's saying.

Sadie implores me with her eyes wide. "Last night. You were upset, and I should've stayed with you instead of going out with Jude."

"Oh god, Sadie. No. This isn't your fault. I'm a grown woman. And—"

"But I wouldn't have let you go to the chapel with him." She leans her shoulder against the tile wall.

"I'm not sure anyone knew where we were going. I don't even remember what happened. But it's fine. I didn't want anyone to know, but now that they do, I just need to keep it away from all the parents so I can get it annulled and forget it ever happened."

Her lips purse, and she looks away from me.

I sigh. "What?"

"Nothing."

This is so Sadie. If I could have an ounce of the patience she has, I probably wouldn't be in this situation. I'm a go-with-my-gut-and-act-fast person, where she's more about weighing the pros and cons with lists and graphs.

"Spit it out." I cross my arms.

"It's just... Brooks is sweet on you."

I roll my eyes and step around her to the sink and mirrors. "He feels responsible for me. There's a difference."

Sadie stands next to me, staring at me through the mirror. "What on earth are you talking about?"

I pull my hair up into a messy bun because the dry heat in Vegas feels as if it's made my hair brittle, and I don't have the patience to deal with it hungover. "Holden is his brother. Brooks clearly is trying to find a way into this family tree, and he can't have me being upset with him because his brother left me at the altar. Brooks is a good guy, and he's just trying to fix what his brother broke."

"Brooks's wanting to join the family is just a joke, Lottie. It's a way for the guys to bust his balls because of how much time he spent there growing up."

I shrug. "Maybe not."

Sadie's forehead creases, and she tilts her head as if she's trying to solve some impossible math equation.

"What don't you understand?"

"I say he's sweet on you—"

"Quit saying sweet on you. What are you, eighty?" I scowl at her through the mirror.

She shakes her head. "Yeah, I blame it on Marge working for me, but I swear she's a chicken whisperer. She just crouches down, whispers a few encouraging words, and they scatter."

Sadie started a pasture-raised chicken farm last year, and Marge is her newest employee—and apparently, a chicken whisperer to boot.

Sadie waves. "Anyway, you understand where I'm going with this."

"That you want to clone Marge?"

She laughs and shakes her head at my usual deflection. "No, Lottie. You know what I'm saying and how you're not making sense. Brooks isn't sweet on you just because his brother is a jackass and treated you like shit. He's sweet on you because he's always been sweet on you."

"Did you purposely use that three times?"

She smiles proudly. "I did."

"I thought so."

"Lottie." Her tone is filled with exhaustion.

"Sadie."

She doesn't take my bait of mimicking her like I knew she wouldn't, just stares at me with that look that says she'll outwait me all day. I glare back, but it's a fruitless venture because I'm too impatient. Hello, this is the woman who waited years to win her best friend's heart. The patience of a preschool teacher, I tell you.

I throw my hands up and turn toward her, eyeing the door to make sure no one comes in. "Do I see the way he looks at me? Of course I do, Sadie, I'm not blind."

"And the protectiveness?"

I blow out an annoyed breath. "It doesn't matter. He's Holden's brother. That's never going to change. I can't even fathom word getting around Willowbrook that I married Brooks."

Sadie's face morphs into an exact replica of that day when she had to tell me they couldn't find Holden anywhere. "Yeah, but—"

"Wait. Are you suggesting I stay married to him?" My mouth drops open.

The hormones must be making Sadie delusional.

"I'm just saying you might have rushed into it, but—"

"I drunk-married him."

She hems and haws, her head moving left and right. "Maybe consider giving it some time before you sever the tie."

"Sadie!"

She throws up her hands in that *hear me out* gesture. I

don't want to hear her out. I want to leave this bathroom, go to the airport, hop on a plane, and hide under my comforter at home until I can forget this whole disaster.

"I want you to be happy."

"I am happy." I plaster on a fake smile so wide it hurts.

She sighs, clearly not buying it.

Taking her hand, I squeeze it. "I am. I promise. I'm really happy for you and Jude and your family, and I'm going to be a kickass aunt/cousin to Daisy and all the other little ones you have. But me? I'm good."

"I wish you'd try again."

"I'm content with my life."

What I don't tell her is that I can't. I can't hand over my heart to someone again—not when I'm terrified they'll leave me gutted and bleeding out all over again.

"Now, come on, let's just go back to the table. I want this over with. You know how I hate being talked about behind my back."

Sadie hesitates, searching my face, but finally nods and squeezes my hand. I guide us toward the private room, pretending I don't feel the weight of everything left unsaid.

She could have said more. I know she wanted to. But she didn't—probably because she sees it too, the cracks I'm fighting like hell to keep from splitting wide open.

Chapter Six

BROOKS

Somehow, we all make it through the lunch and to the airport, but I don't ride with Lottie. Romy and Sadie are acting like a pair of helicopter parents while Jude just gives me the evil eye.

I remind myself I'm playing the long game. Thankfully, I'm a patient guy. I'll bide my time until we land back in Willowbrook—then the rest of the Lottie's family will go their separate ways, back to their lives. Tomorrow morning, when I stop in for coffee—the first fifteen minutes of every day where I cherish my time alone with Lottie—I'll make her see we didn't end up married by chance.

I lean against a pole, head buried in my phone, but I peek up every few seconds to seek her out. Lottie's tucked into a seat across the terminal, nose in her phone, pretending not to notice me. God, even now, this whole damn city could fall apart around me, and she'd still be the only thing I search out.

"Bet you didn't think you'd leave Vegas a married man," Ben says, slapping me on the shoulder.

"Nope."

He shoves his hands into his pockets. "I thought for sure I'd beat you to it."

I chuckle. "Me too. But I'm pretty sure your marriage will last longer than mine."

Ben's gaze flicks over to Lottie as she glances up and catches us staring. Her face twists into a *stop staring or I'll cut off your balls* expression.

God, I love her fire. I love her everything. I'm so fucking screwed.

"I shouldn't have said what I did back at the restaurant," Ben mutters. "I'm sorry."

"Why are you apologizing to me?"

"Because she's the woman you love."

The word hits me square in the chest. *Love.*

"Love, huh?"

He quirks his eyebrow, and yeah, he's right, but saying it aloud feels dangerous, as though I'm giving voice to a secret that could crush me. It's going to be a balancing act. If I push too hard, I'll lose her before I ever get the chance to win her.

"She's your cousin," I say instead, deflecting the conversation away from my feelings.

"Yeah, and I'm pissed at myself. I was an asshole for years, never coming home. I shouldn't be saying that Lottie can't find her way back when I managed to. It's just... don't take this the wrong way, but I fucking hate your brother and what he did to her."

"Shit, man, I get it. I'm related to the asshole." My chest feels tight. I've always felt more at home with Ben and his extended family than I did with my own.

I refrain from mentioning the fight I had with Holden that day or the way I barely tolerate him when he shows his face back home. I'll never forgive him for stealing the light from the girl I love.

He stole her magic. He stole her belief in true love and

soulmates. Most of all, he stole her trust—the idea that a man would stand beside her, shoulder the weight of her burdens with her so they weren't so heavy for her to carry. I want her to have that back. Preferably with me.

"So what's your plan?" Ben sips his drink and eyes me with an expression that says he knows I'm not going to just sign those annulment papers. He knows me too well.

"Other than flat-out refusing the annulment? I haven't figured it out yet."

"You're really going to put your foot down? Not give her what she wants?"

I look at Lottie one more time—her legs crossed in the seat, talking to Romy and Sadie. Whatever she says makes them both laugh, which causes her own laughter. Her head falls back then forward, and that flicker of light she used to always have shines through for a moment. And it fucking slays me. Because I remember that laugh. I remember the girl who trusted the world to love her back. I want to be the man who gives her that world again.

"That's my plan. I'm probably crazy to think it's a sign— that even drunk, she married me—and that it has to mean something."

Ben chuckles and slaps me on the shoulder again. "Why not just tell her how you feel?"

I shoot him a look. "Do you not know your cousin at all?"

He laughs.

"I can tell her my intentions until my last breath, but she'll never believe me. To win Lottie, it's gonna have to be slow. Show her who I am." I search her out again, and she's back on her phone. "Earn one small ounce of trust at a time until hopefully she believes that I'd do everything in my power not to let anyone hurt her. Most of all, me."

Ben just smiles. He knows.

He had to do the same with Gillian when he returned to

town after retiring from professional football. But he didn't do what my brother did. He wasn't cruel.

My brother promised Lottie the fairytale—only to tear it to pieces in front of everyone.

"Step one is that I need this to stay between us. If it gets out around Willowbrook, I might never have my chance."

Again, I keep the thought of my parents to myself. How they would react, since, for some reason I've never understood or cared to, they blame Lottie for Holden's tarnished reputation after leaving her at the altar, causing him to flee town.

I was just happy he left and rarely returns unless Dad summons him home to further his political career.

The boarding announcement for our flight echoes through the terminal. I grab my carry-on and move toward the gate. Ben waves Gillian over to join us.

"I haven't been able to congratulate you," Gillian says, squeezing into the line between Ben and me. "You scored a good one."

"Now I just have to figure out how to keep her."

She smiles softly, glancing at Ben, and I see it—the look that says he's her safe place.

Someday, I want Lottie to look at me that way.

"A piece of advice?" she offers.

"Anything you're willing to give."

She smiles. "It's in the small things. Not the elaborate and big things. *See* her. Discover what she needs to see you and the promise of what you can bring to her life."

"What kind of things do you think I should do?" I'm desperate to get this right.

"I can't tell you that. You have to figure them out yourself. Plus, every woman needs something different. And believe me, you already know. You already like her—probably love her. Just use that big head of yours." She rises on her tiptoes and kisses Ben's cheek. "Now I have to go because, you know, girl code. You understand." She squeezes my forearm. "See you on the plane."

"Hey, wait," Ben says, but he groans when she scurries farther ahead to get in line with the girls. He fishes his phone out of his pocket and presses his password, then studies it for a beat. "Shit."

I stiffen beside him. "What?"

"I'm sorry, man." He passes me his phone, and I see a message from his dad with a screenshot from the chapel website.

It's a picture of a drunk Lottie and me walking down the aisle right after we got married.

God, we're wasted beyond belief, but we're smiling and laughing, arm in arm, our faces so close. And for a second, I forget how wrecked we were, because we look... happy.

I wish I could remember the kiss we surely shared.

Then I come back down to reality and realize—we're screwed... I'm screwed.

"Fuck." I pass the phone back to Ben, and he nods. "By the time we touch down and drive into Willowbrook, everyone in town will know."

Ben cringes, empathy on his face.

This just made my quest to win Lottie a lot fucking harder.

Chapter Seven

LOTTIE

I'm not sure why Brooks is giving me so much space, but he doesn't try to swindle Romy into swapping seats with him like he did on the way to Vegas. In fact, he's kind of stand-offish. Other than while we were waiting for the flight and he was talking to Ben, he hasn't even glanced in my direction. Not even when we had the layover in Denver before our last leg into Lincoln.

He's probably playing a game. Trying to play hard to get or something. Or maybe... maybe he regrets what happened and that fight he said he was going to put up is already diminishing.

Well, good then. I hope that's it.

As the plane lands and we taxi to the gate, it all suddenly seems so real. He's my husband. My freaking husband. A technicality at this point, but I'm tempted to take him right from here to a lawyer or whoever we need to get this marriage annulled. We have to do it in Lincoln with the hopes that no one else finds out about it. I'm pretty sure I can trust everyone who knows at this point. Sure, maybe twenty years from now someone will let it slip to my mom and dad,

41

laughing at the absurdity that I married Brooks Watson in Vegas, but they'll keep my secret for now. At least, I pray they will.

"Hey, Lottie," Romy whispers, leaning closer to me. She has her phone out, and her face is a mix of panic. "You're not going to like what I just received."

I cautiously take the phone from her grip, and my stomach fills with dread. What could it possibly be now?

I look at the screen as the plane taxis toward the terminal. It's a picture of Brooks and me at the wedding chapel, looking as if we drank our way up and down the Strip. I suck in a breath. My stomach freefalls as if I'm on an elevator at the top of the Willis Tower, and someone cut the cables.

It's from Romy's friend, with a text asking her if it's true.

Then I hear the vibrating of phones in the seats around me and any hope that my secret will stay in Vegas vanishes as my phone lights up with a text from my mom.

So I have a new son-in-law?

I turn my phone toward Romy, and she bites her lip to stop herself from laughing. I glare at her, but my heart isn't in it. Although I want to pull her hair like I used to, at the same time, I can't blame her. I'd be laughing too if the roles were reversed.

The plane comes to a stop, and after the tone sounds, everyone unbuckles their seat belts.

"I guess that whole 'what happens in Vegas stays in Vegas' thing doesn't have a shot against the Willowbrook gossip gang. I'm oddly proud to be from Willowbrook." Bennett grabs his carry-on from the overhead bin, looking at me. "Don't think about using Wren to get out of talking to Mom."

"What is the kid good for then?" I'm joking, but he's clearly in no mood.

He shoots me his stern fatherly glare and hands Romy her bag.

"Can you get mine?" I slide to the edge of my seat, although I'm not really in a hurry to get off the plane. I'd be fine staying right here and pretending the outside world doesn't exist for a while.

"Sorry, that's not my job anymore." He turns to face down the aisle. "Brooks, get your wife's bag."

All of my family laughs while the other passengers look at all of us as though we're the loud, obnoxious family. Okay, we kind of are.

"I can get my own bag." I stand from my seat but hit my head on the overhead. "Fuck!"

"That lady swore," a little kid a couple rows behind says.

"Sorry," I mumble, but I swear it was the same spot where I knocked heads with Brooks this morning.

Instantly, my thoughts float back to him.

Brooks naked.

Brooks naked and on top of me.

Brooks naked on top of me about to slide into me.

God, the weight of his body felt so good. Too good. Good enough to ruin me for all other men if I let it.

I shake my head to get rid of the memory that is sure to haunt me for who knows how long.

"Let's go," a deep voice says from the aisle next to me. Brooks stands there, pulling my carry-on out of the overhead bin.

Romy's lips twist next to me. "I'll just be in the terminal, waiting." She ducks under Brooks's muscular arms, shooting me an apologetic look.

Great help she is.

I stay crouched until I'm free of the overhead and put my hand on the handle of my suitcase. "Thank you, but I got it."

As I'm about to snatch it from his grip, my head feels light, and I wobble a bit. My suitcase tips to the side, then both of Brooks's hands are on my hips, guiding me down into Romy's vacant seat. His touch is warm, grounding, and I hate how badly I need it right now.

"Sit," he says and slides into what was my seat. "You've had a couple hard hits today."

He laughs, and I side-eye him. "This isn't funny."

"Come on. It's a little funny. This whole situation is a little funny." He tips his head to look into my eyes.

My lips slowly curl, but I force them to stop. I won't let him make me forget how big a mess this is.

"Brooks... the entire town knows." I hate the whine in my voice, and I blame it on being hungover, traveling all day, and hitting my head twice.

"I got the text." He reaches out but retracts his hand before he touches me.

"What did we do?" I whisper.

"We didn't do anything wrong. Sure, we got drunk and made a rash decision, but it's our business. We don't owe anyone any answers."

He looks so serious. So unlike the Brooks everyone loves. The one who jokes about everything and takes nothing seriously. Although I want to go dig a hole and burrow inside it, Brooks sounds so convinced that we can navigate this together. For one terrifying moment, I believe him. And he's right, it's no one else's business.

"Our parents are going to want answers. Yours are going to ask why you'd marry the woman your brother left at the altar."

His lips thin, and his jaw clenches. The air between us tightens, sharp and aching.

"Excuse me, we need you to deplane." The flight attendant puts her hand on the back of my seat and leans forward. "Thank you."

She walks up the aisle, assuming we're going to listen. I

normally am a rule-follower, but outside this plane is the reality of my decision. I'm going to walk down Main Street only to hear the whispers follow me once again. I can already hear everyone's judgmental thoughts on me being involved with *both* Watson brothers.

Brooks gets out of his seat, and I expect him to slide out around me, but he crouches in front of me. Thankfully, we're in the exit row so there's extra room, otherwise his big body wouldn't fit. "I know you're scared."

I scoff, and he tilts his head. I keep my lips clamped shut, because if I speak, I'll lose it.

"But I'll go with you to talk to your parents. Shit, I'll be your personal bodyguard until we figure this out and things calm down."

I shake my head. "I'll be okay. Just..."

He inches out of the aisle and waits for me to stand. I kind of like that he's not making me vocalize that I need a little help stepping off this plane. Because what I want to do is ask that friendly flight attendant where they're going next and see if maybe I can hide in the bathroom and disappear from my life for a while.

"Let's go. We'll miss our ride, and I don't really want to pay for an Uber all the way back to Willowbrook."

God, he's being too nice, using his usual humor and giving me the out of bantering back and forth with him.

"You're so cheap." I stand and close my eyes for a second, centering myself. Trying to find whatever courage is left in me.

"That reminds me. You owe me for half of the wedding."

Rolling my eyes, I say, "Please, it was your dream come true to marry me."

I step forward while the two flight attendants and pilot watch us with rapt attention, probably wanting us to speed this up.

"If only I could remember it." There's humor in his voice,

but I don't return the same sentiment, instead continuing up the aisle.

"You both have a great day." The flight attendant gives us a little wave, and the pilot and other flight attendant shoot us tight smiles.

Once I'm off the plane and we've walked up the jetway, it doesn't seem so scary. I've totally got this. So what if the townspeople want to talk shit about me again? It was a drunken mistake. I was able to finally not care about them before.

Then again, could I have married anyone worse than Holden's brother? That answer claws at the edge of my mind, but I shove it away. I'm not ready to dissect that truth right now.

We take the escalator down to baggage claim, and I hear the laughter from my family before I round the corner with Brooks right behind me.

My mom and dad stand by our baggage claim with a large sign that reads, *Mr. and Mrs. Brooks Owens,* as if they're our drivers here to pick us up.

Chapter Eight

BROOKS

By the time we reach the escalator, there's an odd feeling in my chest that my small talk with her on the plane was able to make her feel as though we're in this together, a team.

Then she stops at the end of the escalator, hands fisted at her sides. "Mom."

The rest of her family laughs and hugs Darla and Brad.

I read their sign and manage to hold back the smirk that wants to make an appearance.

After everyone has gone to grab their luggage, Darla approaches me, bypassing her daughter's open arms. "I've always wanted a son. Welcome to the family, Brooks."

"Mom, you have Bennett."

Darla squeezes me tightly, laughing in my ear. "Bennett's not a sheriff." She pulls back but holds my upper arms, winking at me. "Where are my get-out-of-jail-free cards?"

I always figured my feelings for her daughter were transparent. I tried for a long time never to let anyone know, but over the years, I've had a hard time keeping them hidden, causing minor slips here or there. Like taking a softball to the groin because I was too busy ogling her ass to notice the ball flying at me.

Bennett comes over with his suitcase. "Gee, thanks, Mom."

She pats his cheek. "You gave me Wren, so you'll always have top billing."

Brad eyes his daughter, then sticks his hand in front of me. "Brooks Owens has a nice ring to it, doesn't it?"

"Is it too late to ask for her hand?"

Brad squeezes my hand a little harder than usual. "Next time just shoot me a drunk text."

Darla and Brad crack up.

He pats me on the back then goes over to his daughter, opening his arms for her to step into. "Oh, come on. Lighten up. You could've married worse." He wraps his arms around Lottie, swaying them back and forth, but she never wraps her arms around her dad.

I don't say anything since I know Brad is joking. At least, I hope he's joking.

"Yeah, he's the sheriff." Bennett raises his eyebrows at his mom.

Darla wraps her arms around Bennett's waist. "Oh, you know where you stand in my line of favorites."

"Not sure I do now," Bennett grumbles.

"Well, I brought you a surprise too." She puts her fingers in her mouth and whistles.

Bennett's daughter, Wren, pops up from behind a row of chairs. "Daddy!"

"Mom, someone could've taken her." He crouches and opens his arms, and Wren runs into them, her arms tight around his neck.

"Please, she was ten steps away, and it's so late no one is even here." She waves off his concern that she'd put her granddaughter in danger.

"God, I missed you." Bennett holds her.

Wren mumbles something into his neck, but I can't catch it. He stands, and she swings her legs around his waist. As I watch, Bennett's words from the hotel room run through my mind. They've got all of us, but I understand what he's saying. If I had a daughter or a son, I'd do about anything to protect their fragile heart, which would mean sacrificing my own wants.

"What about your other daughter?" Romy comes up with her suitcase.

Darla looks at her youngest. "You didn't bring me home a son-in-law." Darla elbows Romy. "Though I heard Zander Shaw was in Vegas this weekend."

Romy's head whips in my direction.

I shrug. "I told you I saw him."

She rolls her eyes, looking exactly like her sister.

"Plus, it's like Lottie gave us all a gift. Brooks." Brad holds his hands out to me as if I'm an award or a prize, like the goldfish at the state fair after spending a hundred dollars to win the game.

"Can we please just stop all this?" Lottie stares at her parents like an annoyed thirteen-year-old girl.

Brad waves her off but swings his arm around her neck. "Let's go. You two are riding with us." He points his pointer and middle finger at Lottie and me.

I'm pretty sure Lottie's getting her wish, and the fun and games are over. Brad has never been weird with me, but Holden used to tell me some stories about Brad drilling him as though he was the lead suspect in a serial killer case. Then again, Lottie was so young, and looking back, Brad had every right. As we walk toward the exit, I just wish that I had some idea what Brad and Darla really think about us marrying in Vegas.

"And what about your other children?" Romy asks.

"You have six cousins here—find a ride. And Bennett, Wren's booster seat is over there." She points toward where it sits next to the chairs Wren was hiding behind.

"So sweet of you, Mother. Remind me to leave you to fend for yourself when you're ninety and senile." Bennett finally releases Wren, and she runs over to Briar and Emmett to congratulate them on the wedding and tell them all about what happened with their infant son, Colter, while they were away.

We leave the airport, but while everyone else heads toward long-term parking, we're led to short-term parking with Brad and Darla. I put Lottie's and my luggage in the back of Brad's truck, then we file into the back seat on opposite sides.

We're not even on the freeway before Darla twirls around and eyes us. "Imagine our surprise to find out our daughter is newly married, and we never even received a phone call?"

"Mom—" Lottie starts, but Darla raises her hand to stop her.

"You're an adult. Your dad and I aren't going to give you some big guilt trip about this giant decision the two of you decided to make while you were drunk." Her eyes widen.

"Except that you kinda are," Lottie says.

Brad's eyes find mine in the rearview mirror, and I hold them because I'm not going to act like some snake and try to hide from what I did. My brother ruined the first time Brad was supposed to walk his eldest daughter down the aisle, and now I've stolen his second opportunity from him.

"I want to apologize." The words are out of my mouth before I wonder if maybe it isn't my place to say anything.

With how fast Lottie turns her head in my direction, I know she'd prefer if I just stayed quiet.

"I'm sorry, Mr. and Mrs. Owens. I shouldn't have... well..."

"Damn, Brooks, I've never seen you this at a loss for

words." Darla pats my leg. "Thank you. We appreciate the apology." She glances at her husband. "Right, Brad?"

"Yeah, sure. But what I want to know is now that you two are married, what are your plans?"

"Annulment," Lottie says.

Darla's shoulders sink, and she eyes me. "And that's what you want too, Brooks?"

I feel Lottie's glare on the side of my face, and I really hope she doesn't have any sharp objects within reach. "Actually—"

"He does," Lottie interrupts.

"You can't speak for the boy. Brooks, what do you want to do?" Brad asks, his line of sight through the rearview mirror on me again.

"I'd rather talk to Lottie about it when it's just the two of us. With all due respect."

Brad side-eyes his wife, and she straightens into the seat. "Fair enough. Keep us in the loop?"

"We're not staying married," Lottie says to me, giving me another evil glare. "We were drunk."

"So what?"

"So we weren't in our right minds."

We've turned toward one another as if we're about to have a face-off. If this were a Western, Lottie would already have her pistol out, and I'd be slumped against the back seat, dead.

"I'm not so quick to agree."

"You cannot do this, Brooks!" She says my name as if I'm a child.

"I get that you're..." I peek at her parents, who have decided to stay out of the conversation for now. "...worried. But can we just talk about it back in Willowbrook?"

She huffs and crosses her arms, sitting straight and pushing back into the truck seat. "Fine, as soon as we're back in Willowbrook, we'll talk."

Darla peeks over her shoulder at me, while Brad looks at

me through the rearview mirror for the tenth time in the last twenty minutes. Then they look at one another and smirk.

I have to admit, I thought I knew the Owens well. I practically grew up on Plain Daisy Ranch with the entire Noughton, Owens, and Ellis families, but this isn't the reaction I thought we'd receive. They seem to be encouraging us to stay married.

All of it makes me a lot more confident in my decision to tell Lottie that I'm not signing the annulment papers until she agrees to do something for me first.

Chapter Nine

LOTTIE

We pull up to Brooks's house. It's an older house on a good-sized plot of land with a big barn where he restores old trucks when he's not on duty.

"Brooks, is that a new one?" My dad points out the window at a truck that looks as if it has sat in the mud for ten years. "You've got your work cut out for you there."

"Yeah, the guy is in desperate need of it for his dad's birthday, so I had him drop it off. I'm off tomorrow, so I'll be looking at it to see what it needs. When he said it was in bad shape, I didn't think he meant that it'd survived the flooding that ravaged parts of our county years ago." He opens up the door. "Thank you for the ride back, Mr. and Mrs. Owens."

"Please, we're Mom and Dad now." My mom giggles.

I inwardly sigh, although I'm sure my expression reveals my annoyance over the fact that my parents are treating this like a joke. As soon as we get back to the ranch, I know they're going to have "the talk" with me.

Brooks's smile is timid as he shifts his attention to me. "Walk me to the door?"

I was hoping for a quick goodbye and that maybe he'd text

me when he wants to talk. But the faster I get this over with, the faster the gossip train will shift onto someone else's track. So I open the door and hop out of my dad's truck.

"We'll be sure to close our eyes," my mom says. Both my mom and dad laugh.

I slam the door. "Make it stop."

Brooks doesn't say anything. I'm sure if I had to guess, his parents won't be as light and jovial about the fact that we got married. In fact, he might just be kicked out of his family.

"At least your dad didn't punch me. He had every right."

We step up on the front stairs leading to his front door.

He drops his suitcase on the porch and leans against the siding of his house. The weight in his shoulders says more than his words. "When do you want to talk?"

"We can talk right now. I want an annulment."

His gaze flows down my body, taking in my crossed arms and wide stance, my tilted head. I'm prepared to fight for this, and all the man does is smirk. That quiet smile that used to unnerve me now feels like a chisel revealing a slow crack in my resolve after this morning.

"Yeah, I'm not talking to you until you sleep and eat."

"What? You can't tell me when I can talk to you about this." My arms fall to my sides, and my fingernails dig into my palms. I remind myself this is what's best.

He crosses his arms, and that smirk still hasn't left his face. "You don't dictate when we talk about our marriage either."

I can't deny that he has a point, so I ask the question I'm most curious about. "Why won't you just agree to an annulment?"

"I never said I wouldn't."

I clench my jaw. I'm sure there's smoke coming out of my ears at this point. Or maybe it's not anger at all. Maybe it's panic. "You keep saying we're going to talk. Let's just do it now."

"Listen, we were up until who knows when last night. It's been a long day, and we've barely slept. I just want a night. I'm off tomorrow, so you name the time, and we'll talk."

How is he able to stay so centered through this situation we've put ourselves in? It's as if he's a monk at peace inside of himself. Meanwhile, every part of me feels jagged, ripped apart in ways I don't know how to stitch back together.

"Fine. Breakfast." I think of where we can go where we won't have every set of eyes in Willowbrook on us. Surely not the house I share with my sister and cousins. Not the Getaway Lodge either. Any place in downtown Willowbrook is a definite no. "I'll be here at eight."

"Eight?" He pulls his phone out, looks at it, and pockets it. "It's late. Ten?"

"You said I get to choose. I choose eight. I'll even bring the doughnuts. What's your favorite?" It's a purposeful dig at him being a sheriff and the fact the man really does love doughnuts.

"Pretending you don't know?" He arches an eyebrow.

I exhale sharply, my frustration slipping out. "Fine, I'll bring you a whole dozen Boston cream doughnuts tomorrow at eight." I step off the porch.

"Don't forget your favorite, a bear claw or two."

I stop and inhale a deep breath, but don't respond.

His chuckle makes me want to stomp back up his porch steps, but instead, I go back to my dad's truck and tuck myself inside.

"That looked like a lovely conversation," my dad says.

"We're talking tomorrow." I buckle my seat belt.

My dad starts to back out of the long drive. I watch Brooks put his suitcase in the house, then head to his truck immediately.

"Is he going to his parents'?" my mom asks.

"How would I know?"

"You *are* his wife." My dad shoots me a look from the front seat, and I mumble an apology for my shitty tone.

"That conversation isn't going to be easy for him," Mom says quietly.

I feel a small piece of guilt that I'm not going with him, but me walking into the Watson house on Brooks's arm would only make the entire situation so much worse.

Chapter Ten

BROOKS

My parents have called me twenty times today, so it's a safe assumption they've seen the picture of Lottie and me at the altar. I've sent them to voicemail every time because I had more important things to take care of. Their lectures could wait. Lottie was my priority—she'll always be my priority. But now that I've asked Lottie to wait until tomorrow to talk, I need to deal with them. It's not going to go well. That much I know.

I park my truck in my parents' driveway. They moved into the heart of Willowbrook once I was out of the house, selling off every piece of my mom's family land that ever meant anything to us. They traded legacy for a mini mansion that screams power and money, two things my father has always cared more about than family.

I hate everything about the four white pillars out front and the red brick and the black shutters. It's a house built for appearances, not to be a home. To remind everyone who holds the leash in our town.

I walk up the brick walkway toward the front door, where a bronze sign sits in the bushes welcoming me to Mayor

Watson's residence. No mention of my mother, of course. Always just him.

My knuckles rap on the door, and I hear the shuffling of feet on the other side. I know who it is. Only one person would get up off the sofa at this hour.

The door opens, and as I predicted, my mom stands there in her matching polka-dot pajamas, robe, and slippers. "We expected you in the morning."

She steps aside, and I stroll in, thinking that maybe I should've come after I showered.

"I figured we could get this over with." I toe out of my shoes and walk toward the family room, where I can hear the nightly news on the television.

"Your dad is tired and upset. You should let him sleep on it." She follows me, but my footsteps don't falter because a night's sleep won't change anything.

My dad pretends he didn't hear the doorbell or my voice in the foyer, and I find him sitting in his brown leather chair, ankles crossed, feet in slippers on the ottoman. He acts as if he's running the whole damn country, not a small town nobody cares about outside our borders.

"Dad," I say, rounding the couch and sitting in the chair on the other side of the room.

My mom passes me and sits on the edge of the couch, as though she's prepared to flee at any moment. The familiar ache settles in as my jaw tightens.

He makes me wait—ten full minutes—watching the weather and sports before muting the television and looking in my direction. His feet hit the floor, and he swivels his chair to face me. "How nice of you to actually show up here after sending us to voicemail the entire day."

His stare is cold, devoid of anything resembling what a father should feel toward his son. So different from the warmth Brad and Darla exude. No wonder I spent all my time on that ranch growing up.

"I was flying home."

He nods, but it's clear he's not accepting my excuse. He's not asking for an apology either—because he knows damn well he won't get one.

"It's an election year." He crosses his arms.

My mom hasn't moved a muscle. She's frozen, just as she always is when things get uncomfortable.

"I'm aware."

His signs are plastered over half the lawns in town. I'm not sure whether people actually want him to be the mayor again or if it's a devil-you-know kind of situation.

"And did you think about how this stunt might hinder my win before you went ahead with it?"

"I'm not sure that what I do, as your adult son, has anything to do with your ability to govern Willowbrook." I lean back in the chair, lifting my ankle onto my opposite knee.

"For fuck's sake, Brooks, don't come into my house and sit there and act like you don't know exactly what this might do to my campaign." He jabs a finger into his chest as though he's trying to punch a hole through to his own heart. Doubtful he even has one though.

"It's my life."

"She's your brother's fiancée."

"Ex-fiancée."

Dad launches out of his seat, pacing like a caged animal, following the tracks in the carpet he's made over the years with his tantrums.

"Really, Brooks, why would you do this?" My mom's voice trembles, her eyes pleading as though I'm supposed to fix this with a few pleasing words. As if I'm supposed to sacrifice my happiness to keep Dad placated.

"I was drunk."

"That's the first problem. Only Emmett Noughton would go to Vegas to get married." Dad shakes his head in disgust.

"Now the entire town knows. You could have been more discreet." Mom's lips thin as though she just sipped spoiled wine.

"We didn't expect everyone to find out. It's this town's incessant need to know everything that's why the picture got leaked."

Dad stops pacing, glaring at me.

"It was sweet of Mr. Torres, wanting to post a picture of Emmett and Briar on the bulletin board at the library," Mom says. "No one expected to find the wedding photo of you and *her*."

"Her name is Lottie," I say, my voice low, tight.

Mom waves me off as if Lottie's nothing.

"She's my wife."

My mom blows out a breath, scoffing so hard I swear it could rattle her knickknacks on the bookshelves.

Dad stops, his hands on his hips, scowling. "You'll post a public statement. Say you were drunk, and it was a mistake. That you're getting it annulled or divorced or whatever the hell fixes this."

I stare at him. Really stare. And wonder how I ever thought he was someone to look up to. "I'm not doing that."

"You will if you give a damn about this family's name."

"This isn't about our name. It's about me. It's about her."

Mom crosses her arms, and her glare matches my dad's. "She wanted out of this town. She used Holden. She's using you now."

My fists clench so hard my knuckles crack. "She didn't use anyone. Holden left her, remember? At the damn altar. Don't rewrite history to suit the lies you tell yourself."

Mom huffs. "She wanted out. She saw your brother's

future and wanted to ride his coattails as far away from here as possible." Her face twists in distaste. "Thankfully, he came to his senses, otherwise could you imagine having the Owens as in-laws?"

"They are your in-laws now." I can't help the smirk that lifts my lips.

"Temporarily." She waves me off.

"She's not temporary," I bite out.

"Are you suggesting you're in love with the girl?" Dad asks, his lip curling in disgust.

My mom narrows her eyes, as though she already knows the answer and hates it.

"Well?" Dad pushes.

I meet their stares, steady, unflinching. "Do you really wanna know?"

My dad roars like a wounded animal. "She's your brother's! She belongs to him, not you!"

"No," I say, standing to my full height, towering over him now. "He walked away. He left her."

"If this is about guilt—" Mom starts.

"Listen," I say, my voice low and even. I'm thankful for my sheriff training so I can be calm when my dad looks as if his head is going to spin around and fly off his body. "Last I checked, I'm old enough to make my own decisions. I'm sorry. No, actually, I'm not sorry. I'm not sorry for any of it. I understand how you would view this as putting you in a bad position, and I wish that picture wasn't spread around. I don't regret my decision though. Give it a few days, and if you can talk in a calmer manner about this, call me. But for now, I'm leaving."

I walk toward the front door.

"We're not done here!" Dad's voice roars after me as I slide into my shoes.

Maybe we aren't.
Maybe we never will be.
But I walk out the door anyway.

Chapter Eleven

LOTTIE

After my parents' late-night talk about how I deserve love and need to open myself up to it, maybe not write Brooks off so fast, I didn't slide into bed until well after midnight. Their words dug deeper than I want to admit.

I've been wondering how things went with Brooks's parents last night. Probably about as well as trying to ride the meanest bull in the rodeo—you're thrown off, trampled, and left breathless.

I'm walking out of the house I share with Romy and my cousins, Poppy and Scarlett, but when I open the front door, Scarlett is there.

She takes out her earbuds and looks me up and down. "Where are you disappearing to so early this morning?"

"You don't want to know." I try to sidestep her, but she matches my move, blocking me.

"Oh, I do."

She's sweaty from her early morning run in her matching outfit. Scarlett's every bit the version of myself I wish I could be—organized, focused, all clean eating and discipline.

"I'm going to talk to Brooks, if you must know. I have to run to the Donut Hut before they run out of Boston creams."

She smiles and steps aside, letting me pass. I step out onto the front porch.

"Getting your hubby's favorite. I love it."

"It's called putting him in a sugar coma, so he agrees to my demands."

She laughs. "You could tie him up and dangle the doughnut in front of him. Tell him to agree or he doesn't get it."

I point at her. "I like the way you think."

She shrugs and unzips her sweatshirt, revealing a matching sports bra. If I ever exercised, it'd be in mismatched shades of cotton, not this Instagram-worthy activewear of my cousin's. "I visualize ways to torment Walker Matthews should I ever decide he's taken the rivalry too far."

"I swear you're going to marry that man one day."

She steps forward as though she's going to tackle me. "Take that back."

I laugh and jump off the porch, not gracefully, nearly rolling my ankle in the process.

She laughs at my clumsiness. "Good luck. I'm thinking you've got a stubborn one there."

I lift my hand because she's right. Brooks isn't going to take this easily. That I know.

I stop downtown at the Donut Hut to get ten Boston creams, a bear claw, and a regular old glazed. See? Brooks Watson doesn't know everything about me. I like glazed doughnuts too. Take that, Brooks.

Naïve me hoped maybe that picture hadn't spread yet, but the minute I walk into the Donut Hut, every set of eyes swings to me as though I'm the main attraction. Great. Exactly the circus I was dreading. An itchy sensation crawls over my skin. Best to tackle this head-on as though it doesn't matter.

I raise my hand. "Hello, yes, it's me, Lottie Owens, and before you ask, I did marry our big ol' sheriff this weekend in Vegas. I'm not really open for questions at the moment, just here to get some doughnuts."

I toss the information out like bird seed, hoping it will give them enough to chew on so I can get my doughnuts and get the hell out of here. But it doesn't stop the whispers.

"Congratulations." Mindy comes around the counter with a box. "My mom and dad made it for you guys. Usually, Sheriff Watson would've already popped by, and they thought..." She blushes. "You know. That he'd be picking up for the both of you."

I open the lid of the box and sure enough—there's a baker's dozen: eight Boston creams, two bear claws, two glazed, and one heart-shaped doughnut with pink frosting with *Mr. and Mrs.* scrawled in icing smack dab in the middle. I close my eyes for half a second, breathing in the sugary scent and the overwhelming realization that this town truly thinks this marriage is the real deal.

"You got a good one there," Mrs. Schmidt calls.

I smile back politely like my mom taught me. "Thanks, Mindy. And please tell your parents thank you."

"He's the best. Anything for you two." Mindy leans closer. "Last year after I got my license, he gave me a warning when I was going too fast out on Route Twelve."

"Nice of him." I manage to keep the smile on my face and turn to head for the door.

"My tire blew out during that torrential rainstorm last year. He stayed, let me sit in his squad car, and fixed it himself. Even offered me his coffee," Mrs. Winslow chimes in, clearly eavesdropping.

"I got stuck in a ditch during that same storm. He gave me his dinner." Mr. Patel smiles widely.

Okay, okay, I get it. He's Willowbrook's personal superhero.

"And with that last name, you can't go wrong," Mrs. Bendle adds, eyeing me as though I just won the town lottery.

A hand lands on my arm as I'm almost out the door.

"Sometimes you have to think someone's looking out for you." Mrs. Parker stares long and hard into my eyes, her meaning crystal clear. "This time, you picked the right Watson."

"Okay, gotta go. Thank you, everyone. Have a great Sunday." I push through the door, desperate for the bell to announce my escape.

Once I'm safely back in my car, I place the doughnuts on the passenger seat and drop my head back against the headrest.

What was I thinking coming here?

After I've gathered myself, I start my car and pull out of downtown, noticing that the *Vote Mayor Watson* signs have doubled since we left for Vegas. Of course they have.

Everyone at the Donut Hut is right about Brooks—he's a great guy. But that's what scares me the most. Because I know firsthand that the Watson family can hide monsters behind their perfect smiles.

I will never forgive them for how they treated me after Holden.

And if Brooks refuses to sign that annulment... if this thing gets dragged out publicly... Mr. and Mrs. Watson will step in. They'll control the narrative, even if it means tearing Brooks down to protect themselves. They'll tear *me* down too —and this time, I might not survive their wrath.

Which is exactly why this marriage has to end today.

I don't care what I have to do to make him see it. I'm doing it for him as much as me, even if he never really understands why.

Brooks deserves the future he wants. One I can never give him.

So I park in his gravel driveway and climb out with the box of doughnuts and my heart hammering against my ribs. As I approach the house, a whistle catches my attention. I glance to the right and spot Brooks in the barn.

"Mack!" he hollers, but the golden retriever beelines for me, ignoring Brooks completely.

"Hey, buddy." I crouch, setting the doughnut box on the gravel, and nuzzle my head against Mack's soft beige fur.

I'm so busy with Mack that I don't notice the shadow fall over us until it blocks the sun.

"Happy to see your new mommy?"

I squint up at him. "Cute."

"I thought so." He bends and scratches Mack behind the ears. "Go on now. Let her be." He throws a tennis ball, and Mack races after it without a glance back.

"I'm here. Let's talk."

He shakes his head. "Come to the barn. I need to figure this truck out while we talk."

I pick up the box of doughnuts and shove it into his gut. "Here's your bribe."

He lifts the lid of the box with one brow raised. "Is this to make up for our lack of a wedding cake?"

"The Brindles did it. Apparently, everyone thinks this marriage is legit." I roll my eyes.

"It is legit. I saved the paperwork if you want to read it again." He keeps walking toward the barn, leaving me no choice but to follow him.

I try like hell not to notice the way his ass perfectly fills out his jeans, but it's nearly impossible.

Once I catch up to Brooks, Mack wedges himself between us, as if he can't bear to not be right by both of us.

"I don't need to read it again. I would, however, love to read the annulment papers so I can sign them."

He pushes his hand through his hair, then puts his ball cap back on his head except now it's backward. God, that looks good on him. "You're not going to calm down so we can talk this out, huh?"

I swallow my reaction to how he looks. "Nope."

"Then I have a proposition for you." He turns to me, the sun haloing him like some untouchable entity.

It's cruel how beautiful he looks. How easy it would be to believe in things I know aren't true.

I have no idea what Brooks could possibly say to make me stay married to him, but I'm out of options. I'm going to have to hear him out before I ever get him to agree to an annulment.

So I walk into the barn, grab a bear claw from the box, and take a big, defiant bite. "Let's hear it, Sheriff."

Chapter Twelve

BROOKS

"Why don't you sit?" I tip my head toward the bench behind her and place the box of doughnuts on the table. It's my workstation when I fix trucks, dodge responsibilities, and apparently, propose deals to the one woman who drives me certifiably insane.

"I don't need to sit." She takes another giant bite of her doughnut, and a tiny piece of glaze catches on her bottom lip.

Jesus. My eyes zero in on it, and I fight the urge to lean in, lick it off, and taste her.

"Just sit. Please."

She huffs, her tongue flicking out, catching the glaze—and nearly making my dick jump. She drops onto the bench with her typical Lottie flare, crossing her legs, chin tilted up, a defiant glint in her eyes.

I open the box, only to get punched in the gut when I see the goddamn Mr. and Mrs. doughnut again.

After getting back from my parents' last night, I second-guessed this whole mess with Lottie. Not because I want the annulment. Far from it. But she deserves better than to be a part of the Watson family shitshow. If my dad wins his re-election campaign and is the mayor for another term, it won't be easy for her to be with me. That's if I could eventually win her over anyway.

Now I'm the idiot staring at a pastry as if it's a crystal ball, envisioning my dream. Wishing Lottie had padded out here this morning in nothing but one of my old T-shirts, hair messy, Mack trotting along behind her, like this was *our* home. Wishing she'd wrapped her arms around my waist and pressed her face into my back as if it was the most natural damn thing in the world.

"Brooks!" Her voice slices through the fantasy, dragging me back to reality—where she's watching me with narrowed, suspicious eyes.

Mack parks himself at her feet, and she absently pets him, her gaze pinned on me.

I clear my throat. "I'll give you the annulment."

She bolts up as though she's been dismissed from jury duty. "Perfect. Thank you. I'll take care of the lawyer and get the papers sent over to you."

Her words are what I expect, but there's no smug smile. No victorious smirk. Just this quiet tension that knots up my gut because I'm not so sure she's as happy as she's trying to appear.

"After you go on seven dates with me."

She freezes mid-step, her mouth dropping open. "What?"

"You heard me." I swallow past the dryness in my throat.

I'm not afraid of Lottie, but this is me putting myself out there fully. Telling her my intentions and giving her the opportunity to crush me. Lottie is part of the Noughton family tree, and I love them like my own. If this goes bad for me, or us, it will change everything. Losing all of them is a hard consequence if I'm wrong about what I think Lottie wants deep down. Although I think even a treasure map wouldn't help her discover what she really wants at this point.

"You can't make me go on a date with you, let alone seven."

I lean back against the truck I've been getting mud off of all morning, arms crossed. "Actually, I can."

"This is blackmail," she accuses, flinging open the doughnut box as though she's going to use a Boston cream as a weapon and whip it at my head. Instead, she snags a glazed and chomps into it as if it's my head.

"No, it's not. You want something, and I want something. We're going to meet in the middle. Think of it as a negotiation."

She wipes her mouth, scowling, then notices the fridge and stomps over to it. Mack trails her like a furry bodyguard.

She slams back a bottle of water and turns, arms crossed. "Why?" Her voice is quieter now. A little rough around the edges.

"You know why." I hold her gaze, daring her to look away first.

Her silence unnerves me. Ben's right, my parents' suspicions are right. I do feel as if I love Lottie, but I have no idea how we'll be as a couple. Will she ever open up to the idea of it after my brother ruined her world for so long? There's so much uncertainty when it comes to us and what we could be.

She shakes her head. "You're crazy."

"Am I?" I grin, letting her see just how little that accusation bothers me. Hell, maybe I am. Definitely crazy enough to want her without knowing if she'll ever admit she wants me too.

She turns her back, and Mack plants himself at her side again. Traitorous bastard.

"Just give me a shot. Seven dates. If you still hate me after, I'll sign the papers. I'll even pay your legal fees."

She circles back around, Mack sticking close, both of them sizing me up as though I'm some weird new animal at the county fair. "What else?"

"What do you mean?"

"Any other crazy conditions? Stipulations? Rules? I want it all out in the open now so we can get this over with."

"I hadn't planned that far ahead."

She plants her hands on her hips. "You have to plan these dates then? Is that the deal?"

I shrug, wishing I hadn't been worrying about this moment so much so that I would have thought further ahead and would have something more to tell her. "Do you want an itinerary?"

"A time limit. No dragging this out for a year."

I shake my head, open the box of doughnuts, and grab a Boston cream before sitting down. I'm pretty sure this will be a long conversation. "Three months."

"Three months?" Her voice ricochets off the barn walls, and Mack's head whips in her direction.

"We're not going to cram them all into a week."

"I'll make myself free every night this week to get it over with. And I should be able to plan a few dates. Actually, all of them."

"No." I bite my doughnut, chew, and swallow, taking my time just to get her to calm down a little. "I plan them."

"I'm sorry." She dramatically looks around the space, even stepping out of the barn for a moment, looking from field to field around us. "Yeah, I didn't think so."

"Think what?"

"I didn't just step off a time machine into the nineteen forties. I'm not going to let you bully me into seven dates."

"Then no annulment."

She picks up the tennis ball and chucks it toward my house. Mack goes running, and she spins around.

"Don't want our fur baby to hear us arguing?" I can't help my grin.

Her eyes narrow. "I'll give you three dates, and I plan all of them."

"Five."

"Three."

"That's one a month."

She shrugs. "We can be done sooner if you'd like. Hell, I'll free up my entire day today, and you can have me for breakfast, lunch, and dinner."

I'm sure when the words came out of her mouth, she wasn't picturing me with my face between her thighs, but that's all I can think of now.

I stand to ease some of the discomfort in my jeans. "Okay, let's go to the house. Don't want the fur baby to see us." I walk out of the barn.

Mack comes back, tail wagging with the ball in his mouth. He drops it at her feet.

She picks it up and chucks it again. "What are you talking about?"

"You said I could have you."

She growls, and her arms go straight, her hands in fists at her sides. "You're impossible. Annul me, Brooks Watson!"

"After five dates."

"Three."

"Five."

"Three!"

"Four. Final offer. You plan two. I plan two. Fifty-fifty."

She glares at me as though she's trying to set me on fire with the purity of her rage. "I don't know what you're trying to prove. This wasn't fate or kismet. Jack Daniels is the one to blame."

"Jose Cuervo, to be specific." It's only a guess, but I

remember drinking a lot of tequila shots before I remember nothing.

Mack drops a slobbery ball between our feet, but neither of us breaks eye contact. I can see it—the flicker of doubt, the tiny *what if* she's trying so hard to crush. I think she's hoping I'm going to back down. Maybe because I usually do when she really wants something, but not this time. This time, I'm taking what *I* want because it's the only way I'm going to show her the man I can be for her. That I'm more than just the Sheriff of Willowbrook. More than Holden's younger brother. More than her cousin's best friend. More than the jokester. I'm the man for *her.*

"Fine."

Relief floods my veins. "You agree?"

"Reluctantly."

"But you do?"

"I plan the first date."

I nod. "Deal."

She blinks, thrown for half a second, before recovering. "Okay then. Four dates, and then you're signing those papers."

"I'll sign... if you still don't want me."

"I won't."

I shrug, cocky. "We'll see."

She huffs, spinning away, marching back to the doughnut box. She yanks out the Mr. and Mrs. doughnut and bites into it as if she can dismantle our marriage with the same ease. "I'll be in touch, Sheriff," she says around a mouthful of doughnut, mock saluting me. "See you, Mack."

"Say goodbye to Mommy."

She flips me off with her finger raised high in the air. "You're going to regret this, Brooks!"

I watch her leave, shaking my head. She's all fire, that one, and I love every little bit of her flame.

I'm pissed I can't remember the night we were together

74

and what happened between us. Did I already have her? But I remind myself I'll have her again. And the next time, we'll both be sober and clear-minded, and it will be so much better.

Relief washes over me that it's over. I've got my shot. Finally. Now all I have to do is make her fall for me the same way I fell for her so long ago.

Chapter Thirteen

LOTTIE

I barely remember the drive back home because I'm so in my head about what just went down.

I'm furious. How can he do this to me? Why won't he just sign the damn annulment papers and be done with it?

Once I'm back on Plain Daisy Ranch, I park at the house and head to the she-shed where I work on my pottery. I grab a chunk of clay, hurl it onto my potter's wheel, and sit on the stool, my fingers already centering the cold, damp mass as though I can work my anger out of my body if I just press hard enough.

He's so full of himself, thinking that four dates are going to make a difference.

I get up off my stool, my rhythm completely shot because of him and this dumb idea. I'm too hot under my sweatshirt, so I strip it off and crank up Florence + the Machine, letting the pounding beat drown out my chaotic mind, and I sit back down.

I let go of all of the thoughts ping-ponging in my head—the future I no longer believe in, all the pain that went down over a decade ago, the baggage I carry around with me every damn day. All the expectations people have for my future that can never be fulfilled.

Everyone in my family wants me to walk into someone's arms and give them a chance to strip away the last part of me that existed before Holden destroyed it all with one fatal blow. Do they think I want to live this way? That I want to feel so lost? To sit in the back pew, wedding after wedding, as my cousins find their happily ever afters, knowing mine will never come?

Maybe if I had shared the whole truth with them, they'd understand better and not think I'm just being stubborn.

I dip my hands in the water, not even sure what I'm about to sculpt, just desperate to ground myself after this disaster.

My fingers move on instinct, digging and molding, my muscle memory taking control as the wheel spins around. I form the base of a mug, the same coffee mugs I always make for my family, but today the clay resists, wobbling under my touch. My hands shake against it, my knuckles whitening from how hard I press, trying to force the mound into submission.

I concentrate on making sure the base is thick enough, the walls steady and even. My nails dig grooves into the wet surface without care. The spinning hum of the wheel and the steady resistance of clay beneath my palms are the only things tethering me.

I'm so lost in the rhythm of trying to perfect this stupid mug that I don't even realize the door to my shed has opened and shut.

My foot lifts from the pedal, and my half-formed mug collapses inward, the clay sagging back into a glob of nothing.

Sadie walks over and lowers the volume of the music. "Hey," she says softly, as if she's afraid of what she just walked into.

I start the wheel again and keep working, my fingers slapping the hunk of clay, unwilling to have the same talk with her that I had with my parents last night.

"I was walking by with Jude and Daisy and heard the music." She sits in the chair by me, her presence warm and patient as always. "I'm assuming you talked to Brooks?"

I nod, the coolness of the water over my hands and the silky texture of the clay the only reasons I'm not melting down like a screaming toddler at what Brooks is demanding in order to give me an annulment.

"So, what did he say?"

She's going to be such a great mom. While I'd bust into my teenager's room, demanding he talk to me, she'll coax teenage Daisy with patience and kindness and get a better result than I ever would.

I stop the wheel, the clay spinning crookedly before slowing to a halt.

She sighs, crossing her legs and getting comfortable.

"He's demanding four dates before he'll give me the annulment. He plans two, and I plan two." I shake my head. "Can you believe him? The audacity."

"You're really mad," she says, as though that's a surprise.

Why wouldn't I be mad? "Of course I am. You know I went to pick up doughnuts this morning—"

"Why would you do that?"

"Because I promised him Boston creams and thought he might repay my kindness with an annulment." My fingers spread out at my sides, and I wiggle my body as if I might collapse from sheer frustration. "But no, he ups the ante. He wanted seven. Can you believe it? Seven dates!"

She bites her lip to stop her laughter.

"Sadie!"

Her hands go up in defense. "I'm sorry, but it's kind of cute, no?"

I scoff. "It's not cute. He's trying to blackmail me..." I

snap my fingers, struggling to find the word. "What word am I thinking of?"

"Bargaining?"

"It's not bargaining. There's only one thing I want."

"That's the point. But he wants more."

I throw my hands in the air. "What could he possibly want?"

She smiles, and my anxiety knots tighter in my stomach. "You. He wants you."

I roll my eyes and spin around, grabbing another slab of clay and slamming it onto the table to avoid seeing that dreamy expression on her face. "It's just because he's always been in competition with Holden."

"No, it's not."

"Well, I'm not some toy to be tossed back and forth."

"Lottie." I hear her rise from the chair, and her shoes scuff softly across the room. "He's not in competition with Holden. He's not asking you so he can join this family. He's asking because he wants to date you."

I always praise Sadie for her calm presence and sweet voice, but right now I could do without it. I circle around and lean my hands on the table behind me, clay sticking to my fingers. "He doesn't even know me."

She tilts her head, the way only Sadie can when she's trying to get me to say what's buried deep.

"There are a lot of things about me he doesn't know." I frown.

There's one thing in particular—one truth—that would change everything. If he knew it, he'd run. Maybe I should just tell him, so he'll leave me alone.

"That's why he wants the four dates. To discover those things about you."

I blow out a breath, a tremor in it I can't hide, and stare at the rows of finished pottery. Mugs that will never see the light of day.

I started working with clay after Holden left me. My hands needed something tangible to rebuild when my heart couldn't be put back together. But other than my family and a few close friends I gift them to, no one knows about my hobby.

I can't deny the thought hasn't crossed my mind—why I don't want to make more of it than just a hobby—but I'm not exactly big on digging into issues. Not ones that could rip me apart if I look too closely.

"Maybe if he wasn't a Watson, I could..." I shake my head, flinging tiny flecks of clay from my fingers. "No. He's too close to all that, and, Sadie, that doesn't just go away with a bouquet of flowers and some sweet words."

She laughs, and it's a light sound floating through my darkness. "Brooks? Sweet? I'm not sure that's something you have to worry about. And flowers don't seem like his thing either. He'd probably bring you a chicken sandwich from The Sprout House before he brought you roses." She chuckles, and I give in with a small smile. "Give the man a shot. He's waited a long time."

She holds my gaze as I think about her words for about a second. And then I remember that Brooks sees a future I can't give him. He's wrong about the life we'd build together. So wrong.

"It's four dates, and I get to plan the first one. How do I sabotage it?"

Sadie shakes her head with a disappointed look and steps away from me toward the door. "Jude and Daisy are waiting for me."

"You aren't going to help me?"

She takes her hand off the doorknob and turns around. "No, I'm not. I've stood by your side and understood all these years. I've watched you hook up with a guy here and a guy there, knowing none of them were going to last more than a few dates. But Brooks is a good man, Lottie, and I really want you to give him a chance."

I sag against the table, the clay drying and cracking against my skin, and think about what she's saying.

"He's a Watson," I say, as if that still holds the weight it once did.

"It's four dates, Lottie. More than you've allowed yourself since Holden. I'm begging you—go into it with an open mind."

Does she have any idea what she's asking me? Of course she does. That's what makes it worse. That's why I feel guilty.

"If after four dates you feel the same, I'll never say another word." She raises her hands in a placating gesture.

I don't say anything, and she reaches for the doorknob again—but the door swings open, almost hitting Sadie before she can step out of the way.

Wren barrels in. "Aunt Lottie, I need your help!"

Sadie ruffles her hair. "Slow down." She shoots me that same look, like she wants to say, *Get it together*, and walks out of my shed.

"What's up?" I ask my niece, pushing away the conversation with Sadie. It would require me to self-analyze, and that's not going to happen.

"I broke the mug," she cries. "I need to make a new one. Before Daddy finds out. I was making him breakfast in bed and..." She sniffs hard and swallows.

I bend down, my heart breaking for her. "Okay, calm down. Which mug?"

She swallows hard, and tears cling to her lashes. Seeing how upset she is, I know which mug she broke.

I quickly clean my hands with the large wet wipes I keep in here and rush back over to her. "It's okay, Wren."

She shakes her head violently. "No, it's not. Daddy is going to be so mad at me."

I run my hand gently down her hair, smoothing back the soft strands, and pull her into a hug. She weeps into my chest, her small frame shuddering against me, every broken-hearted hiccup slicing through me.

The door opens with a creak, and Bennett stands there, the doorknob still clutched in his hand. His eyes lock on Wren in my arms, and he exhales a slow, heavy breath, clearly thankful he found her.

I shoot him a soft look, silently telling him she's okay.

He crosses the room slowly and crouches beside us, grounding all that worry in the steady way only a good father can. He places a reassuring hand on Wren's back. "It's okay, Wren."

She lifts her head, her cheeks damp and blotchy, and looks at me for reassurance. I nod, giving her the little push she needs. She spins around and throws herself into Bennett's chest, clinging to him as if he's her security blanket.

"I broke Mommy's mug. I just wanted to surprise you with breakfast, and it slipped out of my hand," she sobs.

"It's okay. Calm down. Calm down," he murmurs into her hair.

I stand up, giving them space, tucking my arms around myself.

After a few minutes, Wren's cries soften.

"Come here." I wave her over, smiling softly. "I'll walk her home."

Bennett nods, pressing a kiss to the top of her head before rising to his feet.

I position Wren between the wheel and me, the familiar scent of clay and water wrapping around us. For the next half an hour, we work together on a new mug—our hands side by side, shaping something new.

It will never replace the mug her mom once sipped from, but it's a distraction—for Wren and for me.

We don't talk much. Her small hands are steady against the clay while my bigger ones guide her.

When we're finally done, the mug sits on the shelf to dry before I can fire it. We clean up, and I lace my fingers through hers and walk her back across the property, where we find Bennett waiting on the steps of the guys' house, staring at the lake in the middle of Plain Daisy Ranch.

"I think this is yours," I say, handing Wren over with a playful nudge.

Bennett hugs her fiercely. "She sure is." He whispers something into her ear that makes her smile through the last of her tears.

"I'll let you know when it's ready to glaze," I promise, waving goodbye.

As I walk back to my shed, my shoes crunching against the gravel, I realize how good it felt to share that with her.

How Wren pulled me out of my head without even trying.

And that's when an idea springs to mind.

I know exactly how to dodge Brooks Watson and his stupid scheme to get close to me.

He said I get to plan the first date. Well, he's about to find out two can play this game.

Chapter Fourteen

BROOKS

Monday morning, I stop by The Harvest Depot, just like always, except now Lottie's my wife. The door is unlocked, which is a good sign, but as I step inside, Lottie isn't in the front area as she normally is. I spent the entire night counting down the seconds until I got to see her again, so I'm hit with a wave of disappointment even I didn't predict.

But then the back door springs open and shut, and she strolls in, already wearing her apron over a pair of jeans and a long-sleeve T-shirt. She stops in the doorway from the back-room to the storefront. "You're early."

"The door was open." I thumb behind me.

"Yeah. Well..." She seems distracted. "Let me get your coffee." She crosses the room, heading behind the counter to the coffee machines.

I step closer, my hands stuffed into my jacket pockets as if I'm some nervous thirteen-year-old boy in front of his big crush. Before the whole Vegas mess, I felt as though I was getting somewhere with her—sure, it was like following a path of crumbs, but it was something. An easiness had begun to develop between us. Now it's like starting from scratch. The sarcasm's gone. There's no snark or bite. Nothing.

"So, when are you available this week?" I ask, tapping my fingers on the counter.

She prepares my coffee just as always. Her back is to me, and I hate that I can't actually see her facial expressions. Her face always gives her away.

"It's my date to plan. I should be asking that question."

I hadn't realized I was holding my breath until her snarky comment. Finally, the tension in my body loosens a little. "Then ask me."

Turning around, she places my coffee on the counter with *Bully* scribbled on the cup. I shake my head.

"I'm planning a date for Friday night. Do you want me to pick you up or do you want to meet me at the place?" she says.

"If I didn't know better, I'd say you know my schedule." I grin when her expression turns annoyed.

"If you could take Friday night off from going to The Hidden Cave to pick up a woman, we can cross one of these pesky dates off the list."

"Jealous?"

She scoffs. "You wish. Now are you available or not? I have a bunch of stuff to catch up on since I was making shitty decisions in Vegas this weekend."

"You wound me." I cover my heart with my hand.

"Please, you're tougher than that." She leans her back against the counter behind her and crosses her ankles and her arms, as if the million things are going to do themselves now.

"You got two things right this morning. Bravo."

"What are you talking about?" Her lips twist in a pissed-off expression.

"My coffee, and that I am tougher. I've been the victim to your insults most of my life, and I'm still standing here like a loyal dog with my tongue hanging out, begging for your attention."

Lottie rolls her eyes. "So we should add dramatic to your singles ad?"

"I'm not eligible for a singles ad."

"You are, Brooks Watson. This marriage is a mere formality."

I place my coffee down, my pulse kicking up as I round the edge of the counter, cornering her as if I've got every right to. "As of right now, you're my wife, Lottie Owens. So don't stand here and pretend you don't replay that morning just as I do. I saw the way your breath caught when I touched you. The way your skin shivered under my lips. My hands memorized every inch of your body, every curve..."

She inhales sharply because her body remembers too.

"You know how it felt when I pressed into you—when my hips locked between your thighs, my cock hard and aching, seconds from sliding inside you. Hell, I'm getting hard just remembering how soaked you were for me. So don't stand here and lie to me and to yourself—you were ready to let me ruin you."

Her hands flatten on my chest, right over the stitched label that reads Watson. But she doesn't push me away. Her eyes glaze, her lips part, and for one second, I swear she's with me. Remembering. Wanting. Needing. But just as fast, the heat drains from her face, shutting me out.

"That might be your beat-off material, but my vibrator does a better job than any man can."

I laugh low in my throat, stepping into her until there's barely any space between us. She doesn't tell me to back off. So I lower my head and drag my nose along her jaw, slow and deliberate, breathing her in as if I'm starving, and she's the only thing on the menu.

"That little toy might hum a sweet tune, but it doesn't

know that though you put on a good show of being little Miss Independent, what you really want is a man to tell you what to do when he takes you to bed. Don't worry—I will."

I draw back, and yep—her face is flushed as though she just walked through Arizona in the summertime in a down winter coat.

The bell above the door sounds, and she pushes me back so hard I stumble against the other counter, barely steadying myself.

"We're not open," she rushes to say, sliding out from behind the counter, about as far away from me as she can get.

I circle around to find a middle-aged woman with purple-rimmed glasses eyeing every surface. I straighten, my protective instincts on alert as Lottie stops when the woman picks up one of her mugs off a shelf.

"This is it!"

"Excuse me?" Lottie steps closer, and I stay right on her heels. She stops, and my chest bumps into her back. She looks over her shoulder at me. "She's not going to murder me."

"It's always the ones you least expect," I whisper.

"We're in Willowbrook."

"You think crime doesn't happen here? What do you think I do all day?"

She spins around, but I keep my eye on the woman who is now punching out a message on her phone screen.

"From what I hear, you eat doughnuts, drink coffee, and let other people sit in your squad car. Shouldn't that be illegal by the way?"

"Do you want to sit in my squad car, Lottie?"

"I'm not five." She scowls.

"I can turn on the lights for you."

"Your lights don't do it for me."

"Siren?"

"I don't want to be in your squad car."

"Well, you sounded a little jealous." I shrug.

"Oh. My. God. Stop saying I'm jealous."

She whips around, and the lady is now on a FaceTime call, holding up the mug. "I found them! They have the same daisy!"

Lottie glances at me and mouths, "What the hell?"

The mugs aren't even for sale. Lottie puts them up as decorations to hold up books or to put flowers in. She always sticks a plush bunny in one during Easter and a turkey on Thanksgiving.

"Can I help you?" Lottie approaches the woman, but she's completely enthralled, talking to someone on the phone as though she's found a lost Van Gogh at the flea market.

"I'll take a dozen. Do you have more?" Her dark hair flips as she scours the shelves. "Oh, I like this one." She takes the honey sticks out of the green one and picks it up.

Lottie gently takes the mugs from her. "I'm sorry, these aren't for sale."

The woman's lips turn down. "Why not?" Her tone's got the same whine Wren uses when I tell her I won't lock her in a jail cell so she can see what it's like.

"We don't sell them."

"How did you know about them?" I interrupt.

Lottie gives me one of her pissed-off expressions.

Clearly, Lottie doesn't care how the woman found them, because she's going through the store and picking them up as if they're her babies and this woman wants to steal them.

"My friend found two at a secondhand store in Lincoln. We just love them. It's been like a scavenger hunt. There's a group of us who have been trying to figure out where they came from. They're so charming."

Her eyes widen at something behind me. I assume she's watching Lottie collect every piece of her pottery off the shelves.

"Why don't you sell them? They're so beautiful. You should share them." The woman walks by me to Lottie. "I've looked at so many shops for ones like these. It was just by chance I saw this friend-of-a-friend's social media post, and it was in the background. She was talking about your goat cheese or something." She waves her hand as if the woman was nuts for focusing on cheese with this art sitting right there.

"I'm really sorry, but we do not sell them," Lottie says.

"Then why did we find them at a secondhand store?"

Shit. She's not letting this go.

"Someone must not have wanted theirs." There's sadness in Lottie's voice, but she's quick to change her tone as if she heard it herself. "So sorry you made the trip."

The woman stretches out her hand and places it on Lottie's forearm. "Can you at least tell me who makes them? Maybe I could talk to them, and they would reconsider."

Lottie shakes her head. "She won't."

The woman steps back from Lottie, and her shoulders sag. "But..."

It guts me to watch this. Lottie could sell them. Hell, she *should* sell them.

"Here." I go over and pull one of The Harvest Depot business cards and a pen that looks like a flower off the counter. "Why don't you leave your number or email, and if she changes her mind..."

The woman gives Lottie a pained expression, but Lottie doesn't budge.

"Okay. I guess it's better than nothing." She writes down her info, eyes lingering on the mugs now out of reach. "Thank you." She tips her head at me and walks out of the store.

I grab my coffee, no doubt cold now, and break the distance between us. I want to ask a hundred questions. But if I do, she'll just shut down.

"What time are you picking me up Friday?" I ask.

She glances up with a look of relief on her face, and her mask slips back into place. "Be ready at five."

"See you then." I stroll out of the store, gripping my cold coffee, knowing this is something I'll need to address with her at some point, but not today.

I have to remember that I'm in this for the long game.

Chapter Fifteen

LOTTIE

"You want to use my daughter tonight?" Bennett asks from across the table at breakfast in The Getaway Lodge's dining room.

Mom's sitting at the table, giving me the side-eye every few bites of her toast, but staying shockingly quiet.

"I'm not using her." I raise my eyebrows, stabbing my fork into a perfectly ripe strawberry. I have no idea where my cousin Jensen gets the amazing produce he serves us. "I'm asking if I can take her to the fair in Hickory."

"I was planning on taking her since I was gone last weekend."

"If I take her, you can go on a date."

He side-eyes me with a mouth full of Wren's uneaten pancakes. Wren saw Briar in the hallway and bolted, and Bennett said he'd come get her from the yoga studio when it was time for her to leave for school.

"Do you really want to talk about our dating lives right now?" His gaze shifts to Mom at the end of the table, pretending she's not listening. As if she uses her phone for anything other than sending us memes she finds funny.

"Come on, B, what do you want in exchange? Anything."

He leans back in his chair, finishes chewing, and grabs his coffee. "Tell me the real reason why you want to take her to something you hate. Refresh my memory because you swore off fairs after you got stuck on the Zipper in eighth grade."

I groan. "Is there anything you don't remember?"

"It's a pretty significant memory since you threw up on me afterward."

Mom giggles, and when we both turn to her, she buries her head in her phone again. "I'm sending this to you two." She taps her screen as if she's launching a missile. A second later, both our phones vibrate.

I lean in closer to Bennett. "It's important," I say through clenched teeth.

"Bennett, just let her borrow Wren for the night so she can get one of these four dates with Brooks over with. Although he's not going to bat an eye. He loves Wren."

I sigh. "Who told you?"

Mom finally places her phone on the table, screen down as though there would be anything that might pop up on her phone that we shouldn't see. "This is Willowbrook, Lottie. I also know you bought your new hubby doughnuts Sunday morning. I'd hoped it was because you woke up in his bed, but sadly, Scarlett slipped and said she saw you leaving for Brooks's place."

I cock my jaw and look over at Bennett. "I should've moved out of here years ago. Somewhere people aren't all up in my business." Now I glare at Mom.

She shrugs and sips her coffee. "You're the one who married him in Vegas."

"Exactly. I wasn't in the town square in a wedding dress."

A flash of sadness hits her eyes. And just like that, we're both thinking about Holden and how he left me in the church, smack in the middle of the downtown square. The location was his parents' request. As though we were royalty and it was the wedding of the damn century.

"You went to the same chapel as Emmett and Briar."

I throw my hands in the air and decide I'm going to drown my sorrows the old-fashioned way—with carbs.

I snatch Wren's forgotten plate.

"Hey," Bennett says.

"Please. You don't need the extra calories." I shovel a mouthful of chocolate chip pancakes into my mouth as if I'm in an eating competition.

"What the hell?" He looks to Mom for backup, but she doesn't say anything. She's unusually quiet and suspiciously unnosy, which means she's definitely up to something.

I swallow what's in my mouth. "I'm just trying to make sure you stay fit."

"For what?"

I freeze. Crap. My eyes dart to Mom, who's peeking at me over the rim of her coffee mug.

"You know... for... good health and all that." I wave my hand as if that'll distract them from the fact that I almost said *so you can find a woman.* That would've been... too far.

"Right. I gotta go." He stands and grabs Wren's backpack and jacket off an empty chair.

I catch his wrist. "I'm sorry. I didn't mean—"

"You know how you hate everyone pushing Brooks down your throat?" I stay quiet, because yeah, he's not looking for an answer. "Well, I hate everyone thinking I need to find a wife and a mom for Wren." He steps away from the table.

"B, I didn't mean..." But he's already gone. "I'm sorry," I murmur.

Mom laughs again at something on her phone, and mine vibrates with a text. "Adult siblings fighting. Will you ever grow out of it?"

I blow out a breath and ditch my breakfast to try to catch Bennett before he gets in his truck. "See ya, Mom."

"Good girl."

I walk out of the dining room of The Getaway Lodge, and Wren is holding Bennett's hand as they head toward the door.

"B!"

Wren stops and tugs her dad back into the lobby. "Aunt Lottie called you!"

Bennett gives his daughter a tight smile, then lifts his eyes to me. "We're gonna be late."

"Please." I bite on my bottom lip.

He sighs and hands Wren her backpack. "Go wait on the porch. Give me a minute with Aunt Lottie."

"Can I try to find a rock to paint?" Wren asks.

Bennett seems hesitant, but Heidi from reception pops out from behind the desk. "I'll go with her."

"Thanks," Bennett says.

Heidi's smile is a little too wide and too toothy. She's way too young for Bennett.

I close the distance since I know he'll want to stay close enough to keep Wren in sight. He's such a good dad. And he'd be a great husband. But he's right—if I don't want people in my business, I shouldn't be all up in his.

"I'm sorry. I'm an asshole."

"You are." He crosses his arms. "But you're not wrong. I don't want to be alone forever. So maybe I shouldn't keep eating Wren's pancakes just so we don't waste food."

"Still. It was insensitive. And point made about the whole Brooks thing."

He nods. Thank God Bennett doesn't hold grudges. "You can take Wren tonight, but if Brooks asks, you have to say you kidnapped her. I don't want him thinking I helped you cock-block him."

"Thank you!" I throw my arms around his neck. "You're the best brother a girl could have."

Bennett nudges me off him as though I'm contagious. "I want her home by ten."

"Done." I deliver a quick kiss to his cheek.

He checks his watch. "We're gonna be late." He runs into Heidi on the way out.

I watch them for a second before he jogs down the front steps.

Heidi walks back in. "Your brother is so nice. Is he dating anyone?"

I smile tightly. Nope. Not my love life to manage. "I'm not sure. You'll have to ask him."

She rounds the reception desk. "I think I will."

I head back into the dining room to find Mom still there. She's put her phone down but is still watching me like a hawk.

"I take it that smile means you got your way?" she asks.

"He's letting me take Wren tonight."

She leans back in her chair, arms crossed, studying me. "Is that your plan? To sabotage each and every date?"

"The ones I'm in charge of, yes." I shrug.

"Hmm."

"What?"

"Nothing."

I cross my arms. "It's clearly something. Just say it."

She stands, brushes her hand along my shoulder, then down my hair. "I don't have to say anything you don't already know. Have fun at the fair. Love you."

Then she walks away, stopping at another table to check if they're enjoying their breakfast as if she's not casually giving me that mother-knows-best vibe.

Whatever. My plan is perfect.

And I cannot wait to see Brooks's face when I show up tonight with Wren in the back seat.

Chapter Sixteen

BROOKS

Friday couldn't come fast enough. You'd think stopping in every morning for coffee, I would've gotten my fix of Lottie, but it's done nothing but make me crave more time with her. Every part of me wants to convince her I'm the guy for her—even when all week, she's been handing me coffee cups with less-than-complimentary names on them. Turns out, *Bully* was just the start. So far, she's written *Regret*, *Whoops Husband*, and—my personal favorite—*Sin City Slip-Up*.

I'm showered and dressed in jeans and a T-shirt since it's a warm spring night. I opted for no hat. It's weird being on the other side of the dating fence. I've never had a woman plan a date for me before. Now I understand why they always ask what to wear. At least I'm confident Lottie's not planning some romantic restaurant in Lincoln. She's absolutely going to try to tank tonight. I'm half-expecting her to fake a flat tire or feed me something questionable just to end the night early.

Her small SUV pulls into my driveway right on time, and I plant myself in place by the door. I'm not going out to meet her.

She honks her horn.

I don't move.

Then she presses down on her horn again, longer this time.

I stay where I am. If she wants to be the date planner, she can come to the damn door like I would for her.

Then comes the triple-honk—three long, angry blasts as though she's trying to summon the dead.

After I still don't emerge from my house, my phone dings.

I'm here.

I know.

Then why aren't you coming out?

I'm your date, no? Come and get me.

The three dots appear. Then disappear. Then return. I can perfectly picture her rage-typing and rage-deleting. It's pathetic how much I get off on making her angry. I'm hoping there's a day I can piss her off and then kiss her straight after.

Seriously, Brooks?

Dead serious.

Ugh.

A car door slams, then two knocks sound on my door.

I open the door with a smug grin—ready to see her flushed and flustered—but my gaze drops straight down.

"Brooks!" Wren barrels into me, wrapping her arms around my middle like a human seat belt. "We're going to the fair!"

Then she crouches down and gives Mack a hug, rattling off a bunch of questions about his day and our big outing.

I love Wren. I do. I just wish I'd had some warning that my "date" was going to come with a chaperone. Of course Lottie pulled this angle. I told her to plan a date but I never said it had to be one-on-one. I hate that I feel even the tiniest flicker of disappointment. I knew she'd try to ruin tonight, but I guess I was holding out the smallest bit of hope that she wouldn't.

"Aunt Lottie says she won't ride the Zipper with me. Will you?"

I glance at the car. Lottie's sitting in the driver's seat with that smug-ass smirk as if she just dropped a royal flush over my straight flush at the poker table.

I crook my finger at her.

She shakes her head.

Fine.

I look down at Wren. "I'll be right there. Can you ask Aunt Lottie to come talk to me real quick?"

Wren frowns but nods and bolts back toward the car. She and Lottie talk for maybe ten seconds before Wren climbs into the back seat, and Lottie gets out. Her body's all stiff lines and tight shoulders, showing she's clearly not thrilled to be here.

Mack strolls over and nudges at Lottie's hand. She pets him automatically. Doesn't even realize she's doing it, I don't think.

"What?" she bites out through clenched teeth when she joins me at the door.

I was going to say something about her bringing Wren, about how she clearly doesn't want to be alone with me—but when she stepped out of the car, that plan flew out the window. Her hair's a little wind-blown, cheeks flushed. She looks beautiful. And pissed. My favorite combo.

"Where are my flowers?" I ask.

She blinks. "Flowers?"

"You wanted to plan this date, and I'm not feeling very wooed." I lean on the doorframe, arms crossed.

"This is a check-the-box date, and you know it."

"Nope. They're real dates. Not ones where you honk like a taxi and expect me to come running."

She turns her head and stares at my barn as if she'd rather go figure out what's wrong with the truck in there than keep this conversation going. "Are we going or not?"

I grab my keys, get Mack back inside, and shut the front door. "Next time I'd appreciate flowers. And you coming to the door." I walk past her, down the steps.

She lets out a long-suffering sigh while I grin to myself.

"How do you feel about the fair with Wren?" she calls out, a little hopeful, a little hesitant, as though she thinks this might stop me in my tracks.

"Sounds like fun." I stop outside the car's passenger door, waiting.

She doesn't look over.

I clear my throat.

Her hand freezes on her door handle. Her eyes lift and meet mine across the top of the SUV. "Seriously?"

"Deadly."

She mutters something under her breath that I'm pretty sure isn't flattering. Then, to my surprise, she walks around the front of the car and opens my door. "Satisfied?"

"Immensely." I slide into her car, already missing my truck. I practically have to fold myself into this thing.

Lottie slams the door and walks around the front of the SUV while I chuckle.

"Why does Aunt Lottie look so mad?" Wren asks from the back seat, all innocence and big eyes, already strapped into her booster.

"She's just annoyed. She'll get over it when we get to the

fair." I twist to face her. "We have one mission tonight, Wren. And I need a partner."

She leans forward, her curiosity fully engaged.

"We're getting Aunt Lottie on the Zipper."

Her back hits her seat, and she shakes her head. "Aunt Lottie doesn't like the Zipper."

"I know."

"Then why?"

Lottie puts her hand on the door handle.

"Because sometimes," I say, keeping my eyes on Wren, "you gotta face your fears to get what you really want."

Wren wrinkles her nose, and Lottie climbs in with us.

"I wish Mack could come," Wren mutters.

That's a seven-year-old's version of changing the subject, I guess.

"Then one of us wouldn't be able to go on the rides because we'd have to stay with him," I say.

Lottie puts the car in reverse. "Ready?"

"Yes!" Wren throws her hands in the air as if we're about to go down the first hill on a rollercoaster.

Lottie glances at me. Our gazes lock, and I smile.

She rolls her eyes as she always does in my presence.

She thinks she's sabotaging these dates.

She has no idea.

She could bring her whole family and I wouldn't care.

As long as she's next to me?

It's a damn good night.

Chapter Seventeen

LOTTIE

When I came up with the brilliant idea to bring Wren along, I imagined skipping through the fairgrounds. The two of us holding hands, smiling while Brooks trailed behind us like our unpaid babysitter. He'd fetch us snacks and drinks. I'd dodge him all night and call it a win.

Instead, I'm the freaking third wheel.

Wren grabs Brooks's hand while I'm buying the ride tickets. Of course she does. Because he's steady. Because she trusts him. Because he's... him. She's begging him to take her on the Zipper while he tells her they need to "warm up to it."

"Okay, we're all set," I say, holding up the ridiculous fistful of ride tickets as if I just won a game at an arcade and I'm about to turn them in for the top prize everyone wants.

"Let's go!" Wren tugs on Brooks's hand.

He shrugs at me with that lopsided grin. "What can I say? I'm a fun guy." Then he turns his back to me and something inside me twists.

Which is stupid. Why would I be jealous? This was my plan. I was the one who brought a mini chaperone to sabotage this date.

I follow them through the fairgrounds like the forgotten child. Just slap a balloon in my hand and call it a night.

The fair is buzzing. String lights stretch over the walkways, casting a golden glow on everything below. The smell of fried dough, kettle corn, and junk food hangs thick in the air. A distant country song hums from the speakers, challenging the laughter and rise and fall of screams emanating from the rides.

It should feel magical. But tonight, it feels like background noise to the weird ache crawling under my skin.

We stop in front of the Ferris wheel. They hop in the first car together, and I wave them off as if I've mastered being content riding by myself.

I sit solo in the next car, the breeze cool as it rises higher, lifting me above the small town. The view is stunning—sunset dripping pink and purple across the open skies of Hickory. It steals my breath for a second, and I let my mind drift.

There was a time I couldn't wait to leave this place. Now, I can't imagine growing old anywhere but here. Watching my cousins and eventually my nieces and nephews grow up, fall in love, get married, have babies. This is my home. But back then? I would've scoffed at this fair and said I was meant for bigger things.

I think about that girl. The one who wanted out. The one who believed the world owed her something bigger and better than this place. I don't miss her exactly, but I wonder when she stopped being me. Without Holden, would I have become who I am now?

The ride slows. Stop by stop, we lower until I'm finally back on solid ground. My feet barely hit the pavement before Wren comes bounding toward me.

"Did you see the sunset?"

I ruffle her hair. "I did. So beautiful."

"Brooks said that it's because of the light and the

atmosphere, right?" She looks at him with wide eyes as if he invented science.

"Something like that," he says with a deep chuckle.

"Giving her science lessons?"

He shrugs, and there's a tiny flicker of embarrassment in his expression, as though maybe it really matters to him—like maybe he looked it up once just because he was curious.

"It just interests me," he says softly, as if he's confessing a secret.

"Always?"

"Ah..." His voice tapers off, his shyness lingering.

I lean in as if he's offering me a secret. Just like that, I want to know more.

"Come on, there's no line at the Tilt-A-Whirl!" Wren grabs our hands and tugs us forward.

I hand over the tickets to the guy running the ride and immediately notice the full body scan he gives me, not even trying to hide it.

Gross. A shiver creeps down my spine.

Wren's already on the ride, but Brooks pauses, wrapping his arm around the small of my back, leading me over to her. He even looks over his shoulder. The way his strong hand hovers over my hip, his fingertips barely touching, makes me feel as if he's claiming me in front of that creep checking me out. And I hate how much I like it. Hate that it makes me feel safe and secure.

We cram into the arched cab, Wren in the middle. She takes my hand, then Brooks's, and stacks them together with hers on top. "I'm having so much fun." She beams.

Her joy is magnetic.

I look at my brilliant, brave, and resilient niece who doesn't even realize what an inspiration she is. She's already faced so much in her seven years—mourning a mother she never got to know, pushing through questions no kid should have to ask. Still, she loves without fear of the outcome.

How? How does she still believe in love and joy when one of the most important people in her life vanished?

I envy it. I envy *her*.

Brooks's smile is stupidly contagious. "Me too. Great plan, Lottie."

I try to smile back, but it doesn't fully land. The ride hasn't even started, but the drop in my chest is already happening. *Holden*. The wreckage he left in me is still so mangled. I need to be brave like my niece to crawl my way out.

"Yeah, Aunt Lottie, thank you." Wren throws herself against me, and I hug her close, squeezing my eyes shut and soaking her in.

When I open my eyes, Brooks is watching us.

Not smiling. Just... watching. As though he sees beneath my layers and knows what hides there.

The ride lurches to a start, and we're thrown into chaos. Wren shrieks with laughter. Brooks leans his weight to get us spinning faster while I cling to the bar and pray I don't hurl.

For a blissful hour, we jump from ride to ride. Brooks and Wren are a duo, and I trail behind. I wanted distance. I wanted control. Now I'm the third wheel to my own damn plan.

The ache in my chest intensifies because he's so good with her.

Brooks tosses popcorn kernels at her and cheers when she finally catches one. "That's what I'm talking about!" he says, giving her a high five.

The sight thuds against my ribs in a warning. He'll be a great father one day.

"Giddy-up, horsey!" Wren squeals, kicking his side now that she's on his back. "To the Zipper!" Her hand goes up like a general leading the charge into war.

Brooks slows his walk with her cradled on his back and looks at me. "Ready?"

"For?"

"The Zipper. Last ride of the night."

I look at the remaining tickets in my hand. Yep. Enough for all three of us.

"Why don't you two go?" I offer. "I'll just hit the Ferris wheel again."

Brooks stares at me with a look so intense, I almost crumple. It's the kind of look that says he knows I'm not fine, and he hates that I won't say it out loud.

"Kayla!" Wren screeches, nearly tumbling off Brooks's back onto the ground.

"Who's Kayla?" I ask as I help her down.

"My friend from school!" The second her feet hit the ground, she sprints toward another little girl as if they've been separated for six years instead of six hours.

Brooks and I catch up, and I smile politely at Kayla's parents. "Hi, I'm Wren's aunt, Lottie. And this is—"

"Sheriff Watson," the man says, shaking Brooks's hand. The woman shakes mine, then we swap.

Of course they know him. Everyone does.

"How are you liking Willowbrook?" Brooks asks, shoving his hands into his pockets. He gives me a drawn-out stare with a meaning I don't catch. "The Millers just moved to Willowbrook." His tone says I should be cluing into something by now, but I'm not.

"Greg Miller." The man raises his hand. "Mayor Watson's opponent."

"Oh... ohhhh, of course." I nod.

The guy running against Brooks's dad.

This is awkward.

I plaster on a smile, debating on whether telling him "Good luck, I hope you win" is wildly inappropriate.

Before I can decide, Wren tugs on my arm. "Can I go with Kayla? They're heading to the big slide."

"Um..." I look at Brooks, and he nods as though it's okay, they're good people. "We can go too."

"After the Zipper." Brooks steps closer, his arm brushing mine. I ignore the way my body hums in satisfaction.

"No way."

He arches a brow. I don't want to get into a back-and-forth in front of someone who could be the next mayor.

Wren begs while Kayla's eyes look hopeful.

Finally, I give up the fight. "Are you okay if she joins you?"

"Well, I didn't want to go down the slide." Samantha laughs. "Greg will walk them up and go down."

I tear off the tickets Wren needs and hand them to her. "You stay with them, okay? We'll be right over."

Wren thanks me, and we tell the Millers we'll meet them over there. Wren and Kayla fall into a fit of giggles about somebody at school who Kayla already saw here at the fair, and the parents follow them toward the slide.

Brooks turns to me. "You afraid?"

I ignore his question and pose one of my own. "You're talking to your dad's enemy?"

"I'm not talking about my dad tonight." He nods toward the Zipper.

"I don't ride the Zipper."

"You can throw up on me."

And just like that, he's in line... we're in line.

My stomach is in knots. "I haven't ridden this since the eighth grade."

"I'm aware."

"I don't like this ride." I bite my lip and stare at the cages whipping and flipping over.

Three boys turn around in front of us. They're maybe twelve or thirteen years old, all long limbs, bony elbows, and false bravado. The tall and wiry redhead appears to be the ring-leader. His grin is so smug I loathe him before he even says anything.

"You're a chicken?" he asks, loud enough for everyone in line to hear.

"No," I answer evenly, standing taller.

"Then why not ride the best ride here?" His tone is taunt-ing, as though he's on the verge of clucking at me.

My eyes narrow. "I don't have a death wish."

The blond kid with braces who is clearly just trying to be like the redhead, snickers behind the redhead's shoulder. The third boy with darker hair and a freckled face lingers just away from his friends. His gaze shifts from me to Brooks, then down to the ground. Definitely the smart one who doesn't want to get involved in stupid antics like his friends.

They all laugh, but it's the redhead who keeps going. He elbows Braces and says, way too loudly, "Guess the sheriff's dating a wimp."

"We're not dating," I snap before I mentally reprimand myself for engaging this kid.

The redhead smirks, completely unfazed. "Probably regrets wasting his ticket on you."

The brown-haired one diverts his attention. Braces just stares then laughs, a second behind on the insult.

Brooks steps forward, his voice low and stern, instantly commanding. "Watch it. I bite back harder than she does."

The boys straighten. Even the redhead blinks at Brooks's sheriff voice.

And, okay... yeah, that voice does something to me that I don't have time to unpack.

The kids shuffle toward the front of the line, but just before they hand over their tickets, the redhead twists around, eyes gleaming. "Come on, scaredy-cat!" he yells before running into the caged ride.

My whole body flinches.

I see the Ferris wheel in my head again, the sunset, the calm. The version of me from the past who didn't let fear decide everything. Without another word, I hand my ticket to the guy at the gate.

I climb beside Brooks, heart hammering. The guy slams the cage door shut and slides the lock over. Is this what people feel like when they're put in jail?

Panic claws at my chest, a beast demanding escape.

I want to scream. I want to bang on the bars. I want to beg to be let off.

Instead, I stand there frozen, swallowing down my fear.

"You don't have to prove anything to those boys," Brooks whispers, his arm brushing mine, our pinkies so close on the bar, we could link them.

I *want* to reach for him. I *want* to curl into the safety he's offering. But I don't.

"I'm not doing it for them." That's all he needs to know.

The ride lurches upward, and my stomach freefalls.

"I'm right here," he says softly just as the Zipper flips— and I scream.

Maybe I was wrong. Maybe I shouldn't listen to that naïve girl from so many years ago.

Chapter Eighteen

BROOKS

The Zipper cage flips over and over, and all I hear are Lottie's squeals. They're a mix of thrill and panic as if she can't decide if she loves or hates the ride. There's profanity, and my balls are threatened a half dozen times, but when the guy opens the cage and Lottie's feet hit the ground, her smile is brighter than the neon signs scattered around us.

She's happy. Maybe it's relief, maybe it's adrenaline still buzzing through her veins, or maybe it's because she let herself go for once—but her knee hasn't made contact with my balls, so all in all, I call it a win.

I guide her away from the ride, nudging her gently forward and keeping my hand at the small of her back, not ready to lose the excuse to touch her.

She's still catching her breath when the red-haired kid from earlier sprints around us and sticks his head in a trash can to throw up. We both laugh. It hits me how easy this thing between us is when she lets down her walls. Lottie sinks into my side, her contagious laughter continuing on and on.

Without thinking, I wrap my arm around her, holding her close as the red-haired kid's friends glance over. The blond one

113

with braces flips us off, while the brown-haired boy smiles a little before checking on his friend.

"Karma," Lottie says.

"Definitely."

My chest feels light, and for a moment, I see so clearly the couple we could be someday. That's if she'll crack open the gate enough for me to slip past the defenses she locks so tightly. If she could see what I see right now, I know she'd let them down.

This moment alone feels like a crack in her armor. Her laughter, her warmth pressed against me. Hell, it's all a good sign.

"Let's go get Wren. I told Bennett I'd have her home by ten," she says.

I check my watch. It's nine forty. There's no way we're making it, but I keep that to myself.

Wren sits at a picnic table near the big slide, a cloud of pink cotton candy in her hand, laughing with Kayla. The Millers stand nearby, sharing a funnel cake, and I can feel the weight of Lottie's glance. She's wondering how I know them. Of course she is. What kind of relationship do I have with the new guy in town who's running against my dad?

I haven't asked why Greg Miller wants to run a town he's got no real ties to, but he might just have my vote. That part I'll keep to myself.

"Did you have fun?" Lottie runs her hand down her niece's hair.

"The bump was so fun. They got me cotton candy." She lifts the stick in the air—and from the look of her face, I'm not sure any actually made it into her mouth.

"I hope you don't mind." Samantha approaches, and Lottie waves her off.

"I'm the aunt, so those pesky parent rules don't apply to me."

Samantha laughs. "And what about the uncle?" she asks, eyeing me.

Lottie's quick to reject the idea, but I raise my eyebrows as if to say, technically, I am Wren's uncle through marriage.

"I was just dragged here. I have no say." I play it cool, though I'd give anything for a permanent label when it comes to both Lottie and Wren.

Greg chuckles and taps his daughter's shoulder. "We need to get you home before you turn into a pumpkin."

Kayla rolls her eyes. "Dad, it's her carriage that turns into a pumpkin." She looks at Wren like, *Can you believe my dad?*

Wren agrees, though she looks a little lost, watching Kayla sass her dad.

"Okay, you grown-up teenager, let's go. It's bedtime. Is that better?" Greg says.

Kayla stands with her cotton candy, and Wren follows. The girls hug and promise to see each other Monday. Then Wren heads toward Lottie and me. For a split second, it feels as if Wren is ours. I can't help but soak the feeling in like a sponge.

God, I want us walking around the fair hand in hand with our child or children, if we're so lucky. I've always yearned for a family of my own. I used to think family was something you were born into, but as I grew older, I realized that being born into a family doesn't mean there's love and attachment and respect for one another. But this? This makes me believe it's something you can build. No way I'm telling Lottie that right now though. She'd bolt.

We say our goodbyes and head toward the exit.

Wren sidles up between us. "Did you know Kayla lived in Omaha?" Wren looks between us as though Omaha is as impressive as New York City.

"That's cool." Lottie opens the back door of her SUV, and

Wren climbs in, cotton candy still in hand. Lottie shuts the door and glances at me. "Need me to open your door?"

"Nah, I'll get this one myself. But you're cutting it close. Drop Wren off, and I'll find my own way home from the ranch."

"No way." She shakes her head and gets in the vehicle.

She's just started the car when her phone rings with Bennett's name lighting up the screen. She presses the button to take the call over Bluetooth.

"Say hi to Daddy," Lottie says, looking through the rearview mirror at Wren.

"Daddy! I saw Kayla. Can I have her over for a sleepover?"

"We'll talk about it." Bennett's voice is clipped. "Lottie."

"We're leaving now. I just have to drop off Brooks first."

She puts the car in drive. There's a line of traffic crawling away from the fair. It won't take more than twenty minutes, but it's enough to make her even later.

"I told you ten because we have something tomorrow. Zeke and Megan are coming."

"Grandma and Grandpa! Yay!"

I glance over my shoulder to see Wren all smiles, kicking her feet back and forth.

Kristie's parents. They live outside of Omaha by Kristie's sister.

"Okay, we're coming," Lottie says.

"We'll drop Wren off first," I add.

"I got cotton candy," Wren announces, completely unaware she's outing her sugar high.

"Great." Bennett's tone doesn't improve.

"On our way." Lottie ends the call and glances at me. "I'll drop her off and then you. You are my date, after all."

"You guys are on a date?" Wren asks from the back seat. "I don't think I'm supposed to be on the date with you."

I grin at her through the rearview. "We wouldn't have had nearly as much fun without you."

"Yeah, you wouldn't. Thanks again for taking me."

I face forward as Lottie weaves through the traffic.

"So, do you want to tell me about Greg Miller?" she asks.

I figured that was coming, but I don't really have an answer. "Nothing to tell. Their alarm went off. I had to go check it out." I shrug. "He seems like a good guy."

"They have an alarm?"

I laugh. "Might be the only ones in town with one. I guess the 'being from Omaha' thing made them do it."

"Why is he running for mayor?"

"I have no idea. I didn't ask about his campaign. I prefer people not knowing who I am."

She turns the SUV toward Willowbrook. "Speaking of your parents... what did they say?"

I glance back at Wren. She's already asleep, her cotton candy still in her hand, tipping toward the floor of the car. I reach back and take it, stalling. I don't want to tell Lottie what my parents really said about her.

"That bad, huh?" She frowns.

Damn it. I waited too long to answer. "No. Just classic them."

"Afraid I'm trying to ruin their lives by marrying one of their sons again?"

The hurt in her voice just about kills me. Yeah, that decides it. I'm not telling her. Not yet anyway.

"I don't care what they think."

The road stretches ahead of us, quiet and dark. Wren's out cold in the back seat, and for once it's just Lottie and me—and the silence between us.

"Please don't keep things from me," she says. "The last thing I want is to be cornered by your mom and her passive-aggressive comments while she plays fake nice in town. I'm a big girl, Brooks. You don't have to be my bodyguard."

But I want to. I want to protect her from any more pain, especially the kind my family can deliver.

"They're not happy. They want us divorced or annulled."

"Did you tell them they're not the only ones?"

I whip my head in her direction. "It's none of their business. This is between you and me."

"That's the thing—it's not. The second that picture got passed around, it wasn't just between us anymore. This town has opinions. They think I'm hopping from one brother's bed to the next."

I scowl at her. "More than a decade later?"

"Time doesn't matter here, you know that. Once the picture is painted of you, there's no way to paint a new version over it. I'm the slut. I'm the one they'll always think the worst of."

We're closing in on Plain Daisy Ranch, and I don't want this conversation to be cut short because we're dropping Wren off.

"I wish..." I trail off, shaking my head. She's shut herself off again. I can feel it. The ease from earlier, the connection, is gone.

Lottie pulls into the ranch and winds around the drive near the lake. She parks in front of the guys' house. I climb out, unbuckle Wren, and carry her to the porch.

Bennett steps out of the house and takes her from my arms.

"Sorry," Lottie says softly.

"I love it when you bring my kid home dirty and sticky past her bedtime," Bennett says dryly.

Lottie cringes. "We lost track—"

"Did you have fun?" he asks, eyes flicking more to me than to her.

"We did," I say.

He nods. "Good. Have a good night. Thanks for taking her."

I open the screen door for him. "Tell Zeke and Megan hello tomorrow."

"I will. And make sure your date drives you home. Don't feel obligated to kiss her good night just because she paid for your ride tickets." He chuckles, then kicks the front door shut behind him.

"I complain about your family, but mine's no better," Lottie mutters on her way back to the vehicle.

I jog down the steps. "They're wildly different. And just so you know, you're not getting a good night kiss anyway. So don't try anything funny when you walk me to my porch."

Her laughter is unguarded, ringing out into the quiet night.

I'll wait on that good night kiss as long as she keeps laughing when it's just the two of us.

Chapter Nineteen

LOTTIE

After Friday night, I don't see Brooks for the rest of the weekend. There's no morning smirk, no slow swagger as he approaches, no door chime announcing his arrival. It was just quiet. Not that I missed him. I was absolutely, totally fine. Like, throw me a divorce party, I'm thrilled.

I saw him in his squad car down on Route Twelve late Saturday night, so I know he was working. I didn't give him an ounce of my attention. Just breezed on by as if I didn't want to pull my car over and ask him what game he's playing.

Since it's Monday, I mentally prepare for him to come in. I brew the coffee, the arabica one I know he likes best. But at nine o'clock, I change the closed sign to open, and the coffee I made for him sits cold on the counter. I tell myself it's a good thing. A sign. An omen. The Vegas gods have finally granted me a clean break. Maybe the date on Friday night turned him off, and he'll show up with the annulment papers one day this week. I'll sign them so fast I'll get a paper cut. It would be a good thing.

"So sorry I'm late." Saylor rushes in, half running to the

backroom. She's newer, a recent hire after returning to our small town.

I continue straightening out the cheeses, hoping most of them sell before the rush for our goat cheese that's supposed to arrive on Wednesday. That stuff has a cult-like following, I swear.

Saylor is already putting on her apron in the back when I start putting Jensen's famous chicken salad into smaller containers.

"I'm sorry again. I woke up late."

"It's okay. It's not like there's a line outside." I smile to let her know I'm honestly fine with it. "Hopefully there's a good story as to why you woke up late."

She looks confused.

"Like there was a warm body in your bed."

She blushes.

"I'm right?" My voice lifts with surprise. "Who?"

She's already shaking her head before I finish asking. "No one really... I mean..."

The bell above the door rings, and we both laugh.

"Your savior just arrived." I wink at her.

Her smile is nice to see as she disappears into the store-front. She's been a little depressed recently. Coming home after what this town deems a failure is the hardest first step to take. I don't know a lot about her backstory, but honestly, I get it. This town doesn't make it easy to return, let alone lick your wounds.

I overhear her welcome whoever it is to The Harvest Depot. Then I hear the voice. *His* voice. And every nerve ending in my body betrays me. It's as if it wants to drop the ice cream scoop in the bucket of chicken salad and run to Brooks like he just stepped off a Navy ship after months away.

Oh no. Nope. This is not happening. Get a grip, Lottie.

Saylor dips her head into the small cutout window we pass sandwiches through during our lunch rush. "Someone's here to see you." She lifts the coffee mug. "He'd like a fresh cup of coffee."

I bet he would.

Saylor is a smart woman and probably already knows about the Vegas wedding and that Brooks is technically my husband, but she's too nice to ask me directly. I should probably grant her the same favor and let the subject of who rocked her world last night go.

"I'll be right out." I finish the container of chicken salad. Slower than necessary, I fill the plastic containers, weigh them, and slap on the sticker. Just so he knows I'm not at his beck and call.

With my arms full of chicken salad to put in the fridge area, I walk through the doorway, purposely not granting him my attention.

"Black coffee with a little bit of cream and one sugar," I tell Saylor.

"Pawning my coffee off on someone else?"

There he is. Smug in his sheriff's uniform, approaching me as though he already knows the effect he has on me. I need to get it together and fast.

"Saylor makes a great coffee, and it's not like your order is complicated." I distract myself, acting as if I'm way too busy to talk to him. I start arranging the chicken salads, shifting other things around. Anything to seem cool and composed.

Then I smell him. The scent of whatever soap he uses mixed with his natural scent.

"I'm sorry I wasn't here earlier."

I still for a split second before I recover, but I don't look at him. "You don't need to apologize."

"You're obviously upset."

I make the mistake of looking up at Brooks, and it's a fatal error on my part. His smile emerges, and a sudden urge to grab him and take him into the backroom washes over me. Thankfully, my senses return when the door chimes again.

"I told you to stay in the squad car," Brooks says.

I turn away from the man who is starting to star in my masturbation reels and find Deputy Moore with his hands in his pockets and his attention on Saylor.

"You never got my coffee order." He nods to Saylor in greeting.

"You don't get a coffee. You were late this morning." Brooks leans down and whispers in my ear, "The reason I wasn't here this morning, and my coffee is now cold."

I straighten up and blink between Saylor and Deputy Moore, seeing now who the warm body in Saylor's bed was last night. He can't stop staring at her, and she's doing everything to dodge his attention, but her cheeks only grow rosier with every second that passes.

"What would you like, Deputy Moore? I'm happy to make you a coffee. Doesn't seem like good work conditions if this one won't let you have any caffeine. You might want to look for another station." I leave Brooks at the fridge case and round the back counter.

"You'll make his coffee, but not mine?" Brooks doesn't take long before he's at the counter.

"I made your coffee." I slide the cold coffee closer to him on the counter. "It's not my fault you weren't here to accept it."

"Moore," Brooks growls.

Deputy Moore steps up shoulder to shoulder with Brooks, holding up both hands. "Lottie, it was my fault. We're riding over to the county courthouse this morning, and I was late. I'm the reason he couldn't be here."

I look at Saylor, and her face is bright red, her eyes focused on anything but Deputy Moore. I won't be a jerk and ask him why he was late. Not when the blush on her face gives them away.

"Thank you, Deputy Moore." I turn away to make the coffee.

"Go wait in the squad car," Brooks says. "Why don't you walk him out, Saylor?"

I whirl around. "Saylor isn't your employee."

Saylor stops midway across the store, Deputy Moore already holding the door open for her to join him outside.

"I need to talk to you in private," Brooks says through clenched teeth, keeping his voice low.

I glower at him for a second, and his face softens into an expression of *please don't shut me out.*

For whatever reason, I don't have it in me to fight him this morning. "Could you give us five minutes, Saylor?"

She nods and practically runs to the door.

I lean back against the counter, arms crossed, locking down every frazzled emotion. "What do you want?"

He doesn't stay on his side of the counter.

Of course he doesn't.

"Come on. I've come in on time every morning before you open, and the one day I'm late, you give me the cold shoulder?"

I don't mention how he didn't come Saturday either because if I say it out loud, I'm admitting that I noticed. That I cared. That I waited for him to show.

That somehow after one date, one date that *he* begged for, he's discovered I'm not worthy of that pedestal he put me up on.

Oh god, what are we doing? This entire marriage thing, bargaining for him to win me. It's messing with my head, and it's about time I get it together.

"It's fine. I don't care."

"I don't believe you."

I swivel around and make his coffee. "I'm just giving you a hard time. Jeez, I'll make you a new coffee."

I pull out the creamer from the small fridge below the counter, and my ass bumps into his crotch. "Space please," I toss over my shoulder.

His hands fall to the counter on either side of my hips, caging me in. "Please don't do that."

My hands freeze after pouring the coffee into the cup. "I'm not doing anything."

"It's okay to care, Lottie. I'm sorry. Friday night, I got called out of bed in the middle of the night, and I was at the station early for a good part of the day, sorting some shit out. Sunday you're not open—"

"You don't have to tell me this. I'm not—"

"You are," he interrupts. "You are my *wife*. I know it's only on paper right now, but I'm trying to be your husband off paper, Lottie. Thought I'd made that obvious. So, I'm sorry. I should've told you we were running late. But if it makes you feel better, Moore will get my cold shoulder all day for fucking up our morning."

Our. My heart shouldn't react to that word. But it does. Oh god, it really, really does.

His strong chest rests along my back, and he nuzzles into my neck. My eyes close of their own accord.

"Are you free Friday?" he whispers, and goose bumps explode across my back. "It's my turn to plan a date."

I nod.

"Good. I'll pick you up at six. Casual dress." And then he leans in as if I'm his favorite scent and inhales. "I'll see you tomorrow morning, Lottie."

His hand slides between my arm and waist, picking up his coffee, then he's gone.

I wait for the bell to chime to announce that he's left before I release a breath.

I'm in so much fucking trouble because I think I'm falling for Brooks Watson.

Chapter Twenty

LOTTIE

As soon as I flip the closed sign over at The Harvest Depot, I drive my UTV straight to the horse stables. All day long, I've only thought of Brooks. The way his breath ghosted across my skin, the way he caged me against the counter like I was his and he didn't want to let go of me.

I want to be your husband off paper.

That sentence has been looping in my head like a mantra. And every time it replays, my body reacts. My heart flutters, my skin flushes, my chest aches like I'm starved for something I've never allowed myself to want. You'd think I was the lead in some over-the-top Valentine's Day commercial. It's ridiculous.

I need to get a grip.

Normally, when my head's a storm, I retreat to my she-shed. It's my space to breathe, to think, to unravel my anger or sadness. But tonight, it's not anger or sadness I'm dealing with. When I'm emotionally twisted like I am now, I turn to horseback riding to gain some clarity.

What are these feelings stirring inside of me? What do they mean, and why are they so scary?

"You riding?" Nash asks as he steps out of the stall, shutting the door behind him. He's my cousin Jenson's best friend and the horse trainer on the ranch.

I head toward the stalls, and my horse peeks out like she heard me coming before I even said a word. "I'm taking Echo for a little ride."

He runs a hand through his dirty-blond hair. "It's getting late." He hesitates, shifting his weight, sighing like he wants to stop me but knows I won't listen.

"You don't have to take me," I say gently. "I do this all the time."

"But..."

Nash is trouble, mostly. Can't settle down, spends weekends chasing an adrenaline rush on the rodeo circuit. But beneath the swagger, he's a solid guy who cares for my extended family as much as we do him.

"Don't worry about me. I'm fine. Honestly, head home." I enter Echo's stall, my hand trailing down her dark, silken coat.

"Lottie," he says, still clearly torn about letting me ride off alone.

"I'll use the trail and be back before dark. Promise." He exhales a big, reluctant breath, his baby blues that make women fall for him narrowing in concern.

"Go," I say, forcing a small smile.

He shakes his head. "Does Brooks know you're here?"

I frown. "Why would he?"

He chuckles. "I don't know? Because he's your husband, from what I hear."

"It was a Vegas marriage. Are those even real?"

I push down the swirl of new, unwanted feelings rising up whenever someone says his name. Denial is easier than admitting my drunk self might've known something my sober self still won't say out loud. That I... might actually like Brooks.

"I'm pretty sure they are." Nash chuckles.

I step out of the stable and grab my saddle.

"You're really going?"

"I said I was."

He frowns. "I'd hoped you'd change your mind."

"Nash." I walk back in with Echo and start saddling her up. "I'm older than you last time I checked. I grew up on this ranch. I can ride by myself and return safely. You don't need to babysit me."

"The sheriff might think different."

I throw my hands up. "I'm so done with everyone telling me what I can and cannot do. Even if my marriage to Brooks Watson was real, he wouldn't get to tell me when I can or cannot ride."

I take the reins and guide Echo out of the stall. "Now out of my way."

Once I reach the opening of the stable, I climb onto Echo and trot her out onto the trail that winds through our property toward Sadie's, following the creek. Nash doesn't say another word, and I'm grateful for the silence.

The sun is hanging low, glowing and stretching its golden rays across the land. How did I ever think I could live anywhere else? If I had moved to the city, where would I go when my head is this scrambled? A crowded park, boxed in by concrete buildings?

"Oh, Echo," I murmur, running my hand down her neck. "I think I've gotten myself in some trouble."

She doesn't answer, of course, just walks on like she always does, calm and steady—exactly the reason I came here tonight.

"How could I ever be with Brooks?" I whisper into the breeze. "He's Holden's brother. The town... my past... it's all a tangled mess, but I can't stop thinking about him. And why does it bother me so much that he never showed his face the whole weekend? The panic I felt this morning when he was late flared way hotter than I'm comfortable with. These are all very bad signs." I laugh bitterly. "I mean, it was a Vegas drunk marriage."

Echo snorts as though she understands.

"I know. It's not real. Brooks wasn't in his right mind when he agreed to marry me. God knows how we went from a bar to a chapel. He's not a rash guy. There's no way it was his idea, but can you imagine if it was mine?"

Echo's hooves swish through the tall grass. The creek's low murmur lets her know we're close.

I slow our pace and dismount, tying Echo to a tree with enough slack for her to graze. Then I step to the creek's edge and watch the sun sink lower, smearing the sky with shades of amber and honey.

There are so many questions rattling around in my head, and I can't seem to sort through them. Brooks should be in the "do not touch" box—but somehow, he slipped into the "husband" one. How did that happen?

I mean, I know how it happened. I'm not immune to his charm despite what I try to present. I've seen all the good qualities he has. But now there are real, rising feelings that whisper maybe he deserves a spot in the "maybe" box. At the very least, the "dating" one.

I don't know how long I've been standing at the creek's edge. The sun is half gone now, casting a warm buttercream haze over everything.

This wasn't the kind of clarity I expected to find tonight. But one thing is clear—something between Brooks and me has shifted. That flirtation, the teasing we tossed at one another for years, it's turned into something with... weight. And I'm not the kind of person who can ignore that.

Echo whines softly. I glance toward the sound and catch a shadow lengthening behind me.

Brooks.

He's riding Gunner. My whole body tenses.

Fucking Nash.

I pretend to admire the stream, but every crunch of his boots, every rush of his horse's breath, sends those stupid butterflies into a frenzy. God, this is worse than I thought.

"Hey." His voice is deep and smooth like the creek in front of me and laced with that drawl that weakens my knees.

"Did Nash call you?" I cross my arms because the spring air has turned cool as the sun dips further.

A heavy coat settles across my shoulders. The smell of his soap lingers around me, and I force myself not to inhale any deeper.

"He might've passed me and mumbled something, but I was taking Gunner out anyway." He stands beside me, too close for me to keep pretending nothing's happening here.

"Why don't you keep Gunner with you?"

He tilts his head toward the horses. I follow his gaze. Sure enough, Echo and Gunner are brushing noses.

"He'd be lonely."

"I'm sure he'd manage."

"I think Echo might miss him."

"That's presumptuous." I lift my chin.

He raises an eyebrow and looks at the horses, clearly enjoying each other. "I don't think so."

"I don't need your coat." I reach up to shrug it off, but his hand covers mine, gently keeping it in place.

"Humor me?"

"Why?"

He sighs and shoves his hands into his jean pockets. He's still in his sheriff shirt though. Clearly, not dressed to ride tonight.

"Because you're cold, and I'm giving you my jacket to be nice. Just say thank you and leave it on."

There's a frustrated edge to his voice that's not normally present.

"Thank you," I say in a soft voice.

His brows lift, surprised. "Really?"

"You're right. I'm just... bad day."

"You too, huh?" He bends down and grabs a few small rocks, handing one to me. "If you hit the boulder over there, you don't have to tell me about it."

"What if I just don't tell you anyway?"

"What fun is that?" He winks.

I toss the rock because of course I'm going to hit it. The breeze kicks up, and the rock drops short of the boulder, landing with a quiet plop in the water.

"Two out of three?"

He squints, shakes his head. "Afraid not. What happened?"

I shrug. "I don't know how to word it. It's not one thing, but..."

"Us?" he asks, like it's gnawing at him.

I lift a shoulder. "Yeah. I mean, I wish I knew what we were thinking in Vegas. What made us decide to go to the chapel?"

"Me too. For a few reasons. Like knowing what happened when we got back to the hotel room."

"Brooks!" I screech.

He chuckles. "You can't blame me. I've wanted you for a long time, Lottie."

There it is again. Heat rolling through me in waves.

"Well, I guess that and the answer to why we decided to marry one another is locked in our drunken subconscious forever. Sorry to disappoint."

He nods. "I shouldn't pressure you into going on the dates."

I should agree with him and tell him he's right. Say I want to end our agreement so we can carry on with our separate lives, but I don't. Maybe three more dates is a perfect way for me to test these feelings for him.

"Why'd you come here?" I ask.

"Honestly?"

I nod.

"You."

"Were you really going to ride Gunner tonight?"

He shakes his head.

"I was at Ben's. Nash came over to watch the Colts game. He mentioned he saw you at the stables and..." He shrugs, suddenly looking unsure. Like he's worried about admitting he came just for me.

"Thank you." I look up at the sky, the last bit of sun painting it in streaks of blush and gold.

We don't speak, but our gazes meet, the silence between us soft and silent. Comfortable.

"Come on. Let's ride into the sunset," I say, walking toward Echo and Gunner.

"Careful of your words there," Brooks says, stopping beside me. "Want some help?"

I lift my foot into the stirrup and climb onto Echo. "Looking for an excuse to touch my ass, Sheriff?"

He mounts Gunner with the ease of a damn cowboy, smooth and sexy, and there goes another zing straight between my thighs.

"Always."

He nudges Gunner forward, and Echo falls into step beside them. The two of us ride side by side toward the water-color-painted sky.

I have no idea what we're doing, but one thing is for sure. I'm not ready for it to be done yet.

Chapter Twenty-One

BROOKS

I'm in my barn Thursday night after my shift, working on the truck for my client. My thoughts haven't stopped focusing on Lottie since Monday. As much as I'm still ready to take Moore to the ground for making her upset, there's a twisted part of me that's thankful. Because that look on her face? That flinch like she missed me? It cracked her armor. Showed me I'm right to keep pushing for these damn dates. She's not uninterested—she's scared. Scared to start something new. Scared to trust me with her heart.

A car crunches down the gravel path and stops in front of the house. Mack perks up, ears stiff, but doesn't move. The woman getting out isn't someone he cares to greet. Which says a hell of a lot. Mack loves everybody.

She stands, scanning the property, eyes locking on me in the barn doorway. I go back to the truck, tightening a bolt I've already torqued twice. Her footsteps get louder, and just like that, whatever peace I'd carved out tonight evaporates.

My chest tightens. I brace myself. Bet my dad sent her here on some mission to knock some sense into me.

"You're not answering my calls," my mom says, walking in as if this is her property and sitting down at my workbench.

"Your voicemails mentioned why you're calling. I'm not interested in hearing your opinion on my marriage."

She scoffs. "Please, you're not *really* married to her."

"I am." I wipe my hands on a rag. "Want to see the marriage license?"

"This town talks."

And there it is.

I grab another wrench from the set, wishing she'd leave me the hell alone. "Just say what you came here to say."

"You're the town fool."

I shove the wrench back into the drawer harder than necessary, trying not to blow. My parents preach respect but never model it. I was always the disappointment. The loud one. The bruised-knuckle kid brought home in the same kind of squad car I drive now. Always getting the speech about character, the family name, why I couldn't be more like my brother.

"I see you're upset. I didn't come here to upset you. But someone needs to tell you that this is a fool's errand. She's not going to soften toward you. I heard about the deal and the dates. Why the hell are you trying this hard for *that* girl?"

Her voice has changed since my dad became mayor. She wasn't always like this. She used to be *Mom*. The one who wrapped me in hugs after my father's explosions, whispering to Holden and me that we weren't screwups. She took the worst of his cruelty and still found a way to love us. But now? Now she's like him and somehow that feels worse. He's always been who he is, but once upon a time, my mom was a good woman.

I stay quiet. Not because I don't have something to say, but because I might say something I can't take back. She doesn't deserve my restraint, but I give it anyway. I know what weaponized words feel like. I watched my dad sharpen them into knives and throw them at us, not caring where they landed and how badly they hurt. I will never become him.

"I've seen the way you look at her. Since the first time Holden brought her home."

"She wasn't a stranger. She's Ben's cousin. She's lived in this town her whole damn life. Same as us."

She claps her hands for Mack to come to her. He doesn't budge. Good boy. "You know what I mean," she presses. "Your father pitted you and Holden against each other your entire lives, and you see her as some kind of prize—"

"Fucking hell, Mom." I slam my fist onto the top of the truck. That's it. I'm done playing nice.

"Brooks," she snaps, sharp and stern, as if I'm thirteen again.

I don't flinch. "I love her, and you know it. You always have. So stop making excuses as if she's to blame for what Holden did."

She leans back, arms crossed, eyes narrowed. Her silence isn't thoughtful but rather judgmental. "Your father... the election—"

"I don't give one fuck about either of those things."

"That was clear when you were seen talking to Greg Miller."

There it is. Guess I was wrong. This isn't about Lottie. This is about appearances.

"It doesn't look good," she says. "You know that."

"I was at the fair. Wren knows his daughter. That's it."

She tilts her head, smirking as though she knows better. "Did you enjoy playing family? Breaking your father's heart?"

"Spare me."

"I forbid you to do this."

"You *forbid* me?" I laugh, bitter and cold. "I'm thirty-four, in case you forgot. I don't answer to you."

I stalk over to the fridge, pull out a bottle, and crack open a beer.

"You're ruining our image. First you marry the girl who ruined Holden—"

"*Ruined Holden?* Jesus Christ, Mom. *He* left *her* at the altar." I toss the bottle cap in the trash. "He's living his perfect life far away, like he always wanted. If anything, he's the one who got exactly what he wanted."

"He would've come back here if it wasn't for her. But she walks around like he shattered her whole damn life, trying to make everyone feel sorry for her. It's pathetic. Why would you want someone that weak?"

I slam the bottle down so hard beer bursts out the top. Mack jolts up and saunters outside.

"Get out. You're not welcome here." I point out of the barn toward where her car is parked.

"Surely—"

"No, Mom. Out. Lottie is my wife. And until you respect that, you're not a part of my life."

She rises slowly, smoothing her blouse as though she's deciding to leave, and I'm not throwing her out. "Do I need to remind you that I'm your mother?"

"And I'll show you respect the day you show it to me. And to *her*. Until then, don't bother coming around."

She doesn't argue. She just walks away, probably too furious to speak. That makes two of us.

Once she's out of sight, I grab my beer and down the rest of it before pitching the bottle in the recycling bin. Mack creeps back in and curls up at my feet.

I pull my phone from my back pocket and scroll down to Lottie's name, looking for some type of reassurance I'm not the fool everyone is saying I am.

Still good for six tomorrow?

Yep. Ready to cross off date two.

I drop the phone on the table. Not what I was looking for. My phone vibrates, and I pick it back up.

No smart-ass comment back? You're disappointing me, Sheriff.

A small grin cracks my face. God, I needed that. If she was really just checking off boxes, she wouldn't care if I answered.

Do you have time for a walk?

Tonight?

God, I'm putting myself out there, but I press Send anyway.

Yeah.

Does it count as a date?

My mom just left.

The three dots pop up. Disappear. Pop up again.

I'll come to you.

And thre's my proof.

Chapter Twenty-Two

BROOKS

I'm on the front porch with a beer and Mack at my side when Lottie pulls down my drive. She parks and climbs out, Mack climbing to his feet and bolting right over to her. He takes off as though she belongs to him. Hell, we both do.

She's wearing jeans and a Plain Daisy Ranch sweatshirt, her hair thrown into a messy bun and not a stitch of makeup on.

Lottie's beautiful, and seeing her so effortless only makes me desperate for more. She lightens something heavy inside me.

"Hi, Mack." She crouches and, as always, nuzzles her head into Mack's neck, her hands petting him all over. "Sorry about your mean visitor today." Mack eats up the attention, happy to take whatever she'll give.

"Leave Mommy alone," I say. The joke tastes sour in my mouth and is my way to deflect. No one understands my family more than Lottie.

She shakes her head and walks up to the porch, sitting next to me and eyeing my beer. "You have one for me too?"

I pull one out from my side, twist off the cap, and hand it

to her. She takes a sip and sits just like me with her legs spread, forearms on her knees, a beer bottle dangling from her fingertips.

"How bad was it?" she asks.

"I kicked her out."

She blows out a breath. "I'm sorry."

Mack walks up the steps, stops, and looks at both of us, but goes to Lottie's side and flops next to her. Not surprising.

"You have nothing to be sorry for."

She hits her shoulder to mine. "We both know that's not true."

We sit in silence for a few minutes. It was selfish, dragging her into this. But I'm tired of pretending I'm fine. My head is a mess about how I live in this town I love with my parents always breathing down my neck. At some point, I probably need to sever ties to really live without being in their oppressive shadow. I'm either going to burn the bridge or let it rot beneath me.

She rocks her shoulder against mine again. "I thought you promised me a walk?"

I rise to my feet and hold out my hand to her. "You're right. Care for a tour of my property?"

She slides her hand in mine, and Mack is quick to get to his feet, joining us as we descend the steps.

We fall in line, walking between my house and the barn, on a path worn into the grass. We head through the nestle of trees and make our way to the small pond, starting on the path around it. Lottie doesn't try to fill the silence, and I appreciate her for it.

We walk long enough for my nerves to start crawling. Long enough for the guilt to push against my ribs. If I really want her, then I need to show her that she can open up to me about her trauma by showing her my own wounds.

"Did Holden ever tell you about our dad?" I ask.

I don't miss her quick intake of breath, but Holden is my brother, and we can't ignore the fact that once upon a time, she thought he was her forever.

"He said he could be difficult. Had high expectations." She bends to the side and her fingers run down Mack's back.

"My dad would go from zero to one hundred without any warning. And when he got upset, like really mad, he'd rage and say the worst things you can think of. Make you feel about a foot tall because he always knew exactly where the scars were, where to hit so it would hurt the most. It made you feel like you were worthless."

"I know." Her voice hitches, and I instantly grow antsy. For what he might've done to her. What if I wasn't there, and he went after her like he used to go after Holden and me?

"Has he... did he—"

She shakes her head. "No. I just never got a welcoming feeling from him or your mom. They didn't ever seem to like me. Maybe they had dreams of who Holden would marry, and I wasn't her."

I swallow down my irritation with my parents. "I knew they didn't make it easy on you, but they wouldn't make it easy on anyone he brought home, believe me."

We hit the edge of my small dock, where my fishing boat and kayak rest. Lottie sits at the edge, and I sit next to her. Mack rests along our backs like a lower back pillow.

"I'm sure they would love someone from his world now," she says.

Holden never comes up in any conversation with anyone in town, but to my parents, he's seen as the mortal enemy by everyone. He scorned Lottie, and being a part of the extended Noughton family tree and with Plain Daisy Ranch looked upon so highly in Willowbrook, he was cast as the villain. There are a few who believe she wasn't enough for him, but the truth is that he wasn't enough for her.

"They don't even understand his world now." The sun is setting, and the sky is lit up in sherbert shades of orange and yellow. "If you'd rather not talk about him—"

She finishes her beer and sets it next to her on the deck. "I think I spend too much time trying *not* to talk about him. It doesn't really affect me. I'm proud of myself that I've made so much progress. It's hard to explain, but he was a major part of my life for a chunk of time, and everyone dodges his name like a bullet. Honestly, I've been over him for a long time."

I swallow hard, because I've needed to hear that for so long —but part of me worried it wouldn't be the case. That some piece of her was still attached to him.

"I just wish people would stop treating me like I'm about to break at the mention of his name."

"Holden. Holden. Holden."

She laughs and knocks her shoulder with mine.

"Look, you're still in one piece."

"That I am." She smiles, and fuck, she's so beautiful. How did I ever let Holden swoop in and take her like a hawk searching for prey?

Another bout of silence rolls over us.

She says my name.

I finish my beer and place it next to me. "Yeah?"

"You're a really good man."

I turn to her, and my chest loosens at her compliment. I needed to hear it after kicking my mom off my property.

"Don't look so surprised, you know you are. You're nothing like your family, and I want you to know that the reason I'm so hesitant has nothing to do with them. If anything, I feel bad for you."

"Shit, Lottie, don't feel bad for me."

She turns to me, propping one leg up and leaving the other dangling off the dock. "I don't want to play games, so I'm just going to tell you."

146

"What?"

Her hands cradle in her lap, and she takes a deep breath before meeting my gaze. "I like you."

I'm so unprepared, her confession hits me like a sucker punch.

"Oh stop it. You knew I did." She rolls her eyes playfully.

"You hide it well, but yeah, I had a suspicion. I wouldn't force someone to be married to me if I didn't think the feelings weren't reciprocated."

"There's more though—"

But I don't want to hear her list all the reasons she doesn't think this can work. So I lean in and finally take her mouth. Not gently or cautiously, but the way I've been dying to do for years. There's nothing else I want from her in this moment. No more words, no more confessions. I'll handle all that later. Whatever's shattered in her, I'll put it back together piece by piece. I'll stitch her heart back together so tightly, she'll never know it was broken.

Her arms wind around my neck, and the second my tongue brushes her lips, she opens for me.

Somewhere around us, the beer bottles clink and fall with a plunk into the lake. Mack groans as he shifts away. But I barely register it. All I know is the way she clutches me tighter, heat radiating off her as I lift her, mouth never leaving hers, and settle her onto my lap.

She straddles me, her fingers raking through my hair, pushing my hat somewhere behind us. I groan against her mouth when she drags her nails against my scalp, sweet and a tad possessive.

Her body rocks forward, pressing against me, and the contact pulls a curse from deep in my chest. Her core drags along the hard line of me, slow and maybe intentional, because she's not shy about her grinding along my hard length.

I pull back just enough to breathe. Our foreheads are pressed together, and her lips are still parted, swollen and red.

"You have no idea how long I've wanted this," I whisper, voice wrecked. "You. Right here with me."

She bites her bottom lip, and I nearly lose it. "Then stop talking," she whispers.

So I do. God help me, I do.

I have no idea where this is going, but to hell if I'm asking for directions.

Chapter Twenty-Three

LOTTIE

I'm standing in front of my closet, trying to decide between two different shirts. A flowery one that says, "first date," and a low-cut one that says, "kiss me." A soft knock lands on my bedroom door.

Sadie peeks her head in. "Can I come in?"

"Sure. Where's Daisy?" I stare at the hangers as if I'm close to making a decision.

"She's downstairs. The girls are all over her. Heard you were going out with Brooks tonight, and I wanted to pop by and say how sorry I am."

She sits down on the edge of my bed, and I join her.

"You don't have to be sorry. You were right. I was being defensive and letting what happened with Holden keep me from the possibility of a future with Brooks."

Her hand falls to my leg. "I know it's hard. Especially since he's Holden's brother, but they couldn't be more different. I just want you to put yourself out there, but I was being pushy and nosy, and I have no idea what it must be like for you."

"It's been a decade, so…"

She chuckles but stops quickly.

"Sadie, you can laugh. It's okay."

I'm not mentally there yet, but allowing Brooks to kiss me felt really good. I've missed that kind of exhilaration.

"We kissed," I say, needing to tell someone, though I'm still worried how I'm going to feel if this goes south.

She squeals and then covers her mouth. "When? Tell me everything."

"On his dock."

"Love it." She claps her hands together.

I squeeze my eyes shut for a second. "I told him I like him."

She squeals again, tackling me to the bed, her arms so tight, she squeezes the breath right out of me.

"I'm so happy for you." She sits up and slaps my thigh. "Why didn't you call me?"

"It just happened last night. I'm still processing."

It's the truth. Every time I thought about that kiss today, butterflies tore through my stomach. The way his hands ran over my body, the moans that escaped from his throat, and his words that he'd been waiting for that moment for so long...

He asked to hold my hand as he walked me back to the house. The second-guessing didn't come until I was driving home and passed a Vote for Watson sign. That's when the weight of us hit me. Do I want to sign up for his parents' judgment for the rest of my life? Sure, Brooks is upset with them, but in the end, they're his family.

Then this morning, he walked into The Harvest Depot for coffee and smiled at me as if I'm the only thing that matters. His smile lit up the entire store, and he didn't break his stride until he had backed me into the wall and kissed me thoroughly before telling me he'd thought of me all night.

"Look at you. You're blushing."

Sadie's voice pulls me from my thoughts.

"It's scary," I confess.

She nods. "Anything worthwhile is. I can tell you not to worry, that Brooks isn't going to hurt you, at least not on purpose, but my words aren't going to convince you. Just keep moving forward. If you need to pause for a second and just live in the moment, do it, but keep pushing, Lottie. I know you'll be rewarded if you keep pushing yourself forward with Brooks."

I sigh and look out the window just in time to see his truck pulling down our drive. There's no ignoring the way my body lights up, every nerve ending humming with the want to run down the stairs and beg him to kiss me again.

"Oh, you have it bad. Did you sleep with him?" Sadie stands and walks over to my closet.

"No. I'm not ready for that."

She nods, going through my closet. "Understandable."

"I feel like there's more we need to discuss, you know? Both of us are going on attraction, I think."

She laughs and pulls out a blouse, tossing it to me. "No, you're not, but it's cute you think so."

I pull my T-shirt over my head and put on the blouse, then she throws me a pair of jeans.

"Sadie..."

She comes over and drops a pair of boots at my feet. "Listen. All of that will come. Don't get ahead of yourself. This is the best part of starting a new relationship—the butterflies, the exhilaration, the excitement. You don't want to miss it because you're stuck in your head. I know it's not easy, but push all the bullshit away and just enjoy yourself. You deserve to live in the moment. Forget everything except the two of you and how you feel when you're with him."

I stand and hug her. "Thank you."

"I'm still sorry for pushing you instead of listening and trying to understand."

I draw back then hug her again. "Stop apologizing. Thanks for putting up with my stubborn ass for so long."

She laughs, and I sit on the bed to put on my cowboy boots.

"Well, someone has to."

A knock lands on my door. Sadie opens it to find Romy holding Daisy out for her. "She's looking for something I don't have." Then she turns to look at me. "Brooks is here for you, Lottie."

"Sorry about that." Sadie takes Daisy. "Let's go home and get you fed, sweetie."

"You better hurry. Scarlett and Poppy are giving Brooks the third degree about his intentions with you." Romy laughs and scurries down the stairs.

I finish putting on my boots and grab my lip gloss, sliding it across my lips before heading down the stairs.

I'm within earshot when I hear Brooks say, "My intention is to fuck her against my wall tonight. And then take her on the kitchen table. After that, I plan on spreading her on my bed and feasting on her—"

"Jesus, Brooks!" Poppy shouts. "This was all fun and games until you ruined it."

"You asked. I'm just being truthful."

I finish walking down the stairs, shaking my head. Only Brooks sees me because Poppy and Scarlett's backs are facing me where they sit on the couch.

He rises from the chair, holding his cowboy hat against his chest. He's wearing jeans and a T-shirt again, but tonight he's got his cowboy hat with him. Although I didn't mind him in his backward baseball hat the other night, this look is sexier. As if he made an effort to look good for me.

Our shared smile probably reveals my secret—that I'm slowly becoming open to this thing between us. It's weird that we're married when I feel like we just started dating. But I push away that problem for another day.

"Hey." His voice is low and has a seductive drawl that makes my insides quiver.

"All done with the third degree, ladies?"

"Brooks ruined the fun." Poppy pouts, and I laugh, crossing the room, ignoring my sister, two cousins, and Sadie holding a whiny Daisy.

"Are you ready?" I ask.

"Ready and waiting."

He holds out his hand, and I ignore the comments coming from our audience. They sound shocked that I'm being so cordial to him. I accept his outstretched hand.

"Don't wait up, ladies. Remember my intentions. After seeing how hot Lottie looks, I'm adding a shower to the itinerary." Brooks chuckles, opening the front door for me.

"God, you're a buzzkill, Brooks." Scarlett huffs.

On the porch with the door shut behind us, Brooks tugs me into his arms.

"Hi," he says with an even more seductive tone than earlier. "Want me to stop?"

I shake my head, already drunk on him. This is coming so easy, and right now, in this moment, I don't want it to stop.

"Good." His lips land on mine, sweet and innocent. Nothing like the other night or this morning at the store. The kiss ends way too quickly for me. "Ready for your date?"

"Where are we going?"

"That's a surprise." He opens his truck door for me to climb in. "I'm happy to help you. You know, if you need it?"

"No ass touching yet, Sheriff."

He clucks his tongue. "I think I touched your ass last night."

I roll my eyes at him, and he shuts the door before walking around the front of his truck.

He climbs inside and leans over the center console. "Watch the eye rolls, Lottie. I've been waiting for the moment when I can kiss you every time you do it."

Instead of kissing my lips, he kisses my cheek.

"That was disappointing." I roll my eyes again.

His hand slides around my neck and drags me toward him, pressing his lips to mine, his tongue not asking for permission this time. The kiss lasts until he's sucked all the breath out of me, and my lips are swollen and tingling.

"Better?" he says, resting his forehead to mine.

"Definitely."

Brooks straightens and starts the truck, adjusting himself in his jeans. "We need to go before I drive you to my house and do all those things I mentioned to everyone in there." He nods toward the house.

God, I want to. I want to lose myself in him and pretend we're already there in this... whatever this is. But I'm not ready. Not yet. And since I can't seem to keep my mouth—or my body—from reaching for his, I need to say it now. Before I get lost in him completely.

"Brooks..." I say, and his hand stalls on the gearshift. "I'm not ready yet, and I'm not sure when I will be."

He takes my hand, his calluses warm along my palm. "I was just joking with your cousins. I don't want to rush into any of this. I have no expectations. You lead, okay? What I'm saying is, you tell me when you're ready for more."

"Thanks for understanding."

"Always, Lottie." He squeezes my hand, and I believe him. I do.

Am I stupid for believing him? I don't think so.

"Now, tell me where we're going."

He reverses the truck and chuckles. "I feel like we should test this thing, so I stupidly planned an escape room."

My head falls to the headrest, and I laugh. "Maybe I

should have you take me to your house first, because one of us might not make it out of the escape room."

"Nah, we got this."

We share a smile as he looks forward and presses on the gas. He has so much faith in us, and for now, I'll borrow it from him until I find my own.

Chapter Twenty-Four

LOTTIE

Brooks did me a solid by taking us three towns over for the escape room. Far enough that no one in Willowbrook will see us. Although by now, I'm sure the entire town of Willowbrook is getting blow-by-blow updates of our marriage that's more like dating.

I wait for him to open the passenger door, and I accept his hand to help me down. He reaches around me to get the handle of the building door, pulling it open for me to walk through first, then he puts his hand to rest on the small of my back, guiding us toward the front desk.

Every movement he makes, I clock. It stirs something warm inside me.

I tell my brain to shut off, but it doesn't listen.

"Our love couple," the young girl behind the desk says. She looks as though she's probably in high school, and she claps her hands as if we're the highlight of her year.

"We are."

She dramatically checks off his name on the sheet. "Got you. I've been waiting to do one of these. Thanks for filling out the questionnaire. Some men never do, and it makes it so much harder to get all the parts together. You know?"

"You had to fill out a questionnaire?" I ask him.

Brooks nods and gives me a sheepish look as if he's keeping something from me. My stomach twists.

"I feel as if I'm in for a surprise," I say, following the girl toward a room in the back.

"The best kind," she says, circling around on her heel and walking backward.

She stops abruptly before the door, and Brooks stumbles into me, his hands falling to my hips to steady me, and there goes that libido of mine running on its own racetrack. How am I going to hold off on sleeping with this man? Every part of him calls to every part of me.

"Here we are!" She claps her hands again and pulls the keychain bracelet off her wrist. She inserts the key and opens up a room that looks like a lab with hearts and cupids and a big sign that welcomes us to The Love Lock-In.

I glance over my shoulder, and Brooks chuckles. "I just want to note that I signed up for this before last night."

"You guys are going to have so much fun. Hardly anyone does these." Her head bobs right and left. "We did just open last month though." She leans in and cups her hand by her mouth. "I think they're scared."

"Well, our big bad sheriff isn't." I lightly elbow him in the stomach.

"You're a sheriff?" she asks, and from her facial expression, I'd say that doesn't impress her in the slightest. And that's putting it mildly.

"I am."

She hums, and her excitement wanes dramatically. "Okay, well, you each need to get into one of the soundproof rooms to start." She points at them. "As soon as I leave, you'll get your directions. If you need me, my name is Jennie. You have sixty minutes. Good luck."

Then she's gone, and Brooks raises his eyebrows at me, motioning for me to pick a soundproof room first.

"I guess she doesn't like sheriffs," he says with a laugh.

"She's young. Probably gotten some tickets, but at least for once I don't have to worry about someone ogling you."

He wraps his arms around my waist and pulls me into him. "My eyes are only on you."

I pat his chest and push back. "Stop your sweet talk and get into your booth."

Jennie gets on the speaker. "Go to your rooms, I'm starting." Her voice is flat.

This girl is about to let us drown in puzzles with zero hints. I can tell.

We both go to our booths that face one another, and she comes back on the speaker. "Cupid has kidnapped you both and brought you to the love lab. He wants to test if you're truly compatible. The only way to escape? Solve four love-themed puzzles that measure different dimensions of a relationship: communication, trust, memory, and passion. Go."

I stare at my bingo-style boxes with words inside of them, wondering what I need to do to figure this out.

Brooks's voice comes out of the radio hooked on the wall, and I jolt, picking up the small walkie talkie. "Did you read the directions?"

I press the small button. "No."

"We have to work to get our boards to match. Do you have images on yours?"

"No, I have words."

"Okay, I'll explain my image, and you find the word that matches. Ready?"

"I guess." My stomach knots. What if I screw this up?

What if I disappoint him when we can't make it past the first test?

Luckily, we get through that one pretty easily and are able to get free of our soundproof rooms once we each get a code from Jennie to unlock the lockbox with a key in it after we've matched our bingo cards.

"That was easy," Brooks says, glancing at the clock.

"A little too easy."

He shows me the instructions for the next part that he got from his booth that says, *Do you trust your partner?* One of us has to be blindfolded, and the other has to give directions to follow without leading us to the trap.

"I'll be the blindfolded one," I volunteer.

And of course, Brooks guides me perfectly, getting us our next instructions.

"Man, we're breezing through this," Brooks says, way too optimistic because I'm sure the next two are going to be tricky.

We somehow figure out that we have to turn off the lights, then we find a bunch of magnets on a wall lit up from the blacklight. We rush over to see pictures. But I'm not sure I understand what we're supposed to do with them.

A slap bracelet
A broken water balloon
An old school soda glass bottle
A hotel room key
Triple 7s on a slot machine
A ripped-up wedding invitation
Coffee cup

"I don't get this."

Brooks laughs. "They made me fill out a questionnaire that asked about my memories of us. Each of these symbolizes one of them. I'm wondering if we have to put them in chronological order."

"Good job! You're so smart." But then I stare at the pictures again, just as confused. "A slap bracelet?"

Brooks picks it up. "You slapped it on my wrist when I was in the third grade, and it made me bleed. You called me a baby when I got upset. It was the first time I wanted to kiss you."

"In the third grade?"

He chuckles. "Hey... don't judge."

I lift my hand dramatically, then pick up the triple 7s slot machine. "Easy. Vegas." I drop it down below the slap bracelet. "What could the soda glass bottle be?"

Brooks looks embarrassed, and it takes me a second before I realize what the memory is.

"You wrote down the spin-the-bottle kiss in the seventh grade?" I remember playing. There were so many of us cousins we'd always have to spin again to get someone we weren't related to.

"I cherish that memory."

I laugh. "It was a horrible kiss. You were all slobbery, and I was barely opening my mouth."

His forehead wrinkles. "It was my first kiss. Give me a break."

I cling to the picture as if it's actually the same bottle. "Uhh... I was your first kiss?"

He leans in to give me a chaste kiss. "And hopefully my last."

Jennie comes on the speaker. "No kissing until the end, this isn't a porno."

"Damn," Brooks whispers.

I lean forward and lower my voice. "You were mine too."

"Really?" he asks. "I thought for sure you'd already kissed a bunch of guys with how much you guys played. I remember when you asked me and Ben to join, I was so nervous I was going to be a bad kisser."

"You were." I laugh.

He pouts.

"But you're much better now."

Brooks grins. "You too."

I smile, a little stunned. "That's so weird. I had forgotten that until right now."

I place the picture of the soda glass bottle under the slap bracelet, but Brooks picks up the balloon image and sandwiches it between the two.

"What's the balloon?"

"Fourth of July. You had a white T-shirt on, and I purposely threw it at you. You got so mad you poured an entire bucket of water on me."

Jennie makes a sound over the speaker as if she's disgusted.

"I was a horny kid going through puberty, cut me some slack," Brooks says toward the ceiling.

"You're asking for a lot of slack, *Sheriff*," Jennie says.

"I feel like our lives have woven together so much, it's hard to remember the key moments." I stare at the board, overwhelmed by how tightly our histories have braided together over the years. "You did a great job, Brooks." Jennie clears her throat like she deserves the credit, but I ignore her, picking up the ripped wedding invitation. "Our wedding?"

He shakes his head. "It's torn."

I tilt my head, and he tips his head down, staring at the floor. Brooks avoiding eye contact tells me he's avoiding something, which isn't like him.

"I really didn't think this through," he says.

"You sure didn't," Jennie chimes in.

We both ignore her once again.

"What is it?" I slide closer to him and put my hand on his thigh.

"It's you marrying Holden, and me..."

"What?"

He says nothing, so I press again.

"Brooks?"

He swallows and looks at the speaker, taking the picture from me. "Let's just put this here, and I'll explain later."

I frown. "No, I want to know."

"Not here."

"Jennie, we're out. We admit defeat, please let us out," I say a little louder.

"Sorry, no can do. Rules."

I stand. "I believe we have the right to say we quit, and you let us out."

"Come on, this is fun." There's a definite whine to her voice.

"Not really," I say and look over to find Brooks putting the rest of the pictures in order. The torn invitation above the coffee cup, then the hotel key, and last the Vegas wedding.

"The coffee cup should go down after the triple 7s, shouldn't it?" I reach for it, but Brooks puts his hand on my arm, stopping me.

"No, it doesn't."

My shoulders sag. I look at him, heart squeezing at all the blanks in my memory. All the things he clearly never forgot, but I have.

"I swear, Jennie, you let us out or I'm telling your boss," I say, frustration clear in my voice.

"Jennie's not here," she says.

I widen my eyes at Brooks. "Can't you arrest her or threaten to at least?" I whisper, half-kidding. Really, I'm not.

"Not his jurisdiction," she sing-songs. I'd like to know what drugs she's taking up there because this is insane. "And I'm not harming you. You got that one right. Good job, Sheriff. One more and then a kiss, and you're done."

Brooks isn't arguing, and I'm pretty sure it's because he doesn't want to get out of here or explain any of this to me. So, I stop waiting. I go over to the lock, but we have to answer questions, getting over a ninety percent compatibility score. It's all "what would you rather do" questions. I throw them rapid fire at Brooks, pressing down the answers and matching mine even if I think different. Brooks tries to put down a different answer, but I press the same as me. Of course he prefers beaches over mountains. Does it really matter right now?

"Now solve the six-number lock, and you're there," Jennie encourages.

I flip off the camera.

"That wasn't nice," she says.

"It's not nice to lock us in here and not let us out."

"Put our wedding date in," Brooks says. It's the first helpful information he's offered since he went mute during the picture game.

I wind the numbers around and press on the big neon heart. A piece of paper comes out that says, *Seal it with a kiss.*

I put my hands on Brooks's cheeks, plaster my lips to his, and pull back. "Open the door, Jennie."

She laughs. "Good job, guys. Want me to come in there and explain how you could have gone faster?"

"No. Open the door."

The door clicks when it unlocks, and I don't wait for Jennie. I grab Brooks's hand and pull him down the hall.

"Hey, wait," Jennie says.

"Screw you, Jennie." I walk us out the door. At Brooks's truck, I swing him around, surprised he's letting me guide him like a ragdoll. "What are you keeping from me?"

He stares at me, and for a moment, I don't think he's going to tell me. He looks tortured, his eyes filled with uncertainty and longing. "I love you, Lottie. I always have."

Whoosh.

The ground drops out from under me. My heart leaps into my throat and every sarcastic comeback that wants to launch out locks in my throat. But instead, I wait for him to explain further, trying to keep my feet planted on the ground.

Chapter Twenty-Five

BROOKS

"Will you come back to my house?" I'm not going to put my heart on the line while standing in the parking lot of a strip mall after we were basically held hostage by a teenager.

But Lottie isn't a patient person. She pushes when she wants answers. And one day, yeah, it might drive me insane. But I wouldn't change that part of her for anything. It just means right now, I need to be ready for her to push back.

"Okay," she says simply.

Surprise and relief hit me. I've bought myself a little time to figure out how to say all this without scaring her off.

I open the passenger side door, and she climbs up, buckling her seat belt.

Once we're on the road back to my house, I keep the radio louder than normal because I worry that if we start talking, I'll spill it all and freak her out so badly she'll ask me to drive her home.

But as we get closer to my place, she broaches the subject of the weather and the softball season starting. We both complain about Walker Matthews and the Wild Bull Ranch team. How they're always competing with Plain Daisy Ranch and how one day I might be arresting Scarlett on murder charges if things don't change.

Finally, we pull into my drive, and I turn off my truck.

Every step toward the house feels like walking into a storm made from my own emotional turmoil. We've come so far since Vegas, and there's a good chance this will set us back. That she'll go back to talking about annulment, and I'll lose hope of ever making us *more*.

I open the truck door, and she accepts my hand to help her down. Mack is at the door, waiting for us, and she bends, as always, hugging him as if he's hers.

"Mack, we met a crazy lady today. If you thought your grandma was crazy, this girl was ten times worse. I know, hard to believe." She talks to him like a person, and I fall a little more in love with her.

"Want some beer or wine?" I ask, making my way into the kitchen.

She stands and Mack follows her, running his body along hers with every stride.

"You have wine?"

"Just in case." I open my fridge and pull out a bottle of white wine.

"Just in case you bring a woman home?" She sits on the stool at my counter and folds her hands together, lips turned down.

I put the bottle on the countertop, and her mouth drops open. Might as well just start putting it all out there.

"This is my favorite," she says.

"I know."

I watch her reaction. There's a small smile before she lifts her gaze to mine.

"Are you ready to talk now?" Her voice is quiet.

She's being patient with me for once, and it's killing me.

I pour her a glass of wine and grab a beer for myself, signaling for her to head over to the couch. She leads the way, then Mack, then me.

We settle on the cushions, Mack curling up at her feet. My house is more or less like a log cabin with a giant great room and open floor plan where you can see the kitchen.

I lean back in the corner of the sofa, extending my arm across the back of the couch and the other along the armrest. Might as well get right into it. "You didn't know? Really?"

"Know what?"

"You're a smart woman, Lottie."

Her eyes turn to her wine glass, and she twirls it like a little kid trying to make a whirlpool just to keep from looking at me. "I knew you liked me. I mean, I knew you had feelings of some kind for me. I did for you, too, as much as I tried to act like I didn't. But..." She looks at me. "I don't want to assume anything. Can you just tell me?"

I down a sip of beer, hoping for some liquid courage. "Lottie, I've loved you my entire life. Not just since Holden left, but before that." I hold my breath, waiting for her to respond.

"You did?"

The words dig in, revealing what I already knew. I was alone in it for so long. She was always looking past me, at him. Lottie was too hung up on my brother to ever see me. It's a cut I thought had healed, but tonight it feels like someone is picking at the scab.

"I did. I wanted to ask you out so many times, but I thought since I was a year younger that you wouldn't give me the time of day. Then Holden came home after graduating from college."

He saw her, and she had definitely changed that year. Became leaner and developed more curves and overall, just become the version she is now. All the guys were talking about her, and everyone wanted to date her. I wanted to scream at them that I had loved her before she'd developed into a beautiful young woman and that I loved her for who she was, not her body, but I was too self-conscious to approach her.

"He asked me out that first weekend," she says, remembering their romance with clarity. I wish it didn't sting.

"And I stepped aside. You were so into him."

She sets her wineglass on the table and slides closer to me, placing her hand on my thigh. "Brooks, I didn't—"

"I know you didn't. Anyway, you were happy, and I wasn't going to ruin that for you, so I just stayed in the background and hoped you'd find the love you'd always dreamed about."

"Dreamed about?" Her forehead wrinkles.

"You used to believe in fate and kismet like Romy does. You were in love with Holden. You were walking on a cloud, and there was no talking you down. Maybe it's supposed to be like that."

Her eyebrows scrunch, and she frowns.

"You fell fast and hard for him."

"Did I hurt you?" she asks, and I can see the weight of her concern in her eyes.

I place my arm along her shoulders, my hand resting on the back of her neck. "Not intentionally, no. It's not like that. I just... fuck, I sound like a loser. Yearning for you all these years when you never felt the same way."

"No." She shakes her head. "I have thought of you, but you were Holden's brother, and after he left me—the way he left me—I just didn't want everyone talking about me again, so I pushed all those feelings away." Inching closer, she curls into my side, resting her head on my shoulder. "I was really blind, wasn't I?"

I chuckle and kiss the top of her head. "Extremely. I'm pretty sure everyone else already knows. Ben does for sure."

She kisses my jaw. "I thought maybe you were just trying

to get with me because you felt guilty your brother had destroyed me. That, or you wanted to stick it to him by being with me."

I squeeze the back of her neck. "I hate my brother for stealing that light from you. For destroying your belief in true love. My feelings for you have nothing to do with him. But because I've loved you this long, of course I want to cure that for you. I want to show you all men aren't bad."

Her gaze softens, and she lifts her leg, straddling me. "Brooks, I have no idea where this thing between us is headed. I need to keep this casual for now, feel it out and see how it goes."

Lottie's reaction doesn't surprise me at all. I knew going in that it would take time for me to earn her trust. *Really* earn it so that she will trust me with her heart.

"We can go as slow or fast as you need. I'm good with whatever you're willing to give me." My hands find her hips.

"But—"

I lift my hand and place my finger on her lips. "No but, Lottie. I get that I'm already there, and you're not, but I don't want to rush this. I want this to last, and I don't want you ever feeling pressured to feel anything for me that you don't. So, let's just put all this on the back burner and keep going exactly as we have been."

"You expect me to just forget everything you said?" There's a glimmer of something in her eyes that I can't quite decipher.

"If I had a mind eraser, I'd use it on you."

She chuckles, and her forehead falls to mine. "I can't ignore it, Brooks, and I wish things were different, but at the same time, I don't." She draws back and meets my gaze. "Because everything that happened shaped me into who I am. I know my faults. I know I have a brick wall around me, and I don't want it there anymore, but maybe I had to go through all that to really appreciate this." She waves her finger between us. "To appreciate you. I can't forget what you just told me, and I don't want to."

I swallow hard. "So, what do we do?"

"Well, I'd really like to kiss you if you're okay with that?"

A grin teases the corner of my lips. "I'd never say no to a kiss."

She leans forward and places her lips on mine. At first, it's hesitant, a tad awkward after what I just told her, but she slides further onto my lap, and my fingers tighten, possessive and aching, against her hips.

Our tongues tangle, her hands running along the back of my head, tugging me closer as though she's starved for our connection. And there goes all my control—she's in my lap, her mouth hot and hungry on mine. I've wanted this for so damn long, it's been bordering on agony.

I want to claim her, beg her to be mine. She may not be in love with me yet, but there's no denying the physical connection we share.

She strips her mouth from mine, but my lips find her jaw and kiss their way down her neck. "God, you taste too good. Should we stop?"

"Do *not* stop, Brooks."

"Ten-four." I tug at the hem of her blouse, my hands inching the material up. She arches her back, offering herself to me. Fuck, if that's not the hottest thing I've ever seen.

I should be lost in her and not thinking about how lucky I am or how long I've waited. Just taking what she's giving. What I've dreamed about since I was too young to understand why she made my chest ache.

My fingertips graze the sides of her torso and trail over to her breasts, running my thumbs over the thin fabric of her bra and each nipple. She says my name as if it's her favorite sin, and I groan, tugging down the cups of her bra. She strips off her blouse, sitting in my lap in just her bra. The cups shoved down, tits out like a gift I never thought I'd get.

I stare, stunned. It's so much better than I ever imagined. "You just gave me beat-off material for a week."

"I'm not done yet." She reaches behind and unclasps her bra, pulling her arms out of the straps and dangling it from her finger before dropping it to the floor. "Close your eyes, Mack."

I mold my hands to her breasts, inching forward and taking one nipple into my mouth. Her hands hold my head to her, and I continue to devour her by licking, sucking, and tasting every inch of her heated skin, as I've been dreaming about for so long.

She grinds against my hard bulge, and I flick open the button on her jeans before slipping my hand down and under the elastic waistband of her panties. I groan into her breast when I find her soaked.

"Shit, Lottie. I'm so hard right now, and you're so damn wet."

"I know, you feel amazing. Damn it, Brooks." She stares at me as if she wants to swallow me whole. "Fuck me. Fuck me right now. I need you."

Jesus. Her words undo me.

Her arousal coats my finger, and I slide it up and down her center, then circle her clit. When I slip a finger inside, her walls clench as if she's been waiting for me as long as I've been waiting for her.

Her hands dig into my shoulders as she rides my hand. I press my palm harder against her clit, and she grinds faster, chasing that edge. I watch her in complete awe as she's about to come apart because of me. I've never seen her lost, unguarded, or trembling with want, and I'll do whatever it takes to see her fall apart completely.

"God, right there. Don't stop."

"Never."

Her breathing sharpens, her eyes locked on mine, and I hold steady, ready to catch her the second she lets herself go. Her body tenses, sweat trailing between her breasts, and she rocks harder, chasing it—

Knock. Knock.

She freezes as if she's been doused with a bucket of ice water.

I'm going to murder whoever the hell is at my door.

"Ignore them, keep going." My voice is the plea of a desperate man.

She stills, then lifts her leg, pulling my hand from her pants. "It doesn't work like that. Feel free to arrest whoever it is though."

"More like kick their ass," I practically growl.

Chapter Twenty-Six

LOTTIE

Deputy Moore is on my shit list.

Brooks and I were *so* close to having sex when Moore knocked on the door because Brooks didn't answer his phone, and some idiot kids were caught vandalizing down on Wild Bull Ranch. If I ever see him again, I might push him into a mud pile.

My phone dings with a message as I'm getting ready to change into my clothes for our softball game. Every year, the ranches in the area have weekly softball games, and of course Plain Daisy Ranch is part of it.

Can I give you a ride?

Depends

??

What do I get to ride?

And now I'm hard.

I laugh and fall back on my mattress as though I'm sixteen again.

> Sadly, I meant a ride to softball.

I'm ready to hammer out a yes, but then I pause. Us showing up together screams couple. It says we're together. It says we're giving this whole thing a chance.

> Get out of your head. It's only a ride.

> Is it really?

> I'll leave it up to you. I'll stay your dirty secret if you want me to.

For some reason, it pains me that he would think I see him like that.

> It's not you.

> I know.

Giving up the fight the other night and kissing Brooks felt so good. I have liked him for a while, but fear has always held me back. Fear of what people would say, how they'd judge me, whether he'd hurt me.

I sit up in bed and inhale deeply. Wanting to see him and be with him and kiss him trumps any of the things I was scared about now that I've really seen the kind of man Brooks is.

> Pick me up in ten?

> I'm already here.

I bolt up and look out my bedroom window to find his truck idling outside.

> How did you know I'd say yes?

I didn't. But I hoped you would.

> I'll be right down.

I hurry and change into my shorts and Plain Daisy Ranch T-shirt, then open my door and jog down the stairs.

"You ready?" Romy asks me.

"Sorry, I have a ride." I open the front door.

"Cool, I'll just go with you and Brooks." She follows me out onto the porch, and I whirl around.

"Um..."

She steps back and tilts her head at me. "Don't want me to go with you?"

I glance over my shoulder at Brooks's truck. He's waiting, and all I want is my lips on his. The grown-up thing to do would be to give my sister a ride.

"Are we leaving now?" Poppy comes down dressed in her sweatpants and matching Plain Daisy Ranch T-shirt. Her blonde hair is braided to the side. "Is Brooks driving us?"

Romy continues to study me. "I think Brooks is only driving one of us."

Poppy's eyes widen. "Shut up."

"Looks like Brooks has finally won." Romy grins.

"Oh my god, it's new. Don't go labeling it as anything just yet." I take one of the steps down. "I'll see you guys there."

"Didn't the label thing become pointless when you married him in Vegas?" Romy hollers at me, but I don't bother responding.

Brooks's door opens, but I rush to the passenger door and

spring it open before he has a chance to get out. "Stay. I'm good."

He's wearing his usual baseball pants with his matching shirt and belt. I used to make fun of him for always dressing like a baseball player when it's only recreational softball. Now, I like it. It shows commitment, and it says more about Brooks as a person than his fashion sense.

"Do they need a ride?" he asks because Romy and Poppy are still on the porch, watching.

"No. It's just us."

He leans forward to kiss me, but I put my hand in front of his face, not wanting the audience. "We don't want to be late."

He draws back and looks at the porch again where my sister and cousin are still gawking at us. "Okay."

To my relief, he doesn't seem bothered by me putting him off.

We drive over to the softball field and find that we're the first ones to arrive, so I unbuckle my seat belt and climb into his lap, shifting one knee at a time until I'm straddling him in the driver's seat. His breath catches, but his hands lock on my hips.

"How about that kiss now?" I murmur, mouth inches from his.

He groans, low and guttural. "Fuck yes."

I press my lips to his, kissing him hard, and his mouth meets mine with a desperation I'm starting to crave. Our tongues slide together, and he groans into my mouth. His hands roam under my shirt, fingers skimming the skin at my waist before dragging upward. I grind against him, slow and deliberate.

"Jesus, Lottie," he mutters, breaking the kiss, trailing his mouth down my neck. "You're killing me."

"Good," I whisper, pressing kisses along his neck, nipping just enough that he jerks under me.

He pulls me tighter against him, and his bulge tells me how badly he wants me. One of his hands slides to my ass, the other up my spine, anchoring me to him while his mouth devours mine again. My fingers tangle in his hair. His hips lift, grinding against my core as though he can't stand even an inch of space between us.

"Tell me to stop," he breathes against my lips, but his hands still locking me to him.

I shake my head, dizzy with how badly I want him. "Never."

A deep groan slips out of him. The sound rips through me, and I lose all restraint. We're a mess of hands and desperate kisses, making my chest ache and my thighs tremble. I roll my hips once more, and he curses under his breath.

"You have no idea what you do to me," he whispers.

I smile, brushing my lips over his. "I'm starting to."

We close our kiss and laugh, our gazes glued to each other.

Someone pounds on the truck window. "Okay, you two, time to play." We both turn our heads and see that asshole from Wild Bull Ranch, Walker Matthews. "Unless you want to forfeit."

He walks away, and Brooks runs his hand down my back. "I think our secret is out?"

He stares at me with questions in his eyes because Walker Matthews isn't family. He's probably going to tell everyone what he saw as soon as he reaches the diamond, and Brooks looks worried. The way his fingers graze my spine, I swear he feels the anxiety rising inside me.

Before I experienced this feeling with him, I probably would've bolted and said I couldn't play tonight, but he's put himself out there, and it's about time I do too.

"Let's go play." I dodge the subject for a second because words mean nothing. It's my actions that will show him how I'm feeling.

He opens the door, and I crawl off his lap and out of the truck in the most unladylike way.

"We need to talk about your shorts now," he says.

I wiggle my ass as I wait for him to get his bag out of the back. He's the one who brings all the equipment for us. "You can't tell me what to wear."

"I'm only asking for an inch or two longer. Just so I don't get hit in the balls again," he says, swinging the equipment bag over his shoulder.

"Too bad we weren't together back then. I could've nursed your balls back to health."

He looks around, and everyone is still driving into the parking lot. Of course, Walker Matthews is here before anyone else because he scouts the teams. The expression on Brooks's face says he wants to back me up to the truck and kiss me again, but something stops him.

"I think I still feel some phantom pain. Maybe tonight you can soothe it with your mouth."

I push him back against the truck, and he bounces off with the strength I didn't mean to use. Stepping up to him, I rub my hand over his dick.

"People are going to see," he whispers, his gaze somewhere behind me.

"I don't care."

His eyes widen. I inch up on my toes and press my lips to his. His hand slides down my side to my ass and presses me all the way against him as his mouth devours mine.

I'm so lost in the kiss, so lost in him, that it's not until clapping rings out that I realize he's right, I just completely outed us in front of my family and the Wild Bull Ranch players. But I can't find it in myself to care.

Because this feeling with Brooks? It's everything I've ever wanted but didn't have the guts to take.

Chapter Twenty-Seven

LOTTIE

"Shit, you surprised me," Brooks says the minute I close our kiss and step back. Although his hand is still on my ass.

"I know I kind of did a one-eighty on you there."

And he's right. In one truck ride to the softball field, I went from "don't kiss me in front of my sister and cousin" to "I'm going to grab your dick and shove my tongue down your throat in front of my entire family."

"Don't feel bad, I fucking loved it." His hand winds around my neck, pulling me to him for a quick kiss.

"Should we go then? I'm sure they're going to bombard us with questions."

He holds out his hand. "Since you just groped me in public, I'm assuming handholding is okay?"

I laugh and fall into him, my head on his shoulder. He doesn't hesitate to wrap his arms around me, turning me so we can start walking.

Before I realize it, the girls in my family have swallowed me in a huddle, each asking me a bunch of questions at the same time. All except for Sadie, since I had that conversation with her before the escape room date with Brooks.

Instead of going to the dugout, I sit on the bleachers with them.

"You each get one question, but this is where we're at. Brooks and I..." I look over my shoulder to see him stretching on the field. I shake my head. Another thing I used to make fun of him for, but what's the problem with him putting everything he has into something? Isn't that what he did with me?

"Can you focus on us for one second? Brooks and you what?" Scarlett asks, always the impatient one.

"We're..." I glance at him again. "Together. A couple."

"Well, you are married," Romy says, as if I don't remember.

"Yes, but I mean, we're actually dating now." God, I can't believe it. Adrenaline bursts through my veins for a second.

Walker Matthews steps up to the fence line. "Can we stop the high school drama and actually play softball?" His fingers are wrapped around the metal openings, and his cocky smirk is firmly in place on his face. Mostly, his attention is on Scarlett.

"There isn't a start time," Scarlett says.

"Technically, there is. It's six o'clock." He turns his wrist to face him. "And it's 5:58 right now."

Scarlett crosses her arms and pretends to look at her watch. "Then we have two minutes." She shoos him away with her hand. "So go round up your boys who probably don't even work on your ranch."

"Let's remember you have Brooks, and last I checked, he didn't work on your little ranch."

Scarlett's nostrils flare at the word little because it's nothing of the sort.

"Well, he's working *someone* on the ranch." Poppy comes

shoulder to shoulder with her sister as if that's an actual comeback.

Snickers ring out from everyone, and my cheeks heat.

Walker's gaze finds me in the middle of all the women. "That was evident when I found them steaming up the windows of his truck in the parking lot." He steps back and taps his wrist. "One minute, Scar."

She inhales a deep breath and turns around, her eyes rolling to the back of her head. "I swear to God, we'd better beat him today."

"I'm not sure how we got so unlucky that Wild Bull is our first game of the season," Poppy says.

Sadie grabs my wrist before I can leave the bleachers. When I turn around, she's smiling at me. And it conveys everything she wants to say without any words. She's really happy that I was able to step out of my own way and explore things with Brooks. I smile back at her, and she squeezes my wrist before releasing me.

Those of us playing head to the dugout, since knowing Walker, he'll find some loophole and make us forfeit if we step on the field a minute late.

Sadie turns toward the field, and she, Gillian, and Briar—who are all adorned with *Jude's Girl*, *Ben's Girl,* and *Emmett's Girl* T-shirts—clap and cheer for us.

I round the dugout, and Brooks comes over to me, handing me my mitt and kissing my cheek. "I have no idea how I'm going to get through this game without touching or kissing you."

"Who said you had to?"

He pats my ass. "Don't tempt me, or I'll be tugging you down on home plate in front of everyone."

"Can we please focus? This is Wild Bull, for fuck's sake," my cousin Jude groans, clipboard in hand. "I've moved some things around this year."

"What the hell?" Ben says.

"I better be batting third," Emmett says.

Scarlett raises her hand. "Can I not pitch anymore?"

"I don't want to bat. It gives me anxiety." Poppy crosses her arms.

Jude tosses the clipboard on the bench. "You're still batting fourth, so calm the fuck down." He eyes Ben, shifting to Emmett. "You're in the five hole, sorry, but you'll have to work your way up again."

"And when do you go down? I'm not so sure you should be in the third spot." Emmett puts his hands on his hips.

Brooks gets in the middle, putting his hands between the brothers. "Okay, calm down, everyone."

I admire him trying to get between them.

"You want to be higher in the order, practice once in a while," Jude says.

Emmett groans and glances at the bleachers with Briar and baby Colter. Then he shrugs and crosses his arms, ending his argument.

"And Scarlett, you're pitching, you're good at it. Poppy, we don't do pinch hitters, so if you want to play, you hit. Any other questions?"

No one says anything.

"One more thing... Brooks, you've got center field, and Lottie, you're in left."

"I'm sorry?" I ask.

Everyone makes a noise like, *uh oh, Brooks...*

I turn to Brooks and place my hand on his chest. "No offense, but I'm faster."

"Maybe we should race?" Brooks winks.

"I'm still lead off. That says I'm faster." I look back at Jude.

"Are you sure it's not just because I can hit the ball farther?" Brooks knocks his shoulder to mine.

"What?" I face him fully now. "I had the highest average last year."

"Actually, I did." Ben puts up his hand, but I raise my palm at him to say stay out of it.

"From singles," Brooks says, but steps closer to me. "You're a great hitter, babe."

"Babe." Jenson knocks elbows with Bennett, smirking. "They already have pet names."

"Well, *babe*, want to compare how many strikeouts you've had?" I cross my arms.

Emmett raises his hand. "In Brooks's defense, that's mostly because he bats after you, and he's always staring at your ass."

"Those in the five spot can keep their mouths shut," I say, twirling to Jude. "I've always had centerfield."

"Hey, Lottie, you can have centerfield on our team. Let's goooo..." Walker Matthews calls from the other side of the dugout.

"Fuck off, Matthews," Brooks shouts back.

"This is all getting out of hand," Scarlett steps in, shooting Walker a seething glare before concentrating on us. "Does anyone else here want to deal with all the bullshit of deciding who hits where and who plays where?"

None of us says anything.

"Exactly. Jude makes the decisions." She sternly looks at each one of us, waiting for us to nod. "Now, the enemy is that man today. Let's put all our energy into shutting him the hell up." She puts her hand in the middle of all of us.

We all put our hands on top of one another and scream, "Go!"

On our way to the outfield, Brooks runs alongside me. "Want to race to the fence?"

"Want to get laid tonight?" I head to left field, and he follows me, tugging me to a stop.

"Hey, I love you, but I can't have you questioning my abilities in front of everyone. Plus, think of it as we get to be in the outfield together. Side by side. You can kiss me in between innings."

I shake my head, and he just looks at me as though he thinks I'm way too competitive.

The first inning goes well. Walker Matthews is spouting his mouth off at every call, and I'm pretty sure Scarlett tries to actually hit him, but he spins out of the way.

Brooks keeps giving me looks like *relax* from centerfield, which only aggravates me more.

Then Walker Matthews nails a ball right to me. I backpedal toward the fence, screaming, "I've got it." I put my glove up, but then I lose the ball for a second in the clouds before a mitt is in front of my face, catching the ball.

Everyone cheers, and I glare at Brooks, but he's already watching the guy who was on first round second. He throws it to Ben at third, and he gets the tag down. Cheers ring out while Brooks stares at me.

"No kiss and a 'good job, honey?'"

"That was my ball." I jog into the dugout since that was the third out. Of course, Brooks comes alongside me.

"Centerfield has the authority. I called you off."

"No, you didn't."

We're still arguing over whose ball it was when we reach the dugout.

"Kisses one minute and arguing the next. Did we expect anything less?" Bennett says with a laugh.

I flip my brother off and grab my bat since I'm first up.

"Come on, it's just a game," Brooks says, but I go to warm up.

"Go, Lottie!" Wren shouts from the bleachers.

I give her a smile.

Brooks comes out right after, swinging his bat next to me.

"Don't shake your ass, okay? I'll end up with a hard-on out here."

"It would serve you right." I can't fight my smile though.

He lets his bat drop to the ground and tugs me into his arms, taking the invitation from my smile. "I'm sorry. Next ball is all yours." He kisses my neck.

"Jesus Christ, this is a softball game." Walker Matthews walks to the mound. He's always their pitcher against us. "I feel like I'm on some twisted reality dating show."

"They're falling in love. If you had a heart, you'd leave them alone." Scarlett comes out of the dugout just to scream at him.

"Go hit a homer." Brooks pats me on the ass.

I go to the plate and purposely swing my ass a little.

"Lottie," he warns.

I laugh and get set up. On the second pitch, I hit the ball, and it goes right between second and third.

Everyone cheers for me, and I jump up and down on first base.

"Stop, Lottie." Brooks eyes my chest as he steps into the batter's box.

As competitive as I am, I hope he gets a hold of one.

He ends up fouling off two pitches, and then three balls because Walker suddenly can't throw a strike. His eyes are on our dugout, watching Scarlett bend over to tie her shoelace. Hmm...

Walker must not be on his game tonight because his next ball comes right down the middle. Brooks gets a hold of it, and it sails across the infield and outfield, going over the fence.

I jog across the bases, and Brooks ends up catching me. All of our fans are on their feet in the bleachers, and the dugout has cleared out. Brooks and I cross home plate, and he picks me up, twirling me around. I wrap my legs around his waist and plant a huge kiss on his lips, which might be a little too far, to be honest. Especially with Wren present. I hear Gillian say something about covering her eyes.

Brooks closes the kiss and winks. "You know I'm just trying to impress you."

He lowers me to the dirt but doesn't let me go.

"Me too." We both laugh. "Next time, I get the homer."

"If you want some pointers, we can work on it between games."

I shove his shoulder, and he gets swarmed by my family congratulating him. I watch him smile, so wide, and I love that he's already family to the most important people in my life.

Chapter Twenty-Eight

BROOKS

We celebrate our win at The Hidden Cave, the one good bar in Willowbrook.

By the time I reach the outside patio with a cutout silo as the bar, Lottie is already ordering shots.

"Your pick," she yells at me while Tammy waits to pour.

"Tequila?" I tilt my head, since I'm pretty sure that's what we were drinking the night we got married.

"Done." Her smile says she gets why I choose it.

Damn it, I love this thing between us. I even love our bickering at softball.

"So, I heard a rumor," Melvin says from his stool at the end of the bar.

He's the owner's son. Soon-to-be owner, from what I hear. His dad is ready to retire and is actually one of the rare ones who wants to leave Willowbrook for a warmer climate.

"Let me guess." My vision strays to The Canary Wall II.

Melvin's job is to make sure no one rips off the note cards where people write down the gossip about what they see around town. Although, come to think of it, Jude got away with ripping one off once. My guess is it was his last.

"You and Lottie have been filling the board lately." Melvin nods toward it.

"How so?" I sit on the stool next to him. "This is our first time in public."

"Something about a fair and the two of you on a ride. You know I mind my business with the gossip, but it's a staple here, and people love it. So, here I am every night."

The Canary Wall I is inside, locked under glass. You have to hand the card to a bartender to have it posted. But out here, the rules are a little looser. Melvin is the pseudo bodyguard.

"So back to my question."

Tammy, the bartender, slides a beer toward me and nods at Lottie, who winks. "She says you're paying the bill though."

I grin. "Send it my way."

"I know you've always had a thing for her, but you look even more gaga over her now," Melvin says.

I don't strip my gaze off of Lottie. She's passing out shots to all her family members. "Yeah, I'm still in shock, I think. That she's mine."

He chuckles and sips his drink. "You see a lot from this view."

I turn away from Lottie and face Melvin.

"You both have been eye-fucking one another for years. I'm glad she let all that bullshit with your brother go so she can be with the right Watson." He claps me on the back.

"Want to do a shot with us, Melvin?" Lottie comes over, sliding the tequila shot in front of me, the lime on the napkin. "We beat Wild Bull, and this one hit a homerun." She leans in over my lap so Melvin can hear her over the live music.

My hand twitches to grab her ass, but I can't keep groping her in public all the time.

"Congratulations," he says and lifts his own cup toward Tammy. "You guys go celebrate."

"Let's go." I pat her ass. It's as if my hand has a mind of its own.

I grab my beer and shot, and we head over to the tables that have all been pushed together into one large one.

"I really just want to make out with you," I say. "Let's find a corner to disappear into."

She giggles and sways into me. I love that she always seems to want to be around me. The fact she's warmed up to the idea of us being a couple in front of others gives me a warm feeling in my chest.

"To beating Walker Matthews!" Scarlett says, raising her shot glass. "That son of a bitch."

We all take our shots and suck our lime, all of our faces screwing up at how sour it is.

Lottie dances to the music, and soon Romy drags her out to the dance floor to the cover of a Zander Shaw song they're playing. Ben comes up to me with his drink in hand, and I watch Lottie's smile grow when more of her cousins and friends join her and Romy on the dance floor.

"I've never seen you this happy," Ben says. "It's nice."

"I've been happy."

He tips his head right and left. "Not this happy."

He's right. This is everything I've ever thought about— Lottie and me making a go of it.

"So, you're staying married?" he asks, interrupting my thoughts. They're always of her, and now that we're together, I find my concentration is about as good as Moore's.

"We haven't talked about that yet."

"I'm gonna be honest, I can't believe the date thing worked. You got through them all already?"

I laugh and tip back my beer. Lottie catches my eye and crooks her finger at me.

"We got through two," I say.

He nods. "Even more impressive than."

"I've known her my entire life. I think she might've been halfway there, and I just didn't know it. She's got a tough exterior."

He laughs, and I spot Gillian eyeing him from the dance floor. He downs the rest of his beer. "She does, but I think she has a soft spot for you."

"I hope so."

He steps forward as though he's about to leave me, which I now totally understand. He wants to go to Gillian, like I want to go to Lottie. All the shit I gave Ben about always having to be with her, I get it now.

"I just have to hold on to her." I confess the one fear I'm trying to push away. "My parents..."

Ben stalls, shifting back to me. "Yeah..."

I have no friends who have a relationship with their parents like I do. Sure, Ben lost his mom when he was young, and that's hard to deal with, but Bruce is one of those "we're gonna talk it out with sarcastic humor" types. Same as Lottie's parents. They've always been there to support their kids with no judgment.

But watching Lottie, my gut twists, because I can't have a relationship with both her and my parents. There's no universe in which my parents cool down and welcome her into our family.

"What are you thinking?" Ben wouldn't run from the problem. He's a "get it handled and move on with your life" kinda guy.

"I won't lose her for them."

And there it is. The first time I've said it out loud. I'm sure there are things Ben knows. He overheard the screaming when I got in trouble in high school. Even now, he knows my humor in uncomfortable situations is a defense mechanism.

"Whatever you need, I'm here."

"I just... they're assholes, yeah, but to walk away..."

He puts his hand on my shoulder. "It's not easy, and I can't say I understand, but if you love her, and she's it for you, you have a tough choice to make. Maybe they'll surprise you."

"They won't." I frown.

They've never surprised me. Unless Lottie could help them get something they want, they'll never come around.

"I'm sorry, man. You finally get everything you've wanted, and you have to deal with this."

I don't tell Ben it's an easier decision than he probably thinks. But that doesn't mean I have to feel good about it, even if my parents have done nothing but cause me grief my entire life.

Lottie dances over, her eyes only on me, which pulls a smile from me. "Come on, dance with your wife."

As I allow her to drag me to the dance floor, I catch Ben's raised eyebrows. We both know it's Lottie over my parents every day of the week. But pulling that cord is harder than I thought it would be. I can see them doing something rash that might make me end up losing her. Which is the one thing I'll never survive.

Chapter Twenty-Nine

BROOKS

Wednesday evening, I'm cruising down Main Street when I spot Lottie coming out of Laurel's bakery with a box in hand. I tap the siren quick so it squawks, and I pull into the spot beside her car.

She turns and smiles as if she already knew it was me. She better have assumed it was me.

Her happy expression makes my night.

The problem is, now everyone getting off work or heading to dinner turns to look too. My tiny show of affection just bought us an audience I'm not sure she's ready for.

I roll down the window as she steps over. God, she looks good. I wish I was off work already.

"This is a nice surprise," I say.

She lifts the box a little. "I had to pick up the cookies for the store."

"Do you need a lift? You can ride in the back." I nod toward the cage, teasing her.

She checks out the back seat and shakes her head. "I have my car here, but if you promise to use those handcuffs, I might change my mind."

I grin. "You say the word, and I'll bring them home."

Home. That word might scare her. But I can't stop the image that comes to mind. Her shoes next to mine at the door, me pouring her a coffee before she goes to work, waking up to her body curled against mine in bed.

Then again, we haven't slept together yet. We have a long way to go before we get to any of that.

"Maybe we'll incorporate them and a little role play at some point," she says, leaning closer.

I track her gaze when she glances around. We're not exactly in private.

"I assume I can't kiss you."

"Are you allowed to kiss me in uniform?" she asks.

I wrap my hand gently around the back of her neck, my thumb brushing behind her ear, and bring her mouth to mine. "That's not going to stop me from kissing my girl."

I bring her mouth to mine, and I almost nut when she slips her tongue between my lips, as if she's claiming me for everyone around to witness. Damn, it's hot.

"In the town square," a woman mutters from the sidewalk as she walks by.

I glance past her. Mrs. Little, my third-grade teacher. She never liked me anyway.

I mutter the code for meal break into my radio. "Can I take you to dinner?"

"Now?"

"Yeah."

"Does it count as a date?"

I start rolling up the window. If she wants it to count, it counts. If she doesn't, I'm still taking her out. I climb out, and she tilts her head to look at me.

"I think I'd term it an impromptu meeting," I say.

She laughs and lets it slide. I love when she's stubborn until she's not.

"Put those cookies in your car, and then I'm taking you to The Sprout House."

"Oh, yummy," she says, unlocking the door to her SUV and doing just that.

My chest swells with satisfaction at her giddiness because I know she loves the chicken sandwich there, and I'm making her happy.

"How long is your dinner break?" she asks.

"An hour."

She slides her arm through mine and curls her body against me. "We could do a lot of stuff in an hour." She waggles her eyebrows.

I chuckle, but I don't play back this time. I lean in a little. "Not tonight. I'm going to taste every inch of you the first time I have you naked."

Her breath catches. Her body stiffens for half a second—then melts into mine again. And now all I can think about is her under me and moaning my name.

I could take her home now, but I don't want our first time to be rushed. I don't want her slipping back to her place afterward. I want her in my bed for the entire night. In the morning, I want her walking downstairs in my T-shirt, smirking over what I did to her the night before. Hell, I'd take her on the kitchen table. Maybe in the shower too.

"So, you're good with this?" I ask, dragging myself out of the fantasy. If she only knew what I was picturing.

"What?"

"Walking with me. People knowing." I nod at our surroundings.

"I think everyone already does know." She looks around, noticing the lingering stares.

But none of them are mean. No whispers, no glares. Mostly smiles. Willowbrook loves gossip, but they enjoy a love story more.

"They know we're married but not together."

She laughs and leans her head on my shoulder. "The irony, right? I guess we'll have to talk about that at some point. Do I only have so many days to change my name?"

Thinking about her sharing my name spurs a caveman response and it's like she's flipped a switch—I need to have her now. I groan and slide my hand into hers, tugging her faster down the sidewalk.

"Where are we going?" she asks, her steps trying to match mine.

I don't even think. I just take her hand and lead her around the back of the buildings, cutting through the narrow walkway until we're hidden in the alley. She follows without asking any questions.

The second we're out of view, I press her against the brick wall and kiss her, all the desperation inside me that never gets enough of her coming through.

My mouth drops to her neck, to that spot just beneath her ear, and she gasps. My breath is ragged, and I don't bother hiding how much I want her.

"I want to fuck you so bad."

"I don't think an officer of the law is supposed to be naked in an alley."

Her voice has a breathy lilt to it, teasing and turned on, and I only grow harder. I push my thigh between her legs, right up to her center. She clings to me, and fuck me, I feel the heat of her through her shorts when she grinds against me.

Her arms loop around my shoulders, her body grinding down on my leg.

"I want to see you come."

Again, she rolls her hips, slow at first, then more urgent. Her breath hitches with each grind, her nails digging into my shirt, fixing herself to get the friction she needs to get off.

I can't strip my gaze from her. The way she moves, the way

her body knows what it needs. The way she takes it from me is the sexiest fucking thing I've ever seen.

I find her mouth again, kissing her deep and messy. I groan into her mouth. "That's it, baby. Take what you need."

And she fucking does. My thigh tenses instinctively beneath her, and she grinds harder, breathless and wild.

Her voice cracks. "Brooks—"

"Let go for me."

I keep my eyes on her as her head falls back, her mouth parts, and her whole body pulses against me. She comes, right here in the alley, clinging to me as though I'm the only thing keeping her from not collapsing to the ground.

I don't move. I let her ride out her orgasm, keeping my thigh in place, pressing soft kisses to her mouth, her cheek, her temple.

She laughs quietly, still catching her breath. "Holy shit. I hope no one saw us."

"Work up an appetite?" I say, not even acknowledging the possibility that someone did. Because if they did? I don't give a damn.

She eyes me. "What about you?" Her hand slides between us, her palm rubbing my dick.

I grab her wrist and shift my stance. "If you touch me right now, I'm going to embarrass myself."

She laughs. "But—"

"Come on. I'm down to forty-five minutes now."

As we walk out of the alley, hand in hand, she murmurs, "I'm going to reciprocate this weekend."

"And you won't hear any objections from me. Right now, let me get you fed."

Her hand stays in mine as we cross the street, and I glance at her out of the corner of my eye. Her cheeks are flushed, and her lips are swollen. I know exactly what she's thinking about because I'm thinking about it too.

She just came on my leg. In public. In an alley. And I don't think I'll ever forget the way her body ground down on mine, her labored breaths, and the way she whispered my name.

We're almost to The Sprout House when my steps slow, and the air shifts around us.

My parents are talking to some couple on the sidewalk across the street. My dad is too wrapped up in conversation to notice us. But my mom? Her eyes snap to us. Her gaze drops to our linked hands and lingers. Her polite smile falters, judgment written all over her face.

Lottie leans toward me and whispers, "I'm starving." She must not see them because I'm blocking her. Good. I'd like to keep it that way.

I squeeze her hand tighter and angle my body to make sure she doesn't see them. Tonight is not getting ruined because of them.

My mom doesn't look away. Not even as I pull open the restaurant door and place my hand on the small of Lottie's back to guide her inside.

Let her look. Maybe she'll finally realize I'm not messing around. Lottie is my future.

Chapter Thirty

LOTTIE

It's Saturday morning, and I'm pacing around like a teenager crushing on her older brother's best friend, pretending I'm not waiting for him to show up or checking the clock every two minutes.

I glance at the time again. Eight thirty. This is usually when Brooks comes in. My pulse skips, and I hate how hopeful I feel. Hope has been such a foreign emotion to me for well over a decade that it's hard to be comfortable with it when it wells up inside me.

To distract myself, I head into the backroom, pretending to check off my to-do list. But then the door chime rings.

I spin back around as if I haven't been counting the seconds since I got into my vehicle after dinner and messing around in downtown Willowbrook last night. And there he is, strolling in as though he doesn't have a clue that he's completely unraveled me. As if he's oblivious that I'm falling for him.

"How's my girl this morn—"

I don't let him finish. I walk straight over, throw my arms around his neck, and kiss him. I kiss him the way I've needed to since we walked out of that alley last night. Picking us up right where we left off.

Brooks doesn't hesitate. He steps us back, his hands settling on my hips, then slipping lower until he lifts me onto the counter as if I weigh nothing. His fingers dig into me just enough to make my breath catch, just enough to say he's missed me too.

The kiss is slow but full of purpose. A push and pull, a give and take—we're figuring each other out, but somehow it already feels like second nature.

When he pulls away, I lean forward instinctively, chasing more.

"I've been so stupid," I murmur, brushing my mouth along the scruff on his jaw, willing him to stay right here with me forever.

Because I think I could love him. I push away the fear that chokes the breath from me with that thought. If I love him, I'm handing him the power to destroy me, and the last time I did that with a man, he left me in tatters.

"What are you talking about?" he asks with a low chuckle. His hands trail up and down my thighs as though he can't bear to not touch me.

And God, I love that. I love the way he touches me. Both like I'm something delicate to be treasured and something he so desperately wants to manhandle.

"All these years you've been coming in for coffee, and I've been pushing you away. We could have had this." I motion between us, my voice full of regret. "This is really good."

I lean in for another kiss because I can't help it. I want to memorize the way he tastes, the way his breath feels against me.

He meets me halfway, and this kiss is even deeper—sweeter, like a promise. When he finally pulls back, I swear I'm trembling.

His smile is dazzling. That's the only word I can think of to describe it. "Does all this mean I can squeeze another date in?"

I slide off the counter, still breathless, and he helps me down, giving my ass a soft smack as though he knows I'm his.

"What are you thinking?" I head behind the counter to make his coffee, needing something to do with my hands before I start working his utility belt off him.

"I'd like a pottery lesson."

I freeze for half a second, then reach for the pot. "Um..." I pour his cup slowly, heart thudding. "Let me guess, the *Ghost* scene?"

"Obviously."

I grab the creamer and sugar from the fridge and smirk over my shoulder. "Of course."

"Isn't that the whole reason you got into pottery?"

I scribble on his cup and turn around to slide it to him, barely containing my smile. "Yes, that's the entire reason."

Not that he's wrong. Every potter's imagined that scene at least once.

Brooks looks at the cup and frowns a little, curious.

"It was his character's name. I'm guessing you weren't paying attention to that movie except for that scene?"

He sips his coffee and licks his bottom lip, and I swear I nearly combust. "Maybe we can watch it together since I didn't know Sam Wheat was Patrick Swayze's character. I think one of us has watched it a lot more than the other." He taps the little time I wrote on the cup. "I'll be there."

I can't resist circling the counter again. Now that I've opened myself to the possibility of something more between us, I kiss him quick but greedy because I don't want to hold back. He's become the best part of my day.

"I'll walk you out," I say, even though I'm not ready to let him go.

His radio crackles and ruins the fantasy. "I wish I could stay here all day. Maybe I'll stop in for lunch if I have time." We stop at the front door, and he pulls me in close, arm around my waist, mouth brushing mine. "I'll be waiting until tonight."

And I believe him. Because I'll be waiting too.

One more kiss, and he's gone, walking toward his squad car as if he didn't just wreck me for the rest of the day.

"Man, how the tables have turned," Bennett says, coming around the corner with a bucket of flowers. He waves at Brooks. "Flowers from The Perfect Petal. Apparently, I'm errand boy now."

We step back into The Harvest Depot, and my morning rendezvous with Brooks stretches through my mind, warm and comforting.

And just like that, I miss him.

Already.

What the hell is wrong with me?

Chapter Thirty-One

LOTTIE

It's during the lull after the lunchtime rush when the bell chimes at the front door.

Saylor is helping me put away all the sandwich fixings, so I tell her I'll go out front and check on the customers coming in, but as soon as I walk through the doorway to the store, I come to a complete stop.

Brooks's mom is perusing the shelves, and I take a moment to watch her. She picks up one of my mugs, winces, and puts it back down. Her purse hangs off the crook of her arm, probably designer. It's paired expertly with her ankle-length slacks and ballet flats. She doesn't look as if she belongs in Willowbrook, but that's always been our problem. She doesn't think she belongs here and believes she's better than me.

Her gaze lifts, and she tilts her head when she spots me. "Lottie."

My name sounds like it's hard for her to get out.

"Mrs. Watson." I push off the door, smacking on a smile. After all, if I want this thing with Brooks to go the way I do,

I'll need her approval. Or some semblance of it. "Nice to see you."

She makes a sound that implies it's not nice to see me, which makes me wonder why she's even here. That sound alone causes me to brace for the punch in the gut she's an expert at delivering.

"I haven't been here in so long, I figured I'd pop in. It's so charming that not much has changed."

I don't let my smile falter, even though I want to rattle off all the things I've changed since being put in charge of the store. The shelves I chose, the products I've curated, they've turned this store from country bumpkin to Instagram-worthy. But the pride I usually feel here shrinks and shrivels up under her scrutiny.

"Can I help you find something?"

Another one of her noises suggests this is all a ploy. Her arrow is already notched, and her aim will be precise. "You and Brooks really should show more discretion."

"I'm sorry?" I clasp my hands behind my back to hide the fact that they're trembling. Glancing toward the backroom, I beg the universe to send Saylor to my rescue. I'm ready to tag team out.

"I heard you were over at his house, and Deputy Moore was embarrassed when he clearly interrupted something. Saw you two fawning over each other on the sidewalk last night as well."

I clear my throat. I didn't see her last night, didn't realize she was even around. "Well, Brooks *is* my husband."

Her head snaps up, and she scans the length of my body, looking at me as though she's at a flea market and I'm the dirty old blanket no one wants to buy. "I suppose he is. I'm not sure how you were able to swindle yet *another* one of my sons into marrying you." Her gaze zeros in on my stomach.

Bull's-eye. That's one, but I'm sure she already has another arrow ready to fly.

My hands drift to my abdomen.

Her smile is worse than any insult—it's mocking. A slow twist of the arrow. Worse than just shooting me again.

"I'm not pregnant," I bite out, the familiar shame and pain turning my stomach.

"Such a disaster that was. I will say, it's impressive. You trick my first into marriage by getting pregnant, and now you get my second son drunk so he'd marry you. Have you thought about writing a book about all the ways you trick men into marrying you?"

My fists clench at my sides. "I never asked Holden to marry me."

She hems. "You didn't say no when he proposed."

"Because I loved him. The pregnancy was a—" My voice collapses. I won't say mistake. I won't. But I also can't say we'd still be together if I hadn't lost the baby. It all moved too fast. Even though it's the early days with Brooks, I don't remember feeling so myself around his brother.

"Yes, dear, better that it happened early."

At the time, she told Holden the miscarriage was for the best. As though my grief wasn't warranted and losing our child saved her from everyone finding out it was the only reason Holden was marrying me. I have no proof, but I'm pretty sure she tried to talk him into calling off the wedding immediately. It drove her crazy when Holden didn't abandon me after my miscarriage. That he still wanted me. That her version of the story—the one where I trapped him—wasn't proven to be true.

But the girl who once nodded politely while this woman shredded her confidence doesn't exist anymore. I'm not going to let her interfere and destroy what I could have with Brooks.

"Did you come here just to insult me again? Try to scare me away from Brooks?"

"I just wanted you to know that I've figured out your game, and my son might think he loves you, but he just wants to heal you, shelter you... *fix* you." Her eyebrows raise at that last one.

I clench my jaw and tell myself I am not broken.

"Think about it. All the horrible trucks no one wants that he refurbishes. Taking Mack in. You know how he was the runt of his litter and no one else wanted him, so of course Brooks had to have him." She stares at me with a pointed glare, then continues to walk around the store as if she's actually going to buy something.

"I blame myself really. All the nature walks we used to go on... This one time, Brooks found a bird on the ground that we thought was dead. When it moved a little, he scooped it up and took it home. Guess what happened?" She doesn't wait for me to respond before she continues. "The bird just got up and flew away. He fooled Brooks, but of course, like any good mother, I praised him for saving the bird's life. I think that's where his need to take in old, used-up things people don't want came from." Again, her gaze lands on me. She's nearing the door. "I thought maybe he'd be a doctor, but he's just a sheriff. Another fix-it profession. Such a savior complex, that one."

She inches the door open with a satisfied grin. She knows she hit her mark. I'm pretty sure it's all over my face.

"Well, have a great day, Lottie. Tell Brooks to bring you to the house for dinner sometime. I'm sure Mr. Watson would love to catch up." She waves.

I remain quiet because nothing I say will matter. The damage she did isn't fresh. She just reopened an old wound, and she knows it.

"Done," Saylor says, coming out from the back.

Isn't that the truth? I've been gutted in my own store.

"Who was it?" she asks.

I don't answer. I can't. My voice and pride are somewhere locked in my throat, but my sorrow and shame are spilling out of me.

I turn, grab my phone, and type before I can talk myself out of it.

> I'm really sorry. I can't do tonight. I forgot I'm babysitting Daisy.

Chapter Thirty-Two

BROOKS

Fucking hell. I slam my tool drawer shut, and Mack whimpers, moving away from me.

Where is the woman who was all over me this morning? These past couple weeks—hell, this morning it felt real. Felt like maybe she was letting me in. What the hell changed?

"God damn it." I clench my fists, my short nails digging into my palms.

I told her I'd be happy to go with her to watch Daisy, but she said no. Maybe the *Ghost* reference was too much. Too presumptuous. It was a harmless joke. Not that I'd mind her in a white button-down shirt and nothing else as I got behind her and got us all dirty and wet. That image brands into my skull, and I can't stop thinking about it. And now I want to beat off to the image of her. God, I'm pathetic.

My phone dings on the worktable. I pick it up and see that it's Lottie. My stomach flips, hope rising inside me. *Please be asking me to come over.*

Date three is booked. You're off tomorrow, right?

> I'm free right now. 😊

I just got Daisy down and I want to keep it that way. But tomorrow, you're available?

There's an urgency in her texts I don't love. Like she's trying to get something over with, check the box.

> Yeah.

I just scored us tickets to Zander Shaw's show. I know it's last minute, and we have to go to Lincoln, but you good with it?

How the hell did she score tickets this close to the concert?

> Sure.

YAY! I'll pick you up at three. That work?

There's so much more I want to say. I want to ask her to come over after Jude and Sadie get home and spend the night with me. But I also don't want to push her. Maybe she needs a little time to figure out her feelings. She's finally softened. Lottie probably already feels pressured because of my confession about how I've always felt about her. We've gone farther physically in the past few weeks. Maybe she needs to take a step back. More pressure won't help my cause.

> Definitely. See you then. I hope Daisy doesn't wake up.

It's an opening to keep this text exchange going if she wants it to.

Me too. Okay see you tomorrow.

I don't respond, just toss my phone on the table and fall onto the bench. The silence that follows feels deafening.

Mack comes over as though he senses something is wrong and puts his head on my leg. I pet him mindlessly as my mind races like a storm chaser going after a tornado. Will it ever just be easy for us?

At least we're doing another date. That has to be a good sign. Right?

God, I hope so.

SUNDAY AT THREE, IT'S NOT LOTTIE'S SMALL SUV that pulls into my driveway, but Romy's truck.

I give Mack the chance to run down the stairs and greet them all as they file out of the vehicle. They each take turns petting him and saying hello. Lottie lingers behind her sister and cousin, gaze fixed on anything but me. Fear rises to the surface again. Something's shifted between us, and I can't figure out why or if I'm too late to fix it.

"Are you ready?" Romy asks excitedly. She's wearing jean shorts and a Zander Shaw shirt that's shorter, so it shows off her stomach. She's paired it with cowboy boots.

Poppy and Lottie are dressed nearly the same, but it's Lottie's frayed shorts and those legs I want wrapped around my waist that I can't stop looking at. She doesn't come up to me to kiss me though, and it guts me more than I care to think about. I only had her for a matter of weeks and already she's pulling away.

I head back inside and grab my keys off the hook. "I'm driving."

"No, I'm driving." Romy dangles her keys off her finger.

"And what will happen if you somehow swindle your way

backstage?" It's never going to happen, but I'm sure it's a dream she's envisioned already.

"Good point. Okay, let's go. I want to get there early. I'm hoping to find the other groupies and get noticed by Zander." Romy skips over to my truck.

"It's probably never going to happen. You know that, right?" Poppy says, pulling back her long blonde hair into a ponytail.

"Let a girl dream," Romy says, then laughs.

"How did you score these tickets?" I ask Lottie, following her to the passenger side.

"She didn't tell you?" Poppy asks.

"No." She didn't even tell me that it wasn't going to be just the two of us. That stings the worst.

"I was searching online on the off chance there were some available and found them."

"You must have paid a lot." I open the door for her to climb into the passenger seat.

"It's a fun date. Worth the cost." She climbs in and situates herself.

Still no kiss. Barely any eye contact. Zero excitement to see me again. Her walls have been firmly erected once more.

I'm grasping at straws, trying to believe that it's just that she doesn't want to show me affection in front of her family. That once we're alone, she'll lean in again and press her lips to mine.

We drive to Lincoln as Poppy and Romy go on and on about Zander and all the facts they know about him. The biggest thing Romy's concerned about is that he's single. She's living in a dreamland if she thinks she's going to get backstage. Then again, Romy believes in signs and soulmates, so maybe Lottie got these tickets more for her sister than anything else.

"I still can't believe we're going! Tickets sold out within minutes. I'm still upset with that couple for all their damn questions. Our appointment at The Knotted Barn ran long, and I couldn't get online to buy them. They're lucky I didn't miss ordering their cake or something."

Lottie glances at them in the back seat. Her hands are clenched in her lap. "You need to get this crush under control."

"Why? It's endearing that she believes she's meant to spend the rest of her life with the most famous country singer in the nation." Poppy reaches to the front seat and turns up the music. "Let's get ready."

I didn't even notice it was Zander Shaw on the radio.

I lean back in my seat, letting them sing and dance, feeling like the fourth wheel.

I want to ask Lottie what changed. Hell, I want to beg her to look at me like she did yesterday morning. But I keep my mouth shut and let them have their fun.

I'll get her alone eventually. I just hope there's still something left to salvage.

I park, and we file out of the truck and get in line with everyone else. There're more cowboy hats here than at the rodeo. Lottie doesn't pull away when I place my hand on her lower back, and I'm pretty sure she leans into my chest a bit as we wait through the excruciatingly long security line. I tell myself these are both good signs.

Poppy looks over her shoulder a few times, smiling up at me as if she couldn't be happier I won the girl, but she's wrong. This isn't the Lottie I've had on my arm recently. Or from the store yesterday. Hell, she's not even the Lottie from before we got married in Vegas. I've never seen this quiet and reserved version of Lottie. She's lost in her head somewhere. And it's killing me that I don't know where her head is at.

Once we find our way to our seats, Romy walks over to the security people along the edge of the stage.

"We all knew she was going to try," Poppy says, shaking her head.

A couple minutes later, Romy walks back to us with slumped shoulders. "No luck."

Cameras are on everyone, scanning the crowd on the jumbo screen. Even though it isn't exactly comfortable with Lottie at the moment, it's nice to feel the excited energy of everyone here to experience the same thing.

The lights dim, and I take a chance and put my arm around Lottie, pulling her into my side. She doesn't fight me, and I breathe a sigh of relief. The stage lights up and cheers explode around us, but I only look at her, staring into her eyes as though they hold the answers I can't get her to say out loud.

Her hand lifts, and she cradles my jaw. The pain in her eyes hits me like a two by four to the head. She doesn't feel it, and she doesn't want to hurt me.

She's done with me.

I bend down and kiss her forehead, trying like hell to tell her it's okay, even though my heart is cracking into pieces and in jeopardy of splintering apart. Then I lower my head and say in her ear, "Enjoy the concert."

She nods and turns to Poppy, who is jumping up and down to better see the stage.

I release my hold on Lottie and draw in a deep breath.

The three of them scream even louder when Zander comes on stage. The cameras scan the crowd, stopping on a few people who cheer excitedly at their moment in the spotlight.

Romy hops up on a chair, flailing her arms, and when she pops up on the screen just as Zander strums his guitar, he looks at the screen and points out to the audience as if he can see Romy through the mass of people.

Then the concert begins, and I figure it'll be two hours of torture here, and another hour to get home before I can get the space and courage to ask Lottie what's changed between us.

An hour into the concert, Romy is tapped on the shoulder and asked to go with someone from security.

Poppy grabs Romy's arm. "You can't go by yourself."

The security guy looks at Poppy and shakes his head.

Romy waves and holds up her phone as if to say, *I'll text you*.

Poppy jumps on a chair to follow her. Grumbles from the people behind us start, but then the chair buckles, and Poppy goes with it.

Fuck, this night just got a lot longer.

Chapter Thirty-Three

LOTTIE

We arrive at the hospital to find a packed waiting room. Coughs echo throughout. A kid cries while his mom rocks him. It smells like antiseptic and old coffee. When Brooks drops us off, he's silent, his jaw tense as he lifts Poppy into a wheelchair, telling me to check her in while he parks the truck.

His eyes don't meet mine. Not even for a second. And I know I only have myself to blame.

"What's going on with you two?" Poppy asks as we wait in line at the receptionist.

"Nothing. Why?"

"You haven't kissed. You're barely looking at him. After the way you guys were the night of the softball game, I thought for sure you'd be all over each other tonight."

I should probably talk to someone about what Mrs. Watson said to me. Although I'm sure they'd say not to take her seriously. Probably call her a bitch. But they weren't there. They didn't hear her voice, calm and cruel, as though she enjoyed gutting me with every insult. Each word was calculated. Measured. She knew exactly how to inflict as much damage as she could. How do I marry into that and live every day waiting for another blow to hit? The alternative is to be the reason Brooks cuts off his family. It's a no-win situation.

"Did you want me to bang him in the middle of the concert?"

She gives me the look. The one that says to stop being so dramatic and tell her what's bothering me.

"I'm done being the fix-it case," I say.

Which has nothing to do with Mrs. Watson and her pretty much telling me that Brooks looked for the most broken girl to put back together, and I was the winner—as if I'm a charity project. It's the way everyone sees me since Holden left me at the altar. The scorned girl. The broken one. I'm exhausted from everyone looking at me as if I'll never be whole again.

"You're not a fix-it case." Poppy grabs my arm.

What else is she going to say though?

Thankfully, we're next and I check Poppy in to be seen by a doctor. The sound of phones ringing and names being called over the PA system swirls around us like white noise. Brooks joins us the minute we step in, and a nurse comes out of the back to ask the receptionist a question.

"Tegan?" Brooks says, and I turn to him and back to the nurse.

The cute brunette with curly hair glances up. She smiles. It's not a polite, professional smile, but one that says, *Damn, you still look good.*

"Brooks." She takes in that Poppy and I are with him, and suddenly that glow on her face flickers, and she realizes there's more than just her and Brooks here.

Poppy glances at me, but I ignore her stare I'm sure is asking if I know who the woman is.

"How are you?" Tegan asks.

"Good. You?"

I step back as if I've disappeared and been replaced by Little Miss I'll Kiss Your Boo-Boos.

"Working." Her gaze falls to me then Poppy.

Nice of her to notice us again.

"Who do we have here?" She glances at the room full of people behind us.

"We were at the Zander Shaw concert, and she fell off a chair. I think her ankle is broken," Brooks answers for us.

I'm so not jealous. Not at all.

"It might just be sprained," I say, and they all look at me. "I mean, he's not a doctor or anything."

Tegan glances at Brooks like, *Who is this girl?,* and I deny the urge to raise my hand and say I'm the one he's pined for since grade school—so ha.

Jesus. Who am I right now?

"Not a doctor, but I have seen my share of car accidents, and I did carry her through the entire arena, so I'd say my prediction is more than just a guess." Brooks's eyes are glued to mine.

I roll my eyes, turning away from him.

"Is she all done checking in, Rosemary?" Tegan asks.

"Yes, but she's not urge—"

Tegan cuts off Rosemary and opens the door behind them. "We can't take the chance it'll heal wrong. Let's get some x-rays." She winks at Poppy.

Brooks goes to push Poppy's wheelchair, but I slide in front of him and push it down the hallway myself.

"Okay then." He puts up his hands. But his fingers twitch as if he doesn't know what to do with them if he can't touch me. Or maybe that's wishful thinking since I'm so thoroughly messing up this thing between us.

We follow Tegan into a room, and she checks Poppy's vitals. Brooks and I each sit in a chair, the two of us fighting over the elbow room. He eventually relents, and I clasp my hands together.

"So, Brooks, are you still in Willowbrook?" Tegan asks. "How is Mack?"

She knows Mack.

My heart sinks. That's not acquaintance-level knowledge. That's "been to his house, slept in his shirt" knowledge. I turn to Brooks as if he can read my thoughts and is going to answer me, but he continues to face forward. His shoulders are tight, as though he's bracing for impact.

When Poppy gives her a questioning look, Tegan says, "We dated."

The words hit harder than I thought they would. A cold freeze skates over my body. I bolt out of the chair, legs numb.

"Oh... nice." Poppy gives her a wan smile. "Lottie, are you going somewhere?"

Tegan spins on the stool to face me. "Lottie?" She points at me but looks at Brooks as though she's asking, *This is her?*

"I need a drink."

"I can get you some water," Tegan says, feeling Poppy's ankle. "I do think it might be broken. I'll ask the doctor to come and have a look, and then we'll get the X-ray ordered."

She scans her medical card under the computer, and the screen goes blank.

"Thanks," Poppy says.

Tegan looks at Poppy, then me, and lastly at Brooks. "It's really good to see you." Then she looks at me again and squeezes his arm. Her fingers linger before she leaves.

So does his stillness. And it's that stillness I can't look away from.

I scoff, and Brooks crosses his arms. His jaw is clenched, his breathing shallow, his gaze right on me.

"What?" I ask.

"I thought you were getting something to drink."

"My purse is in your car," I sneer.

He stands, crowding me in the small room. His presence floods the space. He's too close, too warm, too everything I can't have anymore.

"Then come on, I'll buy you a drink. Want anything, Poppy?" he asks without his eyes leaving mine.

"Sure..."

I leave the room, and Brooks follows me.

"A Sprite!" Poppy calls behind us.

He falls in line with me as we follow signs to the waiting room with the vending machine. His footsteps are faster than mine, as though he's afraid if he lags even a second, I'll vanish.

"So, how long did you date Tegan?" I try to keep my voice even, but I'm not successful.

"I'm not sure why you're acting so jealous when you pretty much called it quits before the concert even started."

I stop, whirl, and cross my arms. "What are you talking about?"

"That pitying look you gave me? You know, I get it. I threw my feelings out there fast, too fast, but damn it, Lottie, I thought you realized this thing between us is worth fighting for. I thought that's why you've been so open with me these past weeks."

I shake my head. "What are you talking about? I love that you told me how you feel. That you trusted me with that."

"Then why are you dodging me? Canceling last night and making our third date into a group hang? No kissing. No touching. You'll barely look at me. Then we come here, and you play jealous girlf—jealous whatever." He steps closer, looking around before caging me against the wall. His voice drops, ragged and low. "Decide what you want because you say you don't play games, but I feel like I'm trying to win fucking Risk right now."

I push at his chest to give myself some space. "I want to get my purse."

He steps back, and I walk through the waiting room and out the sliding doors into the dark parking lot. The buzz of hospital lights fades into the night air. The door closes behind us.

"What happened? You flipped the switch, Lottie."

"Nothing," I call over my shoulder.

"God damn it, Lottie."

There's so much pain in his voice I nearly crumple to the ground, but I tell myself this is for the best. I can't give him the life he wants anyway.

"I've given you everything. I cracked my chest wide open for you, and you're walking away like it meant nothing. I thought I could get through to you. I thought I could pull that girl you used to be back out of you."

I whirl around. "That girl is dead! Don't you realize that? The girl you knew before Holden, she's long gone." I shake my head and splay my arms wide. "I never will be her again. We can't rewind time and act like what happened didn't shape me into who I am now. We can't go back. We can't undo it. Everything broke, and I rebuilt myself with what was left. Maybe I just don't know how to love you the way you need."

He steps forward, but I put my hand up to stop him. His breath hitches. He swallows hard, as though it physically hurts him not to close the gap between us. "Please, I just want—"

"To fix me." I finish the sentence, and tears spill from my eyes. "Well, I'm not some rusted-out truck or the runt of the litter. And I'm sure as hell not a wounded bird you take home with you who will fly away the next day. I don't want to be fixed."

He tilts his head. I try to memorize the way the moonlight shines down on his brown hair.

His mouth opens as though he's going to speak, but it

closes again. He's shaking his head, slowly, as if he's refusing to believe what he's hearing. "Wounded bird?"

"I'm begging you, Brooks, I can't take this anymore. Just agree to an annulment already."

His lips thin. "Was it her or him?" he asks through clenched teeth.

I shake my head. "How did we ever think this would work? You're his brother. There's too much history. Too much hurt to go around. I'm sorry."

I wipe the tears from my cheeks because letting him go is tearing me apart. But staying means drowning in the doubt every single day.

"Lottie, I swear to God, tell me what happened." His voice cracks. And that sound, more than anything else, nearly makes me fall apart.

He steps in front of me, bending to look into my eyes, but I squeeze my eyes shut and shake my head. "It doesn't matter."

"Yes, it does. You're letting other people ruin this. Ruin *us*." He places his hands on my shoulders. "I love you. I can fix this."

I open my eyes and lift my gaze to his. "That's the problem. You can't fix me. You're in love with a version of me who doesn't exist. I can't give you the life you want."

He stands in front of me, and I touch his chest. My hand rises and falls with his deep breaths.

"Go home, Brooks. I'll handle things here." I step around him and head back toward the hospital entrance.

"I can't believe you're just letting them win," he shouts into the night air.

But I don't turn around because if I do, I'll run right into his arms. And I'm not sure I'd ever be able to let go.

Chapter Thirty-Four

BROOKS

Bennett answers the phone, and I hear Wren in the background, squealing with laughter.

"What's up? Say hi to everyone." He puts me on speaker, and Wren shouts hello.

"First of all, everyone's fine, but I need you to go pick up your sister and Poppy at Memorial Hospital in Lincoln."

"What?" I hear the panic in his voice. "Why are they in the hospital?"

I really don't want to talk about why I can't drive them home, but I have to make sure they get home safe. "I think Poppy broke her ankle."

"Seriously?" Nash says in the background.

"Yeah, Romy is—I have no idea. The entire night was a disaster." The edge in my voice probably gives it all away.

Everything feels as if it's splintering at once. My life is blowing up, and my parents are holding the gasoline and lighter.

"Anyway, just go, please." I swallow hard.

"Done," Nash says. "I'll text Poppy now."

Nash doesn't hesitate. It should calm me but it doesn't.

Nash is a horse trainer on the ranch and the third room-mate in the guys' house. The entire reason we call Bennett Danson is as a *Three Men and a Baby* reference. I've always wondered if Nash has a thing for Poppy, but Nash is Jensen's best friend, and I think that'd be a big problem between those two.

"Thanks, man. I don't want to drag Wren all the way to Lincoln," Bennett says.

"No problem," Nash says, then I hear the door shut.

"I'm gonna go. Thanks." I'm ready to hang up, but Bennett doesn't say anything for a beat.

"You okay, Brooks?"

I blow out a breath. No. I'm not. But I'm not telling him that. "I'm good."

"You're not, and I know it probably has to do with my sister. I just want to... I don't know... tell you she's worth it."

There's a softness in his voice that hits me in that same soft spot I have for Lottie.

"I know."

His voice lowers, and I'm guessing he doesn't want Wren to overhear. "I know you do, but I felt like I needed to say it because I want to see her happy."

"Relax, Danson. She might think she's thrown what we have away, but I'm a goddamn boomerang. There's something I need to clear up tonight though."

"All right, then. Good luck."

"Thanks. See you soon." I click End and tap my thumb on the steering wheel.

I'm seething. My jaw hurts from how tight I'm clenching. My parents—God, they did this. They made her cry. Made her feel less than. And somehow, I've stood by and let them continue to take up space in my life.

This entire time, I thought I was helping Lottie heal. Thought maybe if I could rewind time, bring her back to who she was before Holden, everything would make sense again.

It's not her past self that I love. It's who she is now. Every scar, every bite of sarcasm, every guarded smile. I've only fallen harder for her with every year that passes.

But now she thinks I'm chasing a ghost. That I only love the broken version of her because I think she needs saving, and that's so far from the truth.

I have my work cut out for me. But before I can fix things with her, I need to burn this bridge between my parents and me because they're never going to accept us.

I pull up to my parents' house and walk up the ridiculous brick walkway that's lined with ten different signs about voting for him, as if it's an endorsement when it's your own house. I want to steal the Greg Miller sign two doors down and put it right on their front lawn.

When I try the doorknob, I find it locked, so I ring the doorbell, then knock and ring the doorbell and knock again until the door opens, and my dad stands there in his robe and pajamas.

"What the hell did you do?" I walk in without waiting for an invitation.

"Jesus Christ, Brooks, I'm not in the mood for this shit tonight." He slams the door shut.

"You're fucking with my life, and I'm not going to have it."

My dad shakes his head. "I have no idea what you're talking about. You're the one fucking with mine. All buddy-buddy with Greg Miller. You might as well back him at this point. Now I'm behind in the polls. Tonight is not the night to storm into my house accusing me of bullshit."

He walks away into the family room. I follow. I'm not leaving until this is done.

"You got to her, I know you did."

"Again, I didn't." He slams a piece of paper on the coffee table. "According to this, he's beating me."

"I couldn't give a shit about the election. Tell me what you said to her!" My voice keeps rising. I want it to. I want them to hear my anger.

"I didn't see her. I don't *want* to see her. I never liked that girl." He walks over to the liquor cabinet and pours himself a scotch. Half a glass. Like always.

"Then who did?"

"I did."

I whirl around to find my mom standing there.

"I told you she was trouble. She tricked you, and I won't stand for it. She's ruining our good name, and people are worried to vote for your father because of it. We can't have that. So, I went to that pathetic country store."

I inhale. Deeply. "When?"

"Yesterday. You can't deny you see it, Brooks. First, she's pregnant with Holden's baby, and then you're drunk and marrying her in Vegas. She's manipulating you boys into these marriages."

My hands squeeze into fists at my sides. "I thought I was clear when I left here that night. And when you came to talk to me."

"You went to talk to him?" my dad snaps.

She looks at my dad. "What did you expect me to do? I can't let her get her hooks into another one of our sons."

"How are you not understanding that I love her?" I cut in, chest burning.

"Oh my god." My mom shakes her head and throws her arms up as if I'm a lost cause.

I stand there, trying to think straight, but there's nothing left. This—this is the end of my relationship with them. They're not concerned with what I want, what's best for me, or that their actions hurt me. It's all about them. It always has been.

"Tell me what you said." I try to keep my voice level.

My dad riffles through his campaign crap on the coffee table, ignoring me.

My mom's face tightens. Her robe's striped. I wish they were prison stripes right now. "I told her my thoughts and told her the real reason you're with her."

"The wounded bird story?"

She scoffs. My dad glances up.

"Did you?" My eyes narrow.

"Yes. She's not some wounded bird, but she acts like it. I know you like to help people, and you're very empathetic, but please, Brooks, you need someone different. Someone better."

"That's it. I'm done. You're both out of my life."

My dad stands while my mom jerks back in shock.

"Stop being irrational. Go home and sleep on it and come back when you have your shit together." My dad points toward the door.

"What, did she go and whine to you about me coming into the store?" my mom sneers.

"What don't you get? I'm out."

"Not until this election is over. I need you by my side. So stop being buddies with Greg Miller. I have a plan I want to talk to you about."

"God, you're both crazy. I'm not doing anything. You fucked with my life. You hurt the woman I love."

"Your mother did that. Not me." He turns to her. "What the hell were you thinking?"

I throw my hands in the air. "You don't love me. You don't care what I want. You're actively destroying the one person who means more to me than anything. What does that say about you as parents?"

"You're way too worked up about this." My mom takes a seat on the couch.

I start toward the front door.

"You walk out that door, and I won't endorse you for sheriff," my dad shouts after me.

I spin around and stare at him. This is it. This is who he is. Threats and ego. "I'm not surprised. Just so you're not blindsided—I'm endorsing Greg Miller."

I turn and walk toward the foyer.

"Brooks," my mom says.

I don't turn around. They don't deserve a damn thing from me.

"Get back here!" my dad bellows.

I'm at the door with my hand on the knob when he storms in, my mom trailing, panic etched onto her face.

"You're an ungrateful bastard. I took you in as my own, and this is how I get repaid." He cocks his fist back.

I step aside, and his knuckles slam into the door.

I'm so used to the bullshit he spills when he's angry that it takes a minute for the words to replay in my head.

Took you in as my own.

"Stop it!" my mom cries. "Stop!" She grabs his arm.

He yanks it from her hold. "It's about time he knows. Walking around here like you don't need us, threatening us. Endorsing my enemy after you've been given everything!"

"No. Please don't," my mom begs, reaching for him again.

"You're not mine," my dad spits.

All the air rushes from my lungs like he punched me in the gut.

My mom wails and pushes past him, clinging to me. "Why would you do that?" she sobs.

I'm in shock. Numb. Everything inside me collapses.

He's not my father.

"I—" I nudge her off me.

"Tell him. Tell him how you left me and slept with someone else. That you don't even know who his father is." My father's face is full of rage, but also satisfaction.

I wonder how long he's dreamed of dropping this bomb. How many times he's daydreamed about how much he'd hurt me.

My mom's eyes beg me to stay, but the world has already tilted off its axis.

Everything makes sense now. How he always fawned over Holden. How nothing I did was ever good enough. How I'd catch him looking at me with resentment sometimes.

I wasn't his.

"Then I guess this just made everything easier." I open the door.

"No. Brooks, listen to me—"

"Let him go," my dad spits out.

My mom follows me outside, collapsing onto the bricks, crying as though she loves me. If she really loved me, she wouldn't try to tear apart the woman I love.

I get in my truck, slamming the door, and drive off.

Turns out my whole life was built on a lie, and I had no idea.

Chapter Thirty-Five

LOTTIE

I'm in bed on Monday morning, having already called Saylor to take over my shift.

Brooks never messaged me, and I have no right to think he would have. But I still check my phone obsessively. Still hope. Still hate myself for causing our fight.

Nash came and picked us up at the hospital, and while the nurse wrapped Poppy's ankle, I cried as if it was my ankle, not hers. I cried when the lady from reception brought me my purse, saying the young man we were with had dropped it off. I cried most of the drive home, facing the window so no one would see.

I thought ending it with Brooks was the right choice. That some sort of relief would wash over me afterward. That I'd go back to normal. Whatever that is. That I'd feel how I did before we got married in Vegas. But this feeling eating away at my insides is even worse.

A knock lands on my bedroom door, and when I don't say anything, holding my breath that whoever it is will just go away, the door creaks open. I remain in my bed, hoping if I pretend I'm asleep, they'll leave. The mattress dips, and a hand falls on my shoulder, running down my arm. It's warm and comforting.

Mom.

I should've known but had hoped she was in the middle of the breakfast rush at The Getaway Lodge.

"Sweetie."

I pull the covers over my head. "Not now, Mom."

"Come on a ride with me?" Her hand continues to run down my arm. "I think we're due for a talk."

I push the covers off and sit up in bed. "I don't want to talk."

She nods like she understands, but how could she? She's never destroyed a relationship with someone who feels like home. She pats my knee and stands. "Get up and meet me outside."

"And if I don't?"

She turns around at the door and gives me a soft smile. Her nose crinkles. "I'm not really asking."

Didn't think so.

With a sigh, I toss off the covers and grab some shorts and a T-shirt, pulling my hair into a messy bun.

My mom is already in the UTV when I step onto the porch, blinking into the sun as if it's too bright for the darkness inside of me. I'm happy Scarlett's at work, and Romy and Poppy are still sleeping. I really don't want to see anyone else right now.

My mom pats the passenger seat.

"Why are we doing this?" I whine, but she presses on the gas without answering me.

Totally her.

We drive around our side of the ranch. Past the boys' house, past my parents' house and The Getaway Lodge. We pass the chicken farm and the horse stables until she stops at the base of Daisy Hill.

"Mom," I say, my voice flat.

Daisy Hill is where all of our ancestors—including my cousins' mom—are buried. It's a huge hill planted with daisies, surrounded by a white fence, with a path winding up to the top that we usually take on horseback.

"Come on." She nudges me and turns off the UTV, pocketing the keys and ruining my escape plan.

I reluctantly follow her, and she holds the gate open for me when we reach the top of the hill. It's clear someone's been here recently since Aunt Daisy's grave is littered with fresh flowers.

My mom sits on one of the benches near my grandparents' graves and eyes the empty spot next to her. "Want to talk about it?"

I plop down beside her, and she pats my leg.

"Ever feel like you're just losing it?"

She laughs. "Wait until you go through menopause. It gives a whole new meaning to the words losing it."

"What do you already know?" My voice is barely a whisper.

"Only that one of my daughters went off with some country singer and didn't get dropped off until six this morning. My niece broke her ankle, and my other daughter was crying in the hospital and all the way home."

I bite my lip. "Who told you?"

"I don't give away my sources. Why were you crying in the hospital when you weren't the one who broke her ankle?"

"I basically ended it with Brooks."

Her head rocks back, and she rises from the bench before crouching at her parents' graves, picking around the stones.

"You know, I used to hate the weeds that come in and crowd out the good stuff." She pulls one and tosses it aside. "Did you know daisies are weeds?"

"Why are we talking about weeds?"

"Humor me," she says, searching through the grass for more. "People don't realize that the definition of a weed is just a wild plant that's not wanted in the area. Someone might look at this hill of daisies and only see something undesirable. Others see beauty. It really is just in the eye of the beholder."

"We don't have a future. There's too much that's happened."

"Let's push all the stuff with Holden away. It's been so long, and no one in this town looks at you the way you think they do. Tell me what's really worrying you."

I slide off the bench and join her in the grass. "I thought I was doing well, pushing forward, but then Mrs. Watson came into the store and... well..."

"You'd think a woman with problems in her own home wouldn't go causing them in someone else's." Her voice sharpens. "That's the problem. In my eyes, she's undesirable. Just an unwanted weed."

I laugh a little bitterly, and my mom bumps her shoulder against mine.

"I know I shouldn't listen to her," I say.

"You shouldn't. But there's hurt there, and it's hard to overcome that. Especially with how young you were. Can I speak frankly, sweetie?"

"Don't you always?"

She tilts her head. "Yeah, pretty much. I think you're afraid of feeling unwanted again. Am I right?"

"Are you really comparing me to a weed?" Tears fill my eyes.

"A pretty one. A daisy."

I shake my head, my face crumpling. "He wants a family, Mom." Tears spill freely down my cheeks now.

She puts her hand on my back and rubs slow, steady circles. Not saying anything. Just letting me fall apart in the grass.

"I can't give it to him. He's not going to want me after he finds out. That future he's built up of us in his mind is never going to happen."

"So that's it? You're making the decision for him?"

I pluck out a weed and toss it on the pile. "What choice do I have? He's made it clear he sees a family in his future."

"Okay. So that's that? You just live alone and don't ever put yourself out there? Deny yourself the love you deserve?"

"Come on. I'm a weed. One of those horrible ones that squeezes out all the beauty." I tug on one, but only the leaves give.

"I don't think you're that one. That one's holding on with all its might. You're more like this." She plucks a daisy from the grass. "This one's ready to be moved. To grow somewhere else."

"Thanks for that."

We sit in silence, the sun warming the back of my neck.

"You know," she says after a beat, "I actually would like to thank Holden if I ever see him again."

"What?" I blink, and my forehead wrinkles.

"He gave you a crash course in life when you were nineteen years old. He taught you that nothing comes easy, that people will disappoint you. He broke your trust and your belief in people. You built a damn fortress around your heart."

"Why is that a good thing?"

She sways slightly. "Because only the strong ones will get in past your defenses. You're not giving just anyone the ability to hurt you again. And someone did get in. Someone took down your wall, brick by brick. And now you're trying to tell him he doesn't belong there."

"So, I'm a weed with a wall and Brooks bulldozed it?"

"He didn't bulldoze it. He earned every brick he removed. That's the only way you'd ever let him in." She pats my leg.

239

"You know who he is. But you also assume you know what he wants."

"It's easier this way."

"You think if you don't tell him, he can't break your heart?"

"Yeah."

"And yet you were crying in a hospital and for an hour drive home, and you didn't want to get out of bed this morning. Sounds like you've got it all together."

A bitter laugh slips out of me, understanding her point. "I get it, okay... I do."

"That's because you're my smartest child. But don't tell Bennett or Romy." She laughs, and I laugh with her because we both know she says the same thing to them. "Family isn't just blood. You know that. Brooks was family before you drunk-married him."

I nod.

She adds, "There are a lot of options out there. And from what I know of Brooks, he's not afraid of hard work. Maybe your path to kids looks different, but that boy will be by your side through all of it."

I run my fingers under my eyes. "Thanks, Mom."

She wraps her arm around me. "How'd I do? It's my first official 'get out of your own way and be happy' talk. I was nervous. Went a lot of different directions."

"You mean comparing me to a weed?"

We laugh, and I rest my head on her shoulder.

"I love you," she says softly. "And I want you to be happy and get everything you want."

"I think it's Brooks," I say.

She laughs louder. "Oh, you do, do you? I think you might be the last one to know."

A butterfly floats down and lands on one of the daisies.

"Oh. Oh!" Mom sits up straight. "It's the perfect sign."

"What?" I laugh.

"Butterflies symbolize rebirth. Transformation. It's a sign."

I stopped believing in signs after Holden. But something about today... maybe this butterfly is the start of something new. Something good.

"What a perfect way to seal this all up." She dips her head. "Thank you, little butterfly."

It lifts off the daisy and floats back into the sky.

"You scared it," I say, standing and brushing off my shorts.

"I didn't scare it. It's off to find the next person who needs their life fixed."

"Gee, thanks, Mom."

She stands and slings her arm around me, and we walk down the hill together.

Uncle Bruce is waiting at the bottom. "Came to help in case your mom messed up." He winks.

"I don't need your help, big brother," she says. "I did a great job, right, Lottie?"

"She was saved by a butterfly."

Mom nudges me, and I laugh.

Uncle Bruce pulls me in for a hug and kisses my forehead. "Go get him." He winks and starts up the hill. Probably to see Aunt Daisy.

I climb into the UTV and glance back as Mom starts it.

"Think he'll ever take his own advice?" I ask.

"I hope so." She exhales as we drive away.

I have so many regrets about how I handled all of this because of how scared I was—of my feelings, of his feelings, of the truth. And now I have to wait until Brooks is off work to try to make this right.

But for the first time in days, I don't want to hide, I want to run. Toward Brooks and our future. I guess now I just have to figure out how to win him back.

Chapter Thirty-Six

BROOKS

I never call out from work. I work holidays. I'm on call more than I'm not—but today, I'm off. No badge, no radio. Just me and a whole lot of thoughts I'm not ready to dissect.

My father's words echo through my head every time I let the silence stretch too long—"you're not mine."

The worst part was that it was a semi-relief. Somewhere deep down, I've always been scared I'd turn into him. Now there's a crack in that fear because he created no part of me.

I still believe who you are is more about how you're brought up, what you witness and absorb. Not blood. But it doesn't change the relief that's set in since I found out. But with that relief comes a sense of betrayal too, for keeping the truth from me for so many years.

My mom has called more than a handful of times, but she's crazy if she thinks I'm going to return any of her calls. Not now. Maybe not ever.

I'm on the couch, vegging with a cold pizza from last night and binge-watching *How to Catch a Smuggler*. Mack is sprawled out on the floor as though he's emotionally recovering too. Probably missing Lottie.

Then I hear the crunch of gravel on my drive. I tense, hoping it's not either of my parents. It won't be Lottie, so there's no reason to bother to get up.

Footsteps echo up my porch steps. I wait for a knock on the door I fully plan to ignore. But the doorknob turns, and I glance over.

No one just walks into my house. Except maybe Ben in a crisis. But he doesn't know what went down last night, and there's no way this town has heard the secret. My parents would rather be buried alive than tell anyone that truth. No doubt my dad is regretting his anger-filled rant from last night, worried I'm going to out them both to the citizens of Willowbrook.

Mack lifts his head, then springs up. His ears perk forward, his tail wagging. Definitely not my parents then. Mack doesn't fake his loyalty.

I stand as the door cracks open.

"Hey, Mack. I'm just going to drop these off right here, and then I'll be right back."

She's here. She came.

"Lottie?" I cross the room in a few hard strides, then yank the door the rest of the way open.

She's dressed up with her hair done, makeup on, and arms full of grocery bags. The expression on her face makes her look as though she's been caught.

"You're home." She rocks back as if she wasn't expecting me. "Oh. I wasn't prepared."

We stand, each taking the other in. I'm an idiot for letting her push me away last night, letting her think she could walk out of my life and I wouldn't fight for us.

"I'm sorry." Her voice stumbles out, her eyes wide and glassy. "I'm so stupid. I shouldn't have said those things."

I wrap an arm around her neck and pull her in, pressing my forehead to hers. Her breath hitches and mine stays trapped in my chest until we can get this all cleared up.

"It was me," I murmur. "I'm the one who's sorry. You're right—I should've been telling you how much I love you for who you are today, not trying to rewind time. That's not the woman I fell in love with."

"Brooks," she says softly, pulling back just enough to look at me, "please let me say what I need to first, okay?"

I nod and reach to take the bags from her hands. "Okay. Let me help." I peek inside. "What's all this?"

Her shoulders slump. "I was going to make you dinner. As an apology. Thought I'd be waiting for you to come home, but..."

She walks into the kitchen, Mack trailing her as though she's his everything. Get in line, buddy.

"Why are you home, Brooks?" She unpacks while I carry in the rest of the bags.

"You have more in the car?" I'm dodging her question.

"Just a few. I'll get them."

"No, I got it. I think someone wants your attention." I glance at Mack sitting next to her, tail thumping, waiting patiently.

She looks down and smiles. "I'm sorry, Mack. My mind is all over the place. I'm trying to win Daddy back."

I freeze at the door and look over my shoulder. She looks at me, waiting for my reaction as she's kneeling, running her hands through Mack's fur.

"You never lost him."

Her lips tip up, and that smile undoes all the turmoil inside me. And it guts me in equal measure. She shouldn't have had to come to me. I should've been the one pounding on her door last night.

I jog to her car, grab the remaining bags, and return to find her unwrapping one of those fancy dog treats she carries at the store.

"I didn't forget about you." She hands it to Mack, and he trots off, apparently satisfied.

"I thought he'd never leave us alone." I wrap my arms around her waist from behind, resting my chin on her shoulder.

She leans back into me. "We need to talk. I don't want to sweep the fight under the rug... but why are you home? It's not because of our fight, is it?"

I hold her tighter. "I'd rather talk about us."

My voice cracks on the edges. She hears it. Of course she does. She swivels in my arms, slides her hand into mine, and leads me to the couch.

This is it. The truth I haven't said aloud. The one I'm not ready to own but want to share with her at the same time.

She abandons the groceries and sits beside me, legs crossed, facing me. "What is it?"

I love that she knows something's off. Love that she sees me even when I'm trying to hide.

"I went to my parents' place last night." I take her hand, needing something steady.

She scoots closer, her calf brushing my thigh. I want her in my lap but if she straddles me, this talk won't happen. And it needs to.

She doesn't try to fill the silence but waits for me to speak. I'm probably scaring her.

"I went to tell them to stay out of our relationship. And tell them I was cutting them out of my life."

"Brooks." Her voice breaks.

"My dad was angry. He wanted me to endorse him as mayor, but they wouldn't listen to me. Hell-bent on saying you were..." I frown. "Using me."

She nods. I assume my mother accused her of the same

when she went to see her at the store. I'm sure it doesn't make it any easier for her to hear it again though.

"My dad was pissed after I told them that if they couldn't respect you and our relationship that I didn't want them to be a part of our lives. When I didn't cave, I told him I was backing Miller and... he lost it." I swallow hard.

Her hand flies to her mouth. "No."

I look her straight in the eye. "I do not want them poisoning this. What kind of life could we have if they're constantly trying to destroy us?"

Her hands tighten over my mine.

"Anyway, my dad blew up, forbidding me, and when I didn't bend to his will, he got vengeful and said I wasn't his son."

She gasps, and her eyes widen. "What?"

"Yeah."

"What did your mom say?" She searches my face.

"She was taken aback at first. Upset. Crying. But we both know he did it to punish her."

Lottie's eyebrows draw down. "For what?"

"For going to you. For setting off this whole chain reaction. She went to you, that pissed me off, I confronted them, I pulled my endorsement for mayor. He's already losing, according to him, and me not agreeing to endorse him as I always have in the past would be the final nail in the coffin. He wanted to punish my mom, and who gives a damn who gets hurt in the process? That's how he works."

She throws her arms around me, pressing her face into my neck. "I'm so sorry. How are you handling it?"

She draws back a little and studies my face as though she's waiting for me to cry, or yell, or show anything. Honestly, I think I haven't fully processed it, and maybe I won't, but they weren't my future. I was ready to cut them out regardless.

"This is why you're home?"

I nod.

She kisses my jaw. "Brooks... I'm so sorry. I wish there was something I could do."

I pull her into my lap, just wanting her near me. "You being here is enough."

"But this... this has to be so hard to wrap your head around. It's cruel and careless of him to divulge that truth in the middle of a fight." She climbs off my lap, and I try to tug her back, but she paces, fire in her eyes. "How could they do this? Just drop that bomb in the middle of an argument like a toddler having a tantrum? I hate that I feel bad for your mom... but she didn't deserve that either."

She storms into the kitchen and continues unpacking, each item being slammed onto the counter.

"Lottie." I place my hand on her wrist. "It's not the spaghetti sauce's fault."

She puts up a hand. "Sorry. I'm okay. Just—processing, but I have no right to be the one who's mad." She turns and wraps her arms around my waist. "I'm good now."

I lift her chin. "I appreciate your rage on my behalf. I chopped enough wood last night to start my own firewood company."

"My rage doesn't help you though." She tightens her arms around me, burrowing her head in my chest.

"It does. It makes me feel like you care. Like you're in this with me." I kiss the top of her head and breathe in her scent.

She rests her chin on my chest, fingers combing through my hair. She watches me for a moment, looking deep into my eyes, and I know before she even says the words. "I love you, Brooks. I know I took my time admitting it, but I do."

I smile wide as the weight on my shoulders eases, and something knits together in my chest. "About time."

She punches me lightly in the stomach. "Shut up."

We stand there a moment, wrapped up in one another.

Although we're not talking, I feel as though we're on the same page. I don't want to let her go.

Then I remember... "Didn't you say you wanted to tell me something?"

She hesitates. "This was big enough news. Mine can wait."

"I'd rather get everything out now."

She unwinds herself from me. "Let me make you dinner. You have a lot to think about right now, and you need to deal with that. It's a blow you weren't prepared for, and I'm sure it's going to take some time to figure out how you feel about it."

"Lottie." I walk toward her as she puts some items in the fridge. "It's a shock for sure, but they aren't good people. I was already kicking them out of my life. Sure, I haven't fully processed it, but you and me, us, I need that to be good. So I'd really like it if you told me what you came here to say."

I give her the opening to share with me what's causing her distress, unsure if she'll take it.

She pulls back, rests her hip against the fridge. "You won't let this go, will you?"

I shake my head once.

"Can we walk and talk?"

Mack lifts his head at the word walk.

"We can go wherever you want."

I hold out my hand, and she accepts it. For the first time, it feels as if we're moving forward—together.

Chapter Thirty-Seven

LOTTIE

Brooks doesn't rush me to start talking. He just runs his thumb slowly across my fingers. Our hands are laced together as we walk around his property. Mack trots beside me this time, not wedged between us, like his own quiet confirmation that even he knows there's no space left between Brooks and me anymore.

So much has happened in the short time since we've returned from Vegas.

"I have to tell you something, but to get there, I have to start with Holden. Are you okay with that?"

"I do know you were engaged to my brother." There's a soft tease in his voice as he squeezes my hand.

"Still, I couldn't stand to be around a girl you barely dated without wanting to tug her down by her hair, and I'm asking you to go back to a time when I was going to marry another man."

"Just to note, I like the jealous part of you. And I want this. I want you. So I want to know everything you want to tell me."

I nod, grateful he doesn't make us stop walking. Instead of heading to the dock, he veers us around the small pond.

"Holden and I moved fast. Not as fast as us, but it felt like it at the time." I need to get this all out before I lose my nerve. "I thought I was in the middle of one of those whirlwind love stories—flowers, sweet texts, long talks under the stars. I got caught up in the magical way he painted our future with his words. He was charming and ambitious, but most of all he made me feel chosen, as if I were everything to him.

"I'd barely been out of Willowbrook, and he'd studied abroad in Spain. He talked about the world like it was something you had to see in order to say you'd really lived. Naïvely, I thought we were one of those couples who were lucky to find their forever so young."

I stop and glance at Brooks. I can't imagine being on his side of this, hearing me talk about how I thought another man, his brother, was my everything.

"I'm good. Promise," he says gently. His eyes are on me, solid and patient.

"I was only nineteen. It went from kissing to sleeping together really fast. He was my first..."

His jaw tightens, but he says nothing.

"We were careful... or thought we were. But I got pregnant only three months into dating." I pause, the memories, the emotions crashing in too fast to stop them now. "Your parents had told him to take the summer off before starting job interviews. They probably regret that now."

I fall silent, the memory painfully pressing against my ribs.

Brooks doesn't say a word. He's just there, present. Letting me hold the space how I need to. Letting me tell the story he only knows bits and pieces of.

As hard as I try not to let it happen, I'm taken back to that time, and all the raw emotions claw at me again. Me, crying in Sadie's arms after I took the pregnancy test. Me telling Holden at our make-out spot. Holden's truck door slamming so hard it shook the frame. Him pacing in the moonlight, saying I'd tricked him, that I'd trapped him. And me... trying to swallow the shame and figure out how I was going to tell my parents.

"Holden didn't take it well at first," I say, not needing Brooks to hear how horrible it felt to get that reaction from the boy I was in love with when an innocent baby of both our making was growing inside me.

Brooks inhales sharply beside me. I don't need to say it. He knows what that kind of anger looks like. "Tell me what happened."

"It's not going to change—"

"I don't want any secrets between us. Please, Lottie."

I swallow. "He accused me of doing it on purpose. To keep him in Willowbrook. Said I was ruining his future."

Brooks's chest rises and falls in a wave of restrained fury. He closes his eyes for a second, as though he's trying to breathe through it.

"But the next day... he showed up outside my house on bended knee. Rose petals all around him. Apologized for his reaction the night before, told me I just took him by surprise and that he was in shock. When he proposed, he said we'd prove everyone wrong. Said it didn't matter what anyone thought. And I wanted to believe him so badly that I said yes.

"Our parents weren't thrilled. Irresponsible, they said. Too young. Holden just kept telling me that it was us against the world. He could be so convincing. One moment cruel, the next, reciting poetry. The good outweighed the bad. It was an adjustment for both of us. The baby wasn't planned, but they were still wanted."

"How mean did he get?"

I shake my head. "Just words. I know they can hurt, and they did, but..." I shrug. "It doesn't matter anymore. It's been over for a long time."

We walk again, both silent for a minute. I feel Brooks growing more tense.

"Can we sit?" I ask.

"We can do whatever you want." He guides me down onto the grass, our hands still entwined.

"The wedding was fast-tracked for obvious reasons. Holden started looking for jobs in Lincoln and Omaha. I wanted to stay more local now that we were having a baby, but he sold me on leaving. He was good at getting his way and getting others to agree as if they'd never thought any differently. Soon he expanded his search to Seattle, New York, Los Angeles. He'd spend hours dreaming on Zillow, planning nurseries in cities I'd never stepped foot in. It was like a fairytale."

"Sounds like Holden," Brooks grumbles.

I shake my head, ashamed I was so naïve. "I let my whole world become about him. I never once asked myself what I wanted. If I wanted to go to school. Work. Anything other than to just... be his."

Brooks runs his hand down my leg, a quiet reassurance that I'm not alone in this anymore.

"We were three days out from the wedding when I lost the baby. I started bleeding and cramping. My mom rushed me to the hospital. Holden didn't come for hours. Said his phone died."

"I remember," he says, voice tight.

I look up, startled. "That's right, you were there."

He nods. "I brought him. Found him drinking with his friends in Lincoln."

A lump forms in my throat. I'd forgotten. Or maybe I'd buried the memory.

"You probably remember your parents coming into my room and telling us we didn't have to go through with the wedding anymore. That maybe losing the baby was a sign it wasn't meant to be."

He nods again. "They were horrible."

"But Holden doubled down. Said we'd still get married."

"He never liked anyone telling him what to do. If my dad said stop, he was going to sprint. I don't mean that he didn't want to marry you—"

"It's okay. I think he didn't want to, but the more your parents fought it, the more persistent he became that we'd still get married."

Brooks frowns. "Truth be told, I was really proud of him. I didn't want to watch him marry the girl I wanted, but I was so happy he didn't listen to my parents." Brooks looks away, swallowing hard. "I hated it too though. Watching you be in love with a man who didn't deserve you, when I..."

I squeeze his hand. He doesn't have to finish.

"I wore the big puffy dress. Had my hair and makeup done. Waited inside the church on the square and had my pictures taken in the gazebo in the town square before the ceremony while half the town watched on. Everyone in town was invited. Sure, I had some nerves, but I was determined to marry him."

"You made a beautiful bride."

A sad sort of chuckle leaves my lips. "You didn't see me until after. When I was crying on the floor, dress bunched around me, mascara running down my face."

"I'll never forget that moment," he murmurs.

God, I don't want to do this last part, but I have to. My mom is right—if I don't tell Brooks what happened, then we can't move forward. I straighten and take his hands. Mack presses close, resting his head on my thigh as if he knows I'm about to come undone.

"Something else happened that you need to know about, Brooks. Between the miscarriage and the wedding."

He squeezes my hand.

"Brooks..." My voice trembles. "Brooks..."

Wetness pools in my eyes because I'm about to break his heart. Whether or not he decides to still be with me, he's going to have to figure out if he still wants a life with me based on this new information.

"You can tell me, Lottie." He dips his head to meet my gaze.

"I can't... my uterus... shaped... I can't carry... a baby." I close my eyes and inhale the deepest breath before opening my eyes, tears spilling down my cheeks.

He stills. His hand slips from mine, and the air in my lungs collapses.

"I know you need time to figure out if you can live with that. Take all the time you need, and I mean, obviously, Holden... when he found out, he didn't want me anymore. When I got home from the ceremony that never happened, I found a note he'd left me. It said he'd always dreamed of a family and... more, but I don't remember it all." I take another labored breath. "I know there are some options for children but not ones that don't come with a hefty financial cost and... I get it... I understand if you don't... you know... want this anymore." Tears freefall down my cheeks, toppling over one another as if in a race to slip off my face.

Brooks touches my face. "Hey." His gaze is soft and sympathetic. "It's okay."

"It's not." A sob erupts, and I shake my head. "I will never be able to grow our child. I'll never be able to take your hand and place it on my stomach so you can feel the baby kick. There will be no stomach to kiss or cradle with your hand. No late-night cravings that you have to run out to satisfy. You won't get to experience our pregnancy, watch our baby grow." More tears rush down my cheeks as my breathing labors further. Hiccupping sobs rack my body now.

He slides closer, putting his arm around me. I'm pretty sure I'm not crying about not being able to carry a baby—I've come to terms with that—but the fact that I might lose Brooks because of it is my undoing.

"I know," he whispers.

My head jerks up. "What?"

"I knew. Before the wedding. I overheard Holden and my dad talking about it. I kept it to myself because it wasn't my place to say anything, and I figured it wasn't something you'd want to talk about with me. But I've known all along, Lottie."

Fresh tears unleash down my face. "And it doesn't change anything for you?"

"No. Because I want *you*. If we have a family, we'll figure it out together. Adoption, surrogacy, fostering... or just you, me, and Mack, if that's what life gives us."

"You really mean that?" Hope feels like the first tendrils of a stem poking out of the earth.

He cups my cheek. "I've loved you since before I was allowed to. It changes nothing for me."

"Oh my god, really? Are you sure, Brooks?"

He nods. "Except you reliving that day makes me want to kick Holden's ass all over again."

"Again?" I search his face.

"He was holed up in a hotel two towns over. A story for another time."

I wipe my cheeks. "So, what now?"

"We have one more date. And then you have to decide whether or not you're keeping me."

A smile blooms on my face. "I'm keeping you if that's okay with you?"

He laughs and nudges me down so my back is on the grass. "Hell, Lottie Owens, I've wanted you my entire life. You were the last one to figure it out."

"Figure what out?"

He cages my head between his hands. "That I was the man for you."

"So very true." I place my hand on his cheek. "Thanks for waiting for me to catch up."

"I've been chasing forever with you for a long time. I would've waited as long as it took. It was always you, Lottie."

"Brooks?"

He leans in. "Yeah?"

"Take me to bed."

He stands, offering me his hand with that crooked smile I've always loved. "Thought you'd never ask."

Chapter Thirty-Eight

LOTTIE

Halfway to his house, Brooks bends over and hauls me up over his shoulder.

I shriek. "What are you doing?"

"I need you in my bed, pronto."

He speedwalks us the rest of the way into his house, waiting for Mack to come inside before kicking the door shut and flicking the lock.

"You never lock the door when you're home."

"There will be no interruptions."

"What if Deputy Moore needs you?" I bang my hands on his ass, grabbing a handful with each hand, but he doesn't put me down.

"If Moore interrupts us for some stupid shit today, he's going to have to find another station to work at." He walks us up the stairs and lowers me down the length of his body until my feet touch the floor.

"I'm not sure how slow I'll be able to go." I grab the hem of his shirt, my hands sliding under and up. "Do you think we already had sex?" My fingertips graze over the dips and valleys of his abs. "Because before that morning, I had no idea this is the body you were hiding."

He stares down at me, and the want and lust filling his gorgeous green eyes makes me want to fall to my knees.

"I really hope we didn't that night, but seeing you naked and not being able to touch you that morning? Having to act as if I didn't care? It was pure fucking torture." His hands toy with the hem of my T-shirt, seeming like he's trying to decide if he wants to tug it off completely or tease himself.

"Now you can touch." I move my hands up and his T-shirt rises along with it.

With one hand, he grabs the neckline and tugs it over his head.

My gaze falls down his chest. "Seriously, Brooks, you should've stripped for me years ago, and we could've been here so much sooner." I laugh until his calloused fingers drag lightly along my skin.

"Arms up." His voice is as rough as dried out leather.

I do as he instructs, and he tugs my shirt over my head slowly, gaze dragging over every inch of skin he bares. I thought I'd feel self-conscious, vulnerable, exposed, but I don't. Because this is Brooks. His gaze isn't just admiring—it's reverent. He stares at me as though I'm something he still can't believe he's allowed to touch.

"Shit. Don't think I'm weak, but it's taking every ounce of willpower not to strip you in world record time."

"You should." My breathing is labored.

"I want to take my time."

"I'm not going anywhere. I'm yours for however many times you want me tonight."

He pushes his hand through his hair with a pained expression on his face. "Fuck, Lottie, don't say things like that."

My hand slips down between us, and I run it over the large bulge in his track pants. "I like these pants. No buttons or pesky zippers to get in the way." I run my finger under the waistband, back and forth.

He sucks in a breath, and his dick presses harder into my stomach. He backs me up toward the mattress, then we're lying side by side, flushed with laughter. The next moment, his mouth is on mine. There's purpose to this kiss. No hesitation. No question. He knows I'm all in.

And yet, my heart pounds as if I'm standing on a ledge of a cliff.

It's not a one-night mistake. There's nothing casual about it. We've put the entirety of ourselves out there now, no more secrets.

"You sure you want to do this?" he murmurs.

I nod, throat tight. "I've never been surer of anything."

His forehead rests against mine as he exhales. "God, why am I nervous?"

"Hey, if it's bad, there's always sex books and stuff to brush up on your skills, right?"

He looks at me then, eyes dark and amused, and just like that, the tension lightens. He *gets* me. He always has.

"Baby," he growls, leaning in close, "I promise we don't need any sex books for me to get you to pop off."

And just like that, my breath catches.

He unclasps my bra, and I slide my arms out, taking it off and tossing it to the floor. Again, his eyes speak the words he doesn't, and I've never felt more cherished or wanted in my life.

A pained groan leaves his lips. "You're trying to kill me."

"You're the one with your pants still on," I tease, hooking a finger into his waistband.

"I'm trying to savor this," he murmurs, kissing a line down my throat. "You think I want to hurry? I've waited too long to have you. I plan on memorizing every single inch."

"Is there a test I don't know about?" I suck in a breath, threading my fingers through his hair.

"My own personal one. How many times can I make you scream my name for starters." He lowers his head, lips brushing my jaw, then my neck.

"Show me, Sheriff. Hands-on demonstration only. I don't hand out participation trophies."

He chuckles into my neck. "Oh, I'm starting here."

And then he moves lower, dragging my jeans down my legs along with my panties, his hands firm but gentle. I can feel the weight of this moment—the care in it, the gravity. My body hums with an ache I've never experienced before.

He kneels between my legs, running a hand along my inner thigh. "You should come with a warning label."

I laugh. "Okay, I'll play your game. What would it say?"

"High risk of addiction. No known cure."

I cover my face with my hands, laughing. "Oh my god, you and your lines. Where did you hear that one?"

He lowers his chest to the mattress, spreading my thighs wider with his hand, and rests his chin on my stomach, staring up at me. "Come on, it was a good one."

His mouth finds me without warning, and I cry out, my fingers instantly gripping the sheets. His tongue strokes through my folds with expert precision. He finds my clit with terrifying accuracy, circling and sucking until my hips lift off the mattress.

He moans against me, and the low and hungry sound nearly tips me over.

"You taste like heaven," he murmurs, lips wet. "I might never be done down here."

As if I'm not already clenching to make this last as long as possible, his fingers slide inside me, curling just the right amount, and stars fill my vision. Everything inside me coils tight, tension rising so fast I can't catch up. My thighs shake, my breath stutters, and I come on a cry from somewhere deeper than my throat.

He kisses his way up my body, slow and unhurried, along my stomach, through the valley of my breasts until his mouth meets mine, and I taste myself on his tongue. I never used to be comfortable with this, but with him, it doesn't bother me. If anything, I'm turned on.

"Still think I need a sex book?" he whispers, brushing my sweaty hair off my forehead.

"Cocky, much?"

"Do you know me at all?"

I laugh, breathless. "What else you got, Sheriff?"

He stretches past me and reaches into his nightstand drawer, returning with a condom.

"Whoa, whoa, whoa, it's my turn." I sit up and inch closer to him.

"So is it my turn to grade you on performance?" He quirks his eyebrow.

I've never laughed this much during sex. Never had it be playful. I've clearly been missing out.

"I need you to stand."

He scoots back off the bed. I climb off the bed and saunter over to him. His eyes follow my every step.

I sink to my knees, the heat between us pulsing as fast as my heartbeat. As confident as I look, I'm no expert at this. Brooks watches me with such interest that I grow nervous.

"I—" His voice catches when I tug down the waistband of his track pants, dragging them slowly off with deliberate intent. "Lottie..."

I glance up at him as his cock springs free. It's hard, flushed, and heavy with want. "You said you wanted to memorize me," I murmur, wrapping one hand around the base. "It's time I get to do the same."

He sucks in a sharp breath when I lick a slow path up the

length of him. His thighs tremble before a groan erupts from his throat. When I swirl my tongue around the head, tasting the salt of him, he curses.

"Jesus," he whispers. "You're gonna kill me."

I hum around him and take more of him into my mouth, working him slowly, deliberately, studying his reactions with every pass of my lips and flick of my tongue. His eyes never leave me.

"Lottie..." His voice breaks. Brooks slides his hand into my hair, not forcing anything. "Your mouth—fuck, that feels so good."

I moan around him, the sound vibrating through his body, and his hips jerk forward. I hollow my cheeks and suck harder, letting him slide deeper back. He grips my hair a little tighter. He's so close already.

"You're too good, baby. You're too—" He groans.

I pull back slowly, pumping him with one hand. "What's my grade?"

"A fucking plus, now get off your knees because I'm not coming in your mouth our first time together."

I laugh and stand, my mouth finding his.

He swivels me around, pushing me lightly, and I fall to the mattress. I crawl up as he grabs the condom and rolls it on, watching me the whole time. My chest flutters but not from nerves. More like *this is happening*.

He's *mine*.

"Look at me," he says, positioning himself at my entrance. "I want to see your face as I slide inside you."

I keep my eyes locked on his as he pushes in slow and deep. Filling me in a way that has my entire body clenching around him.

I gasp.

He curses.

"Jesus, you feel—fuck—you're perfect."

He's big, and it's the kind of stretch I'm not used to, but my body hums with satisfaction. I've never felt fuller. So *claimed*. And I want to tell him I was a fool. It should've always been him.

"You feel better than I imagined," I whisper.

"You've imagined me?"

"Only every night since Vegas."

He groans and moves. His thrusts are long and dragging. I gasp each time, my fingernails clawing at his back the deeper he goes.

"You're so fucking tight," he says. "So wet for me. You're making me lose my goddamn mind."

He's everywhere. In every part of me. And it's not just the sex, it's the emotion braided through our movements. The years of longing looks, of restraint, of hoping and wishing.

"I can't believe we waited this long," I manage to say, breath hitching.

"I'd wait a lifetime if this is what I get." His mouth brushes mine. "But now that I have you? I'm never going back."

Our rhythm builds, sharp and deep. I lift my hips to meet him, our bodies moving together in perfect sync. My fingertips graze up his spine.

His hands slide up my arms, placing them above my head, interlocking our fingers. "I want to see you come," he pants. "I want to feel you fall apart around me."

"I'm almost there," I whisper, clenching our hands and tightening my thighs around him.

"Fuck, Lottie."

He thrusts harder, faster, and the pressure explodes. My orgasm crashes through me like a tsunami. I cry out, my body clenching. Brooks follows with a groan, his hips stuttering as he loses all control.

We collapse in a tangle of limbs, our bodies slick and

exhausted. He buries his face in my neck, and I wrap my arms around him.

No one has ever made me feel this cared for. This safe. This *whole*.

Chapter Thirty-Nine

BROOKS

Lottie's draped across my chest, her body warm and soft, legs tangled with mine under the covers. It hardly feels real that I finally get to hold her skin to skin with nothing between us, relaxed and sated.

We don't speak. I just run my fingers through her hair and try to commit this moment to memory. I fear I'll wake up and find this was all a dream. I've never felt this quiet in my head before. My mind used to be racing for ways to win her, to get her to notice me. And now, I can finally exhale.

Lottie shifts, her lips brushing my chest. "How come you didn't say anything? You could have told me you knew."

I stiffen for a moment, but she kisses my chest again. "I wanted you to tell me when you trusted me. It was your business, and I already felt guilty about overhearing it in the first place. Plus, it didn't make a difference, like I said."

"I should've told you this a long time ago..." She scoots up in the bed, and we turn to face one another. "I've liked you for a while, you know."

I smile and run my fingers along her arm. "How long?"

"I'm not sure if I can point to the exact time, but ever since you've been coming in for your coffees probably."

There's no way for me to keep my chuckle at bay. "You always act like I annoy you."

"How else am I supposed to act? Plus, I was scared. Scared of what people would think. Scared of people thinking I was hopping brothers. Scared I'd get hurt again. Scared that I wouldn't be enough."

"Fuck, Lottie, you've always been enough. You're all I've ever wanted." I inch forward and kiss her. She lets me, and I love how easy all this is between us now. How right she feels in my bed, my home, my life.

"Thank you... for... waiting and not judging."

I roll her over and slide on top of her. "I'm not gonna lie, you put up one helluva fight. You're as stubborn as the day is long, but you were worth every therapy session you caused me." I bend and kiss her neck.

"Funny."

"I thought so."

"God, you feel so good. I don't ever want to leave this bed," she says.

"We don't have to."

"Eventually we do."

"Not really. We can quit our jobs and live off the land."

"And die of hunger?"

I dramatically lift my body and look between our bodies, down toward her mound. "I'm not gonna starve."

She slaps my chest and laughs, tilting her head back just enough to look up at me. Her hair is a mess, her lips are swollen, and she's never looked more beautiful. Because she's mine. And I'm hers.

I lean down to kiss her, slow and sweet, and she hums against my mouth. But her legs shift open as if she wants more.

My stomach growls. Too loudly to be ignored.

She pulls back with a snort. "It doesn't sound like I satisfied you."

"So, I guess we'll need to buy groceries." I shrug.

She bites her bottom lip, grinning. "I figured. Why don't I go down and make that apology dinner I promised you?"

"Can I help?"

She slides out from under me and sits up, revealing bare skin that makes my mouth go dry. "Stare all you want. I'm all yours." Her hand touches my cheek, and she kisses me too damn quickly.

"I'm glad we're on the same page there."

She grabs a pillow and throws it at me. I catch it easily, toss it aside, and grab her around the waist, pulling her back down on top of me.

"You're insatiable," she says, curling into me again.

"So are you," I murmur into her hair. "Don't try to pretend like you don't want me to slide into you again."

She presses a kiss to my chest and sighs. "We need to refuel at least. May I borrow a shirt?"

I nod toward my dresser. "Top drawer."

Lottie slips out of bed, not bothering to cover herself, and my eyes track her. She saunters as though she knows I'm watching. She opens the drawer, rummages for a second, and pulls out a plain gray T-shirt with Sheriff on it. It hangs off one shoulder, barely covers her ass, and I don't even bother to pretend I'm not ogling her.

"You look good in my T-shirt." My voice is laced with pure male satisfaction.

"You say that like you're going to try to take it off me again in twenty minutes."

"If I were you, I wouldn't bend down to get anything from the fridge."

She shakes her head and heads for the stairs. I scramble after her, still shirtless, grabbing my sweatpants off the floor.

The house is quiet except for Mack's tail thumping lazily against the floor as he watches us from the living room rug. He probably came down here when we were all over one another.

Lottie opens the fridge and surveys the contents. "I was doing chicken parm, but that seems like a lot of work right now. How about a quick skillet?" She pulls out eggs and sets them on the counter. "You know, other than the stuff I brought, you have nothing here."

I shrug. "I'm never home."

"That might be changing soon."

"I'm not gonna argue with that."

She throws me a look over her shoulder that makes my chest ache. I love her so fucking much.

"All right, Sheriff. Grab a skillet, and I'll beat the eggs."

She searches cabinets for bowls and plates, and I guide her, resting one hand on her hip, reaching for the items she's not tall enough to grasp. We kiss one another as we pass. Hands grazing, fingers brushing. A constant tease between the two of us.

And then it hits me.

This is it.

This is what I've wanted.

Not just the sex—not just the high of having her scream my name in my bed—but the everyday stuff. The kitchen dance between us. The teasing. The fact that she wears my T-shirt as if it's hers.

I lean against the counter, content to watch her for a second.

"What are you thinking about?" She side-eyes me as she pours the eggs into the skillet.

"You know."

She sets down the bowl and saunters over, winding her arms around my waist. "Tell me."

I wrap my arms around her, lifting the hem of the T-shirt and grabbing her ass. "I could get used to this."

She goes still for half a second, then looks up at me. "Me too."

It's been a long damn road to get here, but we're exactly where we're supposed to be—and I don't want to waste another second.

I kiss her again. Slow and familiar, but it's not nearly enough. I swivel us around and prop her up on the counter. She opens her legs for me, pulling me closer, and I kiss her deeper.

I can't hold myself back. Will I ever be able to?

My tongue finds hers. My hands roam her curves. My body's screaming for everything she's already given me.

She moans into my mouth as my hips press against her core. Her fingers weave through my hair, tugging, guiding, pulling me closer. I kiss her deeper and harder, my mouth claiming hers, my tongue brushing against hers again and again.

Lottie wraps her legs around my waist, locking me to her. One hand drags down my back, her heels pushing at the waistband of my pants, and I groan. Fuck, she's not playing fair.

"Brooks," she whispers between kisses, her lips brushing mine.

"What, baby?"

She breathes hard, her forehead pressed to mine. "You can't kiss me like that and expect me to focus on dinner."

I grin, my mouth dropping to her jaw, then her neck, her collarbone, the place just beneath her ear that I discovered makes her shiver. "Good. I wasn't hungry for food anyway."

"Me either anymore." Her voice is all heat, no protest.

I turn off the burner with my lips still seared to hers. Then

I slide my hands up her thighs, under my shirt that's now hers, and she arches, tucking me tighter between her legs.

"I expect you to finish what you start," she whispers.

My hands roam, pressing my length into her, grinding against her until she's soaked and squirming. I want to go slow, but I want to devour her at the same time. One thing's for certain—I never want to leave this house.

Twenty minutes of moaning, grinding, and begging later, and we try making dinner once more.

Chapter Forty

LOTTIE

The door to the store chimes, and Brooks walks in. How was I never this tongue-tied before seeing him in his uniform?

"Good morning, ma'am." He tips his hat at me with a grin, and I swear I just about purr.

"Sheriff, how are you this morning?" I head behind the counter to make his coffee.

"I'm pretty good."

"Just pretty good?" I pour his coffee and bend to reach into the fridge for the creamer.

"It just got better."

I look over my shoulder to see him eyeing my ass. "I'm actually surprised you're still on that side of the counter."

"Is that an invitation?" He's already placing his hat on the counter and walking around.

"You never need an invitation." I turn to face him, and he cages me against the back counter. It's one of my favorite things that he does. "But I must admit, I'm rethinking that after the 'pretty good' morning comment."

He steps closer. "A gentleman doesn't kiss and tell."

"So, it was better than pretty good?"

He chuckles, and I trace the last name on his badge with my finger. God, I could actually make it my last name now. That's something we need to talk about.

"Believe me, getting woken up with your mouth wrapped around my dick is indescribable."

Romy enters the store and covers her eyes dramatically. "Ew. Ew. Ew."

Brooks doesn't move away from me, only securing me to him tighter. "Get used to it."

"Mommy and Daddy, make them stop," she says as the door behind her opens.

"Romy, grow up." My mom comes inside. "Oh, hello, Brooks."

"Brooks, my man." My dad follows my mom inside.

"Can you not speak like that?" I shake my head at my dad.

Brooks releases me, puts his hand out for my dad, and hugs my mom.

"You're ruining our sacred morning tradition," I say, sidling closer to Brooks, like a dog who refuses to stop being petted.

"Sorry to interrupt, but Lottie's been keeping you all to herself." Mom walks around the store, moving things around into different places. "We'd like to invite you over for dinner."

"Um..." I say and shake my head at Brooks.

"I'd love to." He smiles wide at me, and I scrunch my eyebrows. Is he crazy?

"I get that you're doing things a little backward, but we'd like to reverse it now that our daughter has finally come to her senses." Dad smiles at me as though he's proud of me.

"Is this going to be a running joke our entire relationship?"

All three of my family members look at one another. "Yeah," they answer in unison.

Brooks puts his arm around me and kisses my temple, chuckling.

"So dinner at our house next week. Wednesday work?" Dad asks.

"Sounds good to me," Brooks says.

Mom continues moving things around. "Would your parents like to join us?"

Brooks stiffens next to me. I wind my arms around his stomach and squeeze.

I haven't told anyone that Brooks has distanced himself from his parents. Any time I try to bring it up, he just keeps saying they're all dead to him. I can't imagine, with how he's feeling, what it must be like to see his dad's campaign signs on every inch of Willowbrook.

"I'm sure they're busy with the campaign." He kisses my cheek and grabs his hat off the counter, placing it back on his head. "I better get going. See you all next Wednesday."

He nods at my family and walks out of the store.

"Did I say something?" my mom asks.

But I realize that Brooks forgot his coffee, so I ignore her question, snatching it up and rushing out of the store. "Brooks!"

He's already beside his squad car. I hold out his coffee to him, but he doesn't take it.

"I'm sorry. I just... wasn't prepared. I haven't talked to them or about them to anyone but you. I haven't answered their phone calls."

"Hey, it's okay. Let's be honest, my mom was only inviting them to be polite. But I'm more concerned that you haven't really talked to me about this. Not in depth anyway. Maybe you should talk to them. I could go with you."

"Absolutely not." He takes the coffee from my hand.

"Why not? If this thing with us is going to move forward, then—"

"Lottie, you're never going near them again."

I stand back and stare at him with an expression that says he can't control that. "And if she pops into my store again? Or I walk past her on Main Street? Run into her at The Sprout House? I can handle myself."

He kisses me way too briefly. "The answer is no." He opens his car door and steps into the opening, ready to leave me and go to work.

"Last I checked, I was a grown woman."

He groans and says my name with zero patience.

"I'm serious. You've bent over backward for me. You gave me a space to feel safe without any judgment. You've cocooned me in a love bubble, and I love you for it. But it's my turn to be there for you. So deal with it." I step back, ready to walk away from him, but he grabs me by the wrist and tugs me back to him.

His coffee sits on top of the squad car, and he envelops me in a tight hug, burying his face in my neck. "I don't want to fight. It's just hard for me, you know? They've already done so much shit to you. I don't want you to go through any more for me."

"I'm not nineteen anymore."

"I just wish they'd leave Willowbrook, and we could move on without them. How am I going to coexist in this town with them?"

I cling to him tighter. "I know. I know. We can figure this out. But you have to let me in so I can help you."

"It's hard." He sounds like a whiny kid.

"Everything worth having is hard."

"Did you get that from your inspirational quote of the day calendar?"

I push him back.

He laughs, and God, I love that sound.

"If I had one of those, I would've ended up with you a helluva lot sooner."

"Very true." His radio goes off. "I gotta go."

"Okay, be safe out there, Sheriff. You have a woman to come home to now."

He kisses me one last time before climbing into his squad car. I pick up the coffee and hand it to him.

He reads the name on the cup and laughs. "Sir Satisfies-A-Lot. I'm moving up in the world."

I lean into the window, needing one more kiss from him before I have to go the entire day without him. "You sure are."

"Maybe I'll get to be 'Hubby' one day?"

I shrug and stand, backing up a few steps. "Maybe."

I blow him a kiss, and he squawks the siren quickly and drives away.

I watch until I can't see him anymore.

Damn, I have it bad.

Chapter Forty-One

BROOKS

This morning, Lottie wrote a note on my coffee cup.

Kiln Me Softly-7pm

I'm hoping that means she's giving me the pottery lesson I asked for.

That evening, I park at her house and walk the trail to her pottery shed, finding the door cracked open.

"Lottie," I say, pushing it open the rest of the way.

The shed is dark with candles spread throughout the space and soft music playing in the background.

"Lock the door behind you." She comes out from behind a shelf, wearing a white button-down shirt, and I pray nothing else underneath.

"This seems like a date I should plan." I break the distance between us.

"Consider this me making up for our third date." She allows me to pull her to me, and I give her a chaste kiss.

"You didn't have to—"

"I did. But don't worry, date four is all yours."

"I already have a plan." I tap my temple.

She winds out of my arms, and I miss her immediately, as if I don't really breathe unless she's near me.

"Did I dress okay?" I ask, looking down at my jeans and T-shirt.

"You okay getting them dirty?"

"I had hopes I would, but I kind of like this T-shirt." I strip it off my body. "I kind of like that shirt too." I eye the shirt she's wearing, since I'm pretty sure it came from my closet.

"You said you like me in your clothes. I didn't think you'd mind."

"I'd like it better on the floor." She feels too far away, so I weave around the battery-operated candles to her.

"Remember, you're here for a pottery lesson." She holds up her finger when I get too close.

I hold out my arm. "Lead the way."

She sits on the stool and pats the spot behind her. I straddle her from behind, and my hands run up the outsides of her thighs. She leans forward to center the wet lump of clay on her pottery wheel, and her ass hits my dick. I could watch her all day. The way her arms move, how her hips shift slightly on the stool.

"Here." Her wet hands take mine and bring them over to the cool clay.

My lips brush just beneath her ear as I inch closer, pressing against her back.

"You're gripping too tight," she murmurs, winding our fingers together. "Loosen your fingers. There. Let the clay come to you."

I shift slightly, trying to focus on the way her hands

manipulate the clay, but it's impossible to ignore the warmth of the body tucked in front of me, the sweet curve of her breasts, or the way my thighs brace against her. Her voice is low, instructional. I have no idea how she's able to concentrate on making whatever it is we're making when all I want to do is abandon the clay, pick her up, and take her over to one of the tables.

"What do we do next?" My voice is way too eager to get this part over with.

She chuckles. "I'm letting you feel the rhythm of the wheel."

"I'd like to feel something else right now."

"Focus," she says, turning her head toward me. "If we don't control your speed, our masterpiece will collapse." I groan, and my hand lifts off the clay, ready to touch her teasing curves, but she snatches it back and places it back on the clay. "Pay attention to your task, Sheriff."

"You're my task. Or so I hope at least."

"Hey, you asked for this lesson."

"I thought you understood why. I'll leave the sculpting to you, and you leave pleasuring you to me." My lips lick up her neck before I nibble on her earlobe.

"You're not even trying anymore," she whispers.

"Can you blame me?" I glance down through the valley of my splayed open shirt on her. A clear view to her breasts.

Our hands are a muddy mess, my forearms coated in wet clay. Lottie straightens, her hands sliding down my arms, trying to keep me going, but I've lost interest in the clay.

"I'm going to have to call this lesson over soon," she says.

"Do you think I'll complain?" I nip on her ear.

She continues to work the clay, and my fingers manipulate her buttons one at a time as I graze my nose down the column of her neck, sprinkling kisses along her flesh.

"Make me something beautiful," I whisper.

She sculpts, and I watch her hands work, how she's able to use just the right amount of pressure to make the clay do her bidding. Her fingers are fluid as she manipulates it into the shape she wants. Her body is at peace until I flick open another button, and her breath catches for a second.

Lottie's always beautiful, but admiring her here in her element, the place where I assume she calms any voices in her head, is mesmerizing. It makes me feel special that she's sharing it with me.

"You're brilliant."

She laughs, and her head falls back on my shoulder, her movements not faltering. "It's just practice. If you weren't so distracted, you could do this too."

"No, babe, I couldn't." I have no idea the hours she's spent in this shed. The failed attempts, the small successes that encouraged her to keep going. So much rage and reflection has probably happened in these four walls. "Thank you for sharing this with me."

Her head lolls back to my shoulder, and I finally get the last button undone, my hands sliding the cotton fabric open.

Still she has the patience to finish the bowl she's making, dipping her fingers into the water and bringing them back to the clay as her foot knows exactly how hard to press on the pedal. I don't touch her breasts but keep my hands on her thighs, moving them up and down, not wanting to bother her too much.

"Your hands feel so good."

"At least I'm good for something because I'm not doing much to help you here."

"Hmm," she hums.

The bowl is finally shaped, and her foot lifts off the pedal.

I kiss her neck, and after a beat, she gets off the stool and straddles me, thighs pressing outside mine. There's clay smeared along her arms and legs, thanks to both of us.

"Lesson's over," she says.

"Jesus," I mutter, my hands flying to her hips.

She lets the shirt slide down her arms slowly and tosses it aside.

I grip her tighter, pulling her flush against me. "Fuck, Lottie, you're gorgeous. Here, in your element, doing what you love, it brings out a beauty I hadn't discovered in you yet."

"You've done that." Her fingers weave through my hair, nails scraping my scalp. "A lot has gone down in this room, but my body is calm because of you. You bring that out of me, Brooks. Only you."

She undoes me with her confession. Another thing I've always dreamed of has come true.

Our lips crash in a kiss that's all tongue and teeth and pent-up hunger. Her hands are in my hair, mine sliding under her ass, dragging clay as my fingers dive under her silk panties. Her skin's flushed, smeared in fingerprints and streaks of gray, her breathing shallow, and I drag my mouth down her throat, over her collarbone, across the swell of her breast.

"Brooks," she gasps, arching into me as I suck on one nipple and tease it with my tongue. "God—"

She rolls her hips and grinds down, and I swear I could come in my pants. She flicks the button on my jeans. It's a little frantic, her hands wet with clay while she's full of awkward laughter and cursing. I inch up and finally get my pants removed, then her panties. Somehow, we manage for me to line myself up to her core and drag her forward.

"Shit, condom?"

"Oh god, yeah, of course," I say.

"Brooks, I was tested after my last partner, and I'm on the pill since I don't want to get pregnant by accident."

"Me too. I came back fine, and there hasn't been anyone since."

She smiles at me, "So, we're good."

"You sure you're okay with it?"

She nods and wraps her arms around my neck, holding me to her. "Yeah, I don't want anything between us."

She sinks down slowly, and I almost black out.

It's everything. Heat and pressure and her mouth falling open in a gasp, my name tumbling from her lips. I grip her hips and thrust up, watching her fall apart above me. She chases the friction and control she wants.

She rides me slowly at first, drawing her pleasure out, her lips brushing mine, her fingers digging into my shoulders. I thrust up harder and faster, and her moans grow louder.

I really hope no one is walking by outside.

Her climax rips through her, and I follow right behind her, groaning into our kiss as my release hits me.

She stays in my lap, and I run my fingers along her skin, our bodies connected until our racing hearts calm.

Eventually, she laughs against my shoulder. "Maybe we should be choosing activities where we're far apart in proximity."

"Appears so." I chuckle.

"You couldn't even hold out to make a bowl."

"Next time I'm going to sit in front of you in nothing but my boxer briefs, and we'll see how long you hold out."

"Hey, I made a whole bowl with your hard dick pressed to my back and your lips on my skin. I deserve a reward."

"Didn't I just give you that?"

She laughs and lifts off me. I miss her immediately.

There's wet clay on the floor, the stool, the table. My clothes lay wet and ruined on the floor. But my favorite part is the flushed look on her face as she brushes damp hair out of her eyes.

Hours later, after two more rounds, we lie on the ground, a blanket under us and the lights casting our flesh in a soft glow. She nuzzles into my chest, and I keep my arm around her shoulders, addicted to touching her soft skin.

"Can I ask you a question?" I worry about broaching the subject that could ruin our night.

"Sure."

"That morning with the woman from Lincoln... she wanted your coffee mugs, and you acted like you weren't the potter?"

Her finger traces the dips and valleys of my abs, running up my chest, though her eyes never meet mine. "I'm not sure I can handle the criticism."

"She was in love with them, so disappointed she couldn't buy them. That says something."

Lottie picks up her head and rests it on my chest. "I started throwing pottery after Holden. I wanted to control something because my body and my mind felt so out of control. It kept me going, so it's hard to share."

"But you give them as gifts and put them in the store."

She nods and lays her head on my bare chest but tips her head up to me. "They're safe there. It took me years to even do that. If you haven't noticed, I have a bit of a fear of not being good enough, and there're a lot more talented potters than me."

"I don't think so."

"Well, you probably haven't been into the pottery world. There are."

"Would you ever think about selling them?"

She laughs. "I never wanted to before, but I will admit after that lady, I have thought about it. I just have to get over my fear. But now that I see what my reward was after putting myself out there a little, I'm debating it."

"What was your reward?" My forehead wrinkles as I look down at her.

She kisses my chest, inching up. "You, silly."

She kills me with her confession, and I keep her lips on me, deepening the kiss until I roll us back over and take her again.

I'll never forget tonight. But I hope that it's just one of the many memories I'm going to make with Lottie over a lifetime.

Chapter Forty-Two

LOTTIE

Brooks parks at my house before dinner with my parents. Since we all live on the property, it's just as easy to meet up here and walk over to their place. Romy went over to my parents' house earlier to help my mom with dinner, although I'm sure she's sitting eating the appetizers instead of helping.

Wearing a sundress, I walk out onto the porch with a sweater in hand in case it gets cold on our walk back after dinner.

"Why don't we turn around, and you can show me your room?" Brooks twirls his finger in the air.

"Hey, is that any way to talk when you're about to have dinner with my father?"

I slowly step down the porch stairs, and by the time I hit the bottom, Brooks is there waiting for me. He pulls a bouquet of flowers from behind his back.

"For me?" I take them from him and inhale their scent.

"They're actually for your mom," he says with a straight face. I take him for his word until he laughs. "Kidding. I have another bouquet for her in the truck."

"I should put them in water." I turn back around and go

into the house, where I pull out a vase and fill it with water. Once the flowers are inside, I place the vase beside the sink and smile.

When I circle back around, Brooks is there. "Will you come home with me tonight? I'm off tomorrow because I have to finish that truck I've been working on. I can drive you to work though."

I draw closer to him, fiddling with the collar of his button-down shirt. "Maybe I can swindle a day off too. Be sweet to my mom tonight."

We kiss quickly, then he takes my hand and guides me out of the house, over to the path by the lake.

"Will you miss it here?" Brooks asks as we're passing the guys' house.

"The ranch?"

"I'm not trying to be presumptuous, but if we stay married, or if you marry someone else—"

"Wait what?" I stop him, and he looks down at his feet before lifting his gaze to me.

"I don't want to assume anything."

"Assume away!" I say, my tone more forceful than I mean it to be.

"Well, we haven't talked about it." He tries to slide his hand from mine, but I grab his big palm.

"Have I not been clear?"

"Lottie, you can't get mad. We got married in Vegas. Drunk. I swindled you into some dates to keep you from getting the marriage annulled. We're here, and I love where we are. My head is a mess, and I just want to give you options. I don't want this to end, and I know you don't either, but I don't know if you want to be *married* to me."

I release his hand and turn toward the lake, wrapping my arms around me. I'd assumed we were on the same page. "I don't want options."

He slides his arms around my waist and puts his chin on my head. "Does that mean you don't want to annul me?"

"We still have one more date, but I wasn't going to call the lawyers or anything."

He chuckles, and his arms tighten across my middle. I rest my hands on his arm.

"It's crazy, right? I mean, where do we go from here? We kind of started at the finish line."

I circle in his arms, sucking in a big breath. "I'm going to be really brave right now and tell you where my head is. And if yours isn't there, Brooks, I'm begging you, please tell me. You've been so forthcoming with your feelings for me, and I want to do the same, but I don't want you to pity me or anything."

"God, Lottie, I would never pity you. I'll always be truthful with you." He tucks a wisp of hair the breeze has caught and blown across my face behind my ear.

I inhale and exhale, staring into his eyes. Eyes that I've learned show everything he's feeling, and I know I can trust him with my heart. "When I woke up married to you, I wasn't completely disappointed, despite how it may have seemed. I mean, it was insane, but I was way more worried about what people would say than I was worried about my life with you."

He smirks, the same one that drew me to him in the first place, but also the same one that drove me crazy when he was fighting the annulment so hard.

"Oh god, think you can keep your ego in check? Can I continue?"

He waves for me to keep going, still grinning. "Please. So far, I love where this is going."

"I thought you would. Anyway, I wanted the annulment because I didn't want to let you get close to me. I didn't want to give you the chance to crack my armor and risk feeling all that pain all over again. But you're a stubborn bastard, so you did it anyway, and somewhere along the way, I fell madly in love with you. You couldn't just do what I wanted you to, huh?"

He chuckles and tugs me into him, securing me in one of his hugs that always makes me feel so safe and taken care of. "So, what do you want now, Lottie Owens?"

"I love you, and you don't even know my name." I circle out of his arms and throw my arms in the air. "It's Lottie *Watson*."

He doesn't say anything, waiting for me to say the actual words. I've delayed it enough and need to put it out there.

"I want to stay married. I want to move in together. I want to have a big reception and celebrate our love with all our friends and family. I want to make you crappy dinners you swallow down, pretending to like them, and I want to make you honey-do lists. Most of all, I just want Mack."

"Always the dog." He shakes his head, smiling.

"But if you want to wait and see—"

He puts his finger on my lips and stops me saying anything else. "I've wanted all those things for as long as I can remember, and I want to give them all back to you. Well, except Mack. He's already mine. I guess I'll share him."

"So, we're on the same page?"

Brooks nods. "We're on the same page."

He gives me a kiss as if we're sealing our agreement.

I draw back for a second. "We're going to be late, but all I want to do is make love to you right now."

"I'll still be here after the dinner. We have all night after we're done at your parents'." He takes my hand and guides me farther along the path.

"A quickie at my house?" There's no way I can wait.

"You have no idea how fast I can be." He swoops me up over his shoulder and runs back to my house.

I'm sure we won't miss anything. Romy's probably eating all the appetizers anyway.

By the time we walk in the door at my parents', everyone is seated at the dinner table, with annoyed expressions on their faces.

Whoops.

Chapter Forty-Three

BROOKS

A rriving late isn't exactly the impression I wanted to make on her family now that I'm officially Lottie's husband in more than name alone.

And damn it, after all that, I forgot Darla's flowers.

"See, I told you Romy would have eaten all the appetizers." Lottie walks in and sits down at the table. "Sorry we're late."

"My chicken is cold now," Wren whines, which isn't like her.

"Sorry," I mumble.

"It's okay, I remember those days." Darla looks lovingly at Brad.

"And if we didn't live on this ranch, there would be more." Brad picks up his fork and cuts into his chicken.

"What days?" Wren asks, but Bennett tells her to eat her food.

"I'd like to hear about Romy and where she's been disappearing to lately." Lottie changes the subject fast.

Her relationship with her siblings is so different from mine with Holden. Nowadays, I never even talk to him. Guess I can add my parents to that list as well now.

Romy looks at Wren. "Just hanging out with a friend."

"I have a new friend," Wren says, smile bright.

"Kayla, right?" I wink, putting a piece of chicken in my mouth.

"Is that the Millers' girl? I've heard he's really converting some voters over to his side." Brad glances at me.

"The girl we met at the fair?" Lottie asks. "She's nice. You like her?"

"Not her." Wren shakes her head. "I like her, but she's not my new friend."

"Oh, who?" Bennett's wrinkled forehead tells me even he's in the dark about it.

"Leia," Wren says. "Kayla and I asked her to play with us at recess."

"So, you have a trio, that's cute." Romy smiles at her niece.

Wren tells us how Leia is from California, but her grandparents live here. When she says her last name, it doesn't sound familiar to any of us though.

"I guess we've had a few transplants recently," I comment since I know most of the people who come and go in the area.

"Everyone wants to live in Willowbrook." Darla smiles at us, and I quickly feel as if I'm in the hot seat. "So, Brooks, how are things progressing?"

"Don't, Mom. Stay out of it." Lottie's hand falls under the table and squeezes my thigh.

"Hands where I can see 'em, Lottie," Darla says, and I slide my leg to the side.

Lottie's hand falls off my thigh, and she grunts. "I'm thirty-five."

"If I can't talk about it, you can't touch him." Her mother gives her a look.

I refrain from laughing because I know it would earn me a swat from my wife.

My wife.

Jesus, that sounds good.

Lottie picks up my hand and puts it around her shoulder. "But he can touch me?"

"No one is touching anyone," Brad says, pointing his fork at me.

Maybe Holden was right about Brad not being as easy-going as he seems.

The rest of dinner is relaxed. They talk about nothing major but all have major reactions. All the siblings bicker as I expected, and Darla makes inappropriate jokes while Brad eats mostly and only mumbles something here and there. I love every second of it.

It beats the dinner tables I grew up with that were nearly silent unless my dad was holding court. Mostly my mom, brother, and I kept our mouths shut because we were never sure what might set my dad off.

When we're finished eating and have cleared the table, I figure this is the time for me to pull Brad aside while Lottie is distracted by coloring with Wren. This wasn't my plan tonight, but after my talk with Lottie, I feel as if I need to do this sooner than later.

"Brad, can we chat on the porch?" I ask, my hand shaking.

"Sure. Want a beer?" he asks.

"Love one."

Once we have our beers in hand, we step out onto their big porch that overlooks the lake on Plain Daisy Ranch. Ben, Emmett, and Jude all have their houses on the other side of the lake. This side is dedicated to the Owens and Ellis families, but right now, all the girls live in one house and all the guys in another.

"Sit." Brad points toward a chair.

The night has a chill in the air, but it's growing warmer every day. The sun has almost set, the sky just still barely lit up.

"Should I pretend this isn't *the* talk?" Brad asks when I'm quiet for too long.

"Lottie and I talked on the way over," I say. "She seems to want the same thing as I do."

He nods, sipping his beer. "That doesn't surprise me."

"Mr. Owens, I know a long time ago, my brother came to you and asked for Lottie's hand, and I'm sure you don't love that here's another Watson doing the same. It takes a lot of trust on your part, but—"

"Your brother never asked me."

"What?" I frown. There's no way. How could he not have talked to Lottie's dad before he proposed, especially with how young she was?

Brad shakes his head. "Just knocked her up, and when she lost the baby, the bastard abandoned her."

"Jesus." I push my hand through my hair, chest tight.

He sits on the edge of his seat. "Listen, I'm not really a hard ass. I definitely don't want to be one of those fathers-in-law who cleans his gun any time you're around. I'm not going to tell you that if you hurt her, I'll break you. Hell, your brother got off scot-free."

"I—"

"I don't like being interrupted though."

"Sorry," I mumble, and he eyes me before chuckling.

"I've been a fan of you for a long time, son. A lot of years went by where I just wanted to lock the two of you in a room together. I meant what I said at the airport, you're already family, so there's no welcoming you because you're already a part of us. Have been for a long time. I would never hold what your brother did over your head. I trust you with my daughter, and I hope I never regret that one day. I'm fairly sure I never will though. So go ahead and ask the question so I can say yes, and we can enjoy our beers."

"Sir."

"Not sir, and not Mr. Owens, just Brad."

"Brad, may I have Lottie's hand in marriage? I love her and—"

"Yes, you can. You don't have to give me all your reasons. I know why you love her, and I've seen how much you care for her written all over your face for years. So, go ahead and take her off my hands. *Please*." He chuckles and tips back his beer.

"Thank you." I have to swallow hard past the emotion clogging my throat. I'm not used to this feeling... acceptance. Feeling as though I'm enough just how I am.

Darla walks out with a glass of wine. "What's going on out here?"

"Don't try to act like you don't know," Brad says.

"Did you give him a hard time?" Darla sits in the chair next to Brad.

"Why would I? He married her behind our back anyway."

"Please, I was drunk, and I never would—"

"Relax. I'd like the Brooks who existed before he was married to my daughter. Can you bring him back? Stop tiptoeing around us and just be yourself?" Brad asks.

I lean back in the chair. "I can."

"Good. Now tell me how upset Walker Matthews was after you guys beat him at softball."

And just like that, the conversation moves on, and Brad is the same Brad I've talked to a million times before.

Lottie ends up coming out with Wren, and they blow bubbles along the porch, circling around and around until Lottie gets dizzy and sits in my lap.

Brad builds a fire in the fire pit, and we all sit around and bullshit about nothing and everything.

It's so different from my family, and I realize it's a family I'm blessed to be a part of.

I didn't just win the jackpot with Lottie, but with her family too.

Chapter Forty-Four

LOTTIE

For his final date, Brooks drives us into Lincoln. I'm surprised we came all the way up here, but I'm not complaining. It's time with Brooks, and that's all that matters.

Although we've already decided we're not getting an annulment, Brooks was adamant that we finish all four of our dates. The funniest part to me is how many things we've done that could be considered dates anyway.

He made me go home and get changed even though I've been staying at his house every night for the last week.

Brooks is dressed in jeans and a T-shirt with his baseball hat on. I opted for a dress with my cowboy boots, thinking that we'd be going to a restaurant.

"Am I too dressed up?" I ask.

"You look perfect." He turns the corner once we're in Lincoln, obviously knowing exactly where he's going.

"Where are we going?" I ask.

"A farmers' market."

"Oh fun." I straighten and look around to try to see what it will look like. "Good date idea."

He pulls into a small area with a sign that says vendors.

"Oh, I don't think we can park here," I say, pointing at the sign.

Brooks parks his truck anyway, turns it off, and grabs my hands.

"What's going on?" I look at him warily because now he seems a little nervous.

He dodges eye contact, looking out the window at people with carts and bags walking into the farmers' market area. "First, I want to say, you don't have to do this. You say no, and I'll turn this truck around."

"Why are we in the vendors area?" My stomach is like a rubber band of anxiety.

"In the back of the truck, I have all the pottery you've stored on your shelves. I know I went behind your back, and you can be mad at me if you want. I'll completely understand, but Lottie, you're so talented, and I'm really hoping that all you need is a little push. Kind of like marrying me in Vegas."

I roll my eyes and can't help the small smile that lifts the corners of my lips.

"You know what that does to me, and we're in a very public place." His voice is low.

I shake my head. "Be specific. What are you asking?"

"I rented a booth for today. I have your stuff, I've bought displays, I've gotten business cards made. Briar designed a logo and said if you hate it, you guys can go over it after this and change it, but we felt like you needed something to hand out here."

I bury my head in my hands. "Seriously, this is crazy." I turn in my seat and look out the window. "And in Lincoln? You could have done it in Hickory."

"I figured the farther away, the better. It's like dipping your toes in the water. Like a first date."

"Brooks, stop comparing this to us."

"Why? Look at what a success we are. We got married

drunk and fell in love. We won after taking that risk, and I know you're going to win at this one too."

I flop back in my seat. "I'm not sure I want to stay married to you. You're one of those 'go big or go home' guys, and I'm more of a 'don't show your cards at all' person."

"Maybe that's why we're so good with one another." He waits patiently as I chew on my bottom lip.

"What did you bring?"

He smiles as though he's won already. "Everything I could pack. Mostly the coffee mugs, but also some bowls and vases. You can pick what you want, obviously. We don't have to put it all out."

"And you're not dropping me off, right? You'll be there the whole time?" I move my hands to my stomach because it has that tingly feeling.

"Right at your side."

"And you won't leave me." I meet his gaze.

He takes my hands. "Never."

I nod and blow out a breath. "Okay."

"Really?" His smile is wide, eyes twinkling.

"Why do you sound so shocked? You did all this, and you really thought I'd say no?"

He shrugs. "I was eighty-twenty you'd go through with it." I arch an eyebrow, and he chuckles. "Okay, ninety-ten... maybe ninety-five, five."

"All right, let's do it then."

We climb out of the truck and meet around the back.

Brooks has everything nicely packed in crates. It takes us an hour to get set up, and I send Briar a thank-you text for the logo she created and the business cards.

Right before the market opens, I wrap my arms around Brooks's neck and draw him as close as I can, inching up on my tiptoes. I take his baseball hat and slide it onto his head backward so I can kiss him.

"Thank you for doing all this. I'm so lucky to have you." I kiss him, and he holds me tightly.

"No matter what happens today, remember, you are talented. You create beautiful things. Now, chin up, shoulders back. I'll just be your eye candy behind the table." He flutters his eyes.

I laugh and kiss his cheek. "I love you."

"I love you more."

"Oh, no, we're not starting that as a competition."

Then I notice the woman with the purple glasses who was in my store that one time eyeing my table, and all the nerves double in my stomach.

Chapter Forty-Five

BROOKS

I'm too busy laughing to notice a woman with purple glasses eyeing our table before she smiles and weaves through the crowd toward us.

"The mugs?" she says, voice full of excitement as she picks up one. "The daisy."

I step back and let Lottie be the center of attention as she should be. She talks to the woman, apologizes, and openly confesses her fear of putting herself out there. It's endearing to watch, and I'm so proud of the chances she's taken in the last little while.

I saw her broken and shattered well over a decade ago, but she's shown how strong she really is.

For the entire day, I admire Lottie from afar, helping her pack items when necessary, but never interrupting unless I'm directly asked a question. I try to be the strong wind at her back, although I'm not sure she needs me because she's soaring all on her own. A constant stream of people come up to her and rave about her items.

After the last straggling customer leaves, she tackles me in a hug. Thankfully, I'm stronger than her. "Thank you so much. This was perfect and the push I needed. God, I'm so lucky to have you."

"You would have done it at some point."

She falls down to her heels and takes in the almost sold-out table. "I'm so happy I could burst."

"Does this mean you might not be making me coffee every morning?"

She leans her head on my shoulder. "I'll always make your coffee."

"Good." I kiss the top of her head. "Let's go to dinner here in Lincoln and celebrate."

"Sounds perfect."

I couldn't be happier with the way the day has turned out.

I'd been so scared, asking Romy to help me keep her distracted until I could get everything packed up in my truck. I now owe Bennett, Emmett, and Ben a night out at The Hidden Cave on me.

We pack up all her stuff, and I'm just shutting the tailgate of my truck when my phone vibrates.

I open my door, and Lottie's already in her seat, putting on her seat belt. "I'm kind of sweaty and gross, so can we go somewhere not too nice? Maybe a bar-b-que place where we can eat outside."

I pull my phone out of my pocket to look up a place nearby and blink when I see the message.

"What is it?" Lottie asks.

I turn my screen to face her, and she leans forward to read the text I just got from Ben.

> Hey man, I know you're in Lincoln, but I just wanted to let you know that I just saw your brother with your dad in town. Looked like he might have been campaigning with him or something.

Lottie's face falls, and I'm sure mine is lined with anger. My dad called Holden home, I can almost guarantee it. The question is whether he's just here for my dad or if he plans on messing with me too.

Chapter Forty-Six

LOTTIE

Brooks tosses his phone into the center console of his truck and jams the key into the ignition without a word. His hand lands on the back of my headrest as he looks over his shoulder to back out, never once looking at me.

Talk about going from the highest of highs to the lowest of lows.

Holden is back.

He's returned home a few times over the years of course, only ever for a brief time. As if we came to some unspoken agreement, we've both stayed on opposite sides of town until he left.

But now everything has changed. I'm in love with his brother. Hell, I'm *married* to his brother.

As Brooks drives, the silence between us grows, making the cab feel small and ripe with tension.

"Thank you for doing all this for me today. I really appreciate it."

He links his hand with mine, bringing my knuckles to his lips and kissing them. "It's going to be okay."

I shouldn't be surprised he can hear how unsettled I am. He can always read me, knows what I'm not saying.

I put my other hand on top of his. "Why do you think he's back?"

The idea of Holden becoming a wedge between us makes my stomach turn. If Brooks and I are going to last, really last, we have to face this together. There can't be anything between us.

"My dad. The election. Voting is Monday. Some people in town may not like him, but there are a lot of newcomers who weren't here when everything went down between you two. You know how charismatic my brother can be. I'm sure my dad is hoping he'll help him win over some of the residents who don't know him. It's the final card he has to play."

"But…" I hesitate, trying to find the right words.

In small towns, sides get taken based solely on bloodlines. My family has had the largest ranch in Willowbrook for generations, and a lot of folks took it personally when Holden left me the way he did. Maybe if he'd walked away before I was in my wedding gown and the guests had arrived, it wouldn't have turned into such a public betrayal.

"He wants to show a bonded family. Since I'm endorsing Miller, that's a stain on my dad. Plus, you know Holden. He charms everyone. Makes you feel like you're the most important person in the room. He'll help my dad, but I'm pretty sure he'll still lose." Brooks tightens his fingers around mine. "But I'm going to handle this. You don't have to worry. It's my issue."

I turn in the seat to better face him. "It's *our* issue. *Our* problem."

He doesn't glance in my direction. "Lottie, I want you as far away from this as I can get you."

"Um… who do you think you're married to?"

He huffs and side-eyes me. "You don't need to be dragged

into it. I'm going to handle it. I'll call Holden tomorrow and meet him for a beer. Tell him that while he's here, he can stay the hell away from us."

Brooks's in full protective mode, and I get it. Deep down, he's scared this will shake me—maybe even revert me back to the girl Holden left behind.

"This has nothing to do with me thinking you want him," Brooks says.

I laugh. "Good because you would be stupid if you thought that."

He glances at me, pulling onto the highway toward home. "I'm just saying, I'm not trying to keep you from him because I don't believe in us or the fact that you love me. It's purely to protect you."

"I can protect myself." My tone sharpens. I'm not going to let him play the white knight and shove me behind the castle walls as if I'm some damsel in distress.

Brooks pulls over to the side of the highway.

"What are you doing?"

He throws the truck in park and turns in his seat. "I know you're a badass. I know you love me. I know where we're at with our relationship. I'm not afraid of losing you. I'm not afraid you're going to run away with Holden. Those are not my fears." I open my mouth, but he shakes his head. "Let me finish. Please."

I remain silent, heart twisting at the edge in his voice.

"But I also know my family. Holden learned it from my dad, and if you think I'm going to give him another chance to hurt you with his vengeful words, I won't do it. I'm not trying to handle it for you because I don't think you can. But words stick with people a helluva lot longer than a bruise. Years later, they'll just pop back up in your head and make you second guess yourself, even if it's for a millisecond. So, I'm begging you, Lottie, just please let me handle this."

I exhale slowly, staring at this man who looks as if he'd fight the whole damn world to spare me an ounce of pain. His jaw is clenched, but his eyes... they're pleading.

I lean forward and place my hand on his cheek and move in to kiss him. Right before my lips land on his, I say, "No."

He says my name with a frustrated sigh.

But he should know me better than that by now.

"You got your chance to speak, so listen to me now. I hate that you grew up in that house, and no one told you that your father's criticisms, the words he called you, picking on you when you were young, that he was wrong and cruel and weak for doing so. I hate that you might have for one second believed any of the things he said. And I understand you wanting to protect me from that. But I have you. You don't even have to tell me that whatever they'll say is wrong because you counter all of that by just the way you look at me. So, Holden, your dad, your mom, they can say whatever they want about me. I don't really care, and I sure as hell don't believe them. You've taught me that. So, I'm really sorry, but we're a team now. When you drunk-married me in Vegas, that solidified that it's you and me. Not just you. Not just me. *Us.*"

He stares at me long and hard, his hand now cradling my cheek like I cradle his.

A semi barrels by and shakes the truck.

"God, you're amazing," he says.

"Same."

He presses his lips to mine. There's no urgency in it. No attempt to deepen or dominate the kiss. Just his lips, soft and steady, pressed to mine.

I feel him relax, and he ends the kiss slowly and rests his forehead against mine. "Okay."

"I wasn't asking your permission."

He chuckles lightly and kisses my forehead. "I figured."

"Come on, let's go have some fun with our friends rather

than eat here in Lincoln. Romy texted me, and they're all watching the ballgame at The Hidden Cave. It will be good for us to be around our people tonight." I need to escape this weight, if only just for today. We can face all the shit tomorrow.

"I really just want to take you home."

"After we watch the Colts win."

He sighs since he's a Kansas City fan. "How the hell did you become a Chicago fan?"

"We all are." He kisses me one more time and situates himself in the driver's seat. I keep my hand on his thigh. "We've always been. I think our great-grandpa just wanted to be different, but sorry, the Colts are going to beat KC tonight."

He shakes his head, and the mood lifts.

We'll push it all aside for tonight.

Chapter Forty-Seven

BROOKS

There are times I think I have this all figured out, how Lottie and I will be as a couple, and then she schools me in the front seat of my truck and surprises me all over again.

We walk into The Hidden Cave when I really just want to take her home and remind her how good a team we really are. I guide her by the hand, and she holds on tight as if she wants to make sure we don't get separated in the crowd.

Outside on the patio, our friends and family are sprinkled among a few tables. We raise our hands in hello but stop at the bar to grab some drinks.

Melvin is having a very stern talk with someone I assume might've been trying to take something off The Canary Wall II. Tammy slides us our usual drinks of choice—me a beer and Lottie a margarita—then we join everyone else.

Ben shoots me a look, but I shake my head. I'm not going to ruin tonight by allowing my brother to wedge his way in.

"I brought your shirt and shorts," Romy says, tossing Lottie her Chicago Colts shirt.

I groan. "I might have to tear that off you tonight," I whisper in her ear.

Lottie kisses my cheek. "I'll just buy a new one. I heard a rumor that Foster Davis might be getting traded to the team. Maybe I'll get his jersey." She pats my ass. "I'll be back."

"Oh, I'll go with you," Sadie volunteers, her eyes finding mine as she walks by.

I guess I'm to assume more than Ben has seen my brother around town. No doubt Sadie's number one priority is to see how Lottie's doing with the news. I'm glad Lottie has her as a friend.

When Lottie comes back, she's in jean shorts and her Chicago Colts T-shirt with BAILEY on the back. Easton fucking Bailey. The best thing that's happened to the Colts in years.

Hours later, Lottie's in my lap, rubbing in that the Colts are beating Kansas City by three runs.

"Lots of time left," I say, patting her outer thigh.

It's a great night and just what I needed after hearing the shitty news about my brother that I really should have predicted. Of course my dad would summon him home. And forever the obedient son, he comes.

Ben knocks his elbow against mine and nods behind me.

Lottie's laughing with the girls about how crazy Poppy seems to be about the tattoos on the players, and Lottie's hand runs along my arm where mine are. I glance over my shoulder. I'm not sure if I still or something, but Lottie straightens and turns around to look at me, sensing somehow that something is amiss.

"Tomorrow just became tonight," I say, and she looks over my shoulder to see Holden at the bar with his friends.

"The Colts better win," she mumbles, lifting off my lap, but I place my hand around her middle to keep her where she's at.

"We don't have to give him any attention."

She tilts her head in a way to say I'm crazy, but she doesn't fight me or get off my lap.

No more than two minutes later, a familiar voice sounds from behind us. "Look who we have here."

"I knew it," Lottie grumbles under her breath.

Holden rounds our table to come front and center. "The Noughtons. I feel as if I should bow." He actually does bend at the waist like an asshole.

No one smiles. No one laughs. They all look as if they'd like to tie him up and get a swing at him.

"I see Dad commanded you home?" My voice is flat.

"Can you blame him? His other son just leaves him high and dry. Endorses the competition."

I don't bother telling Holden I'm not his son. He'll find out, or he won't. I really don't care.

Holden's gaze falls to Lottie. "Hi, Lottie." He holds his arms out to his sides. "Hear I should welcome you to the family."

"Just go off with your friends, Holden," Jude says.

"Come on. I haven't seen my brother for a few years. He never comes to visit me. Now I hear he's marrying my sloppy seconds."

"Fuck," Ben says with a sigh, knowing this is about to escalate.

I tap Lottie's ass, but she's already getting up, and I follow suit.

"Go to hell, you piece of shit." Lottie pokes Holden in the chest. "Crawl back in that hole you squirmed your way out of."

He releases a condescending laugh. "That's fresh coming from you." He looks her up and down and gives her a look like she comes up lacking.

I fight the urge to step in. Sadie's kind of giving me a look like I should. Ben stands on one side of me and Bennett comes up along the other. My guess is the rest of the guys are close. I keep telling myself that Lottie needs this, with the safety of all of us here, but damn I want to push her out of the way and beat the shit out of my brother just like I did the night of their wedding that never happened.

"I figured you married her just because you wanted to be a Noughton. I didn't know it was because you were mad at me for stealing the girl you always wanted. Dad and Mom filled me in when they broke the news that my little brother married the girl I left at the altar."

He's purposely choosing his words to inflict the most damage.

"Oh, Lottie, you'll like this—did you know your little knight in armor beat the shit out of me that night? Is that how he got you to agree to marry him? Told you he defended your honor all those years ago?"

Lottie turns to me. I've alluded to that but never told her the full story.

"So, tell me, how long did you want Lottie? The entire time I was fucking her?" Holden crosses his arms and gives me a smug look.

"You act like I stole her from under you." My fists are clenched at my sides just to keep me from using them.

He laughs again, but nothing about it is genuine. "Well, we all know that's not the case because it's been well over ten years. You took a long time to take your shot, little brother. But I never expected anything less. You always were the weaker one of us both."

"Get the fuck outta here, Holden." Ben points toward the door.

"Look at this guy." Holden looks around our table as if they're his friends. "Mister pro football player who left his girlfriend behind to fuck every other woman who stroked his ego."

"You don't know what you're talking about," Romy says. "You don't belong in this town, so just leave."

"I can tell you one thing I know." Holden leans in, his face close to Lottie, and it's all I can do not to snatch her around the waist and pull her back into my chest. "I bet you've kept it your little secret, haven't you? You're both fucking with my life, so why shouldn't I fuck with yours a little?"

Lottie leans back, her head hitting my chest, and I place my hands on her hips. *I'm here*, I hope my touch conveys. But I also hope it says, *You say the word, and he's on the ground.*

"Are you threatening me?" Lottie lets out a caustic laugh. "This is what you don't understand, Holden. I'm not that enamored little girl who naïvely believes anything you say. You're just a loser, a snake in nice clothes, and a pretty package. Romy's right, you have no place in this town anymore."

He keeps his eyes on Lottie but talks to me. "So you told him? You know, little brother? That big family you always wanted? Our family name to be carried down generations... that's not going to happen with your new bride here."

My fingers flex on Lottie's hips, but her hands fall to mine, and she squeezes.

"Because she can't have kids. Did you tell my brother that before you tricked another Watson into marrying you?"

Before I can even get Lottie out of the way, she's gone from in front of me, her fist cocked back before she lands a punch square to Holden's right eye.

"Oh, damn!" Ben hollers, and our entire table roars with cheers for her.

Lottie lowers her face to him as Holden bends down, holding his eye. "Your brother does know, asshole. He's a better man than you. He's in it for me, not for what I can give him. It's funny, you know? I wasted so much of my life thinking about what you did to me. So much time feeling like I was worthless. But you're the worthless one. You're the one

317

who will never find what I have with your brother because you can never love someone more than you love yourself."

"Save me the holier-than-thou speech." Holden stands and looks past Lottie. "All you are is a slut who jumps from brother to brother."

"Sorry, Lottie." I nudge her out of the way.

Then I punch him in the right eye and the left. He lifts his gaze. I've seen that look so many times before. From the age of four, whenever we'd fight, I'd see that anger flare inside him. He tackles me to the ground and a chair or table falls to my side. I roll us over and straddle him, landing punch after punch.

"Don't you ever speak to my wife that way again."

Holden's hands come up and push at my chest, but I get another blow to his face before someone pulls me off him.

"I'm calling the police," Holden says, stumbling to his feet.

I yank myself out of Ben's grip, chest heaving.

Lottie comes over and touches my face where Holden got in a couple hits of his own. "Your lip," she says, touching it lightly, but I flinch.

"He is the police, you idiot," Romy shouts at Holden.

I really appreciate the sister vibe she's giving.

Holden ignores her and pulls out his phone. "I think it's about time the town golden boy gets knocked down a peg." He puts his phone to his ear. "Sheriff Watson just assaulted me, and I want to press charges."

As if my family couldn't do anything more to hurt me.

Chapter Forty-Eight

LOTTIE

Brooks sits on a chair, our entire family around us as Holden sits in another chair with the few friends he has in this town.

Melvin walks out from the inside bar, Deputy Moore behind him.

Deputy Moore takes in the scene. The knocked-over furniture that no one has picked up. The drinks spilled on tables. Everyone who is still here is here because they no doubt want to see the drama that's about to unfold.

The gossip will spiral into false stories like the two brothers were fighting over me, or something so much worse.

Tammy brought Brooks a towel with ice, and I'm holding it to his eye as he holds another one to his hand.

"Are you mad?" he mumbles around his swollen lip.

"Absolutely not." I shake my head.

"You know I had to do it, right? I'm not suggesting you couldn't have handled it, but—"

I kiss his forehead. "I understand. Did it feel good?"

"Fucking fantastic. You?"

"The best."

We both laugh as Holden groans.

Deputy Moore comes up to Brooks first. "What happened?"

It's clear there was a fight. They're both beat up. And I won't be able to bear it if something happens to Brooks's job over this.

Deputy Moore takes out his notebook and pen. "Did you hit him?"

Brooks's arm is draped around my middle and his hand tightens on my hip as he tries to get up. "Moore, can we talk outside?"

"It was purely self-defense," Scarlett interrupts. "They had to protect themselves. Holden came in here like a madman."

"Yeah, practically foaming at the mouth." Poppy stands alongside her sister.

I smile at my family.

Holden puts his arm in the air. "They're a bunch of liars! Ask anyone here."

"It was the older one," Mrs. Parker says from a table nearby.

"From where I sit, that boy caused the ruckus. He swung first," Mrs. Schmidt next to her says.

"They're lying. First Lottie Owens hit me and then Sheriff Watson." Holden stands and comes closer to us.

"There is no Lottie Owens here, just a Lottie Watson." Romy rolls her eyes. "He can't even get his facts right."

"Melvin?" Moore turns to him where he stands at The Canary Wall II as if the notecards are going to crawl away.

"I asked Holden not to come in," Melvin says. "I knew he'd cause trouble just like when he was younger."

I'd forgotten until now how Holden would cause fights every time he came to The Hidden Cave after he returned from college. I wasn't old enough to get in, but he'd come here with his friends and was usually nursing a black eye or busted lip the next day.

"You've gotta be fucking kidding me." Holden looks around at everyone.

Moore does too. "Did anyone see anything different?"

"Nope," a table of guys who work down at the auto body place say in unison.

"Exactly as Mrs. Parker said," a table of teachers from the elementary school add.

All around the room, people confirm that Holden is the one who started it, and it was purely self-defense on Brooks's part. Not even Holden's so-called friends speak up on his behalf.

Brooks looks up at me, and I smile down at him, touching his cheek, tears filling my eyes. All of these people know what a good man he is and are supporting the two of us. His head falls to my chest, and I run my fingertips through his hair.

"Melvin, are you pressing charges or seeking any damages?" Moore asks.

Melvin waves off his question. "Nah, we're good."

"Sheriff? You want me to take him down to the station?"

Brooks looks at his brother, who is staring right at him, eyes full of anger. It still breaks my heart that they'll never have a proper sibling relationship. At least not for a very long time. My suspicion is they never will. Maybe that's okay because Brooks has my entire table as his family. My brother and sister are his siblings, along with my cousins.

I'm fortunate to have blood relatives, but blood doesn't mean family.

"No. I'm sure Holden has to get back to Texas."

"This is bullshit," Holden says.

Moore walks over to him and reaches for his arm. "I'm going to escort you out. We can do it with you in handcuffs or not. Your decision."

Holden shrugs his arm out of Moore's hold. "You deserve each other," he spits at us as he passes by.

"Ah, thanks. I think so too." I kiss my husband gingerly, so I don't hurt his busted lip.

My family starts picking up all the cups and tables, putting everything back together.

Afterward, I corner Brooks along the wall. "Take me home."

"I thought you'd never ask."

We say goodbye to my family, and with his arm around my shoulders, we walk out of The Hidden Cave, finally feeling free of the weight of any demons that could hurt us now.

Chapter Forty-Nine

BROOKS

The next morning, I'm out in my barn, finishing up the guy's truck because he's coming to pick it up this evening.

I left Lottie in bed to sleep off last night.

I suppose what happened with Holden means I've severed my ties with all of my family members. My dad's election will be held tomorrow, and from what I've heard, he's going to lose. I'm not sure what my parents will do afterward, but I don't really care.

Lottie is my family.

The Owens are my family.

As are the Noughtons and Ellises.

The only thing bothering me is my last name. Technically, it's not mine. I have no idea what it should be.

Two arms wrap around my waist and a head falls to my back. "I don't much care for waking up alone in bed."

"You had Mack." I circle around and give her a warm hug.

Lottie's in my T-shirt with no pants on. One major plus about not living near anyone.

Mack sits down next to her, and we hold on to one another, breathing each other in.

"Are you okay?" She tips her head up to look at me.

I stare down at her and brush her morning hair out of her face. "I'm good."

"You looked like you were thinking hard. You didn't even hear me come up." I shrug, and she straightens her head. "What is it?"

"Watson. I'm not really a Watson, you know?"

She nods and doesn't say anything at first. She's not quick to tell me I'm being stupid, or I should be okay with that, and I appreciate her for it.

"Your last name doesn't dictate the person you are. You're not Mayor Watson's son, or Holden Watson's brother. You're Sheriff Brooks Watson. A man who looks out for others before himself. A man who helps others whenever asked, and sometimes when he's not." She gives me a lopsided grin. "You're my husband, and I'm proud to be Lottie Watson. Not because it's your family name. Not because of who your ancestors were or what they did in their lifetime, but because it means I'm attached to you, a wonderful man whom I love very much."

I place a kiss on her lips. "God, I love you. That's the first time I've heard you call me your husband. Kinda like it."

"Well, I showed you how much I appreciated your 'my wife' moment from last night when we got home."

"Yes, you sure did." I grin.

"All that aside, if you want to be Brooks Owens, we could make it happen." She laughs, and I tighten my arms around her, resting my cheek on top of her head.

A car driving up my gravel driveway interrupts us, and we both look to see my mom's car parking near my truck.

"Of course, I'm only in your T-shirt." Lottie moves to get out of my arms, but I hold her tightly.

"Don't go."

She rises on her tiptoes and kisses my cheek. "This will go much better if I'm not here. Make peace. I'm not saying forgive her, just do what you have to in order to find peace here." She taps my heart and steps back.

She turns toward the house, Mack trailing at her side, not giving my mother one ounce of his attention. Lottie gives my mom a wide berth as the two of them cross paths. I catch my mom glancing, wondering if Lottie will give her a welcome, but she doesn't. She keeps her head down. Good girl.

I wait for my mom's snarky comment about Lottie wearing only my T-shirt, but she stops at the entrance to the barn, as if she's waiting for an invitation.

"Can I come in?" she asks when I don't welcome her in.

"Sure."

She sits at my workbench. Obviously, she just came from somewhere, since she's all dressed up in a pantsuit.

"I heard about the fight," she says in a soft tone as if she's not sure why she's even here.

I'm not sure why she is either.

"And?" I cross my arms.

"I know you're angry, but I didn't bring you boys up to make such a scene. The entire town is talking about it. Your father is already losing the election, thanks to all of this drama." She waves her hand. "All of this couldn't have come at a worse time."

"Are you looking for me to apologize?" I take the rag and wipe my hands before tossing it on my tool case.

"No. I'm here to explain myself. I should've started with that first." She sits and stares into her lap, gazing at her big wedding ring my dad upgraded after they sold her family's land. "I left your father when Holden was still young. I ran away."

I suck in a breath. So she's going to tell me who my father is. That's why she's here. Of course she is. She's not one to leave things unsaid or open-ended. She needs closure. Maybe I do too.

"I don't need to explain to you what your father is like. You know how he is. The words he uses like weapons. He can be cruel and downright mean. One night it got really bad, and he raised his hand to me. He didn't hit me, but the threat was there. So, I saw him off to work the next day, then left. I wrote him a letter and said I didn't deserve to be treated like that and told him I was leaving him."

I say nothing, not wanting to fill the space with questions.

"I was gone for three months. I found a waitress job, and my parents were sending me money. I met a married man and became pregnant. He wasn't going to leave his wife. I never even told him I was pregnant with you. Your father came for Holden and me, after convincing my parents he was a changed man and he wanted his family back. So, I told him I was pregnant with another man's baby. And he said he'd raise you as his own. And I believe he has."

"Unfortunately," I let slip.

She nods, mouth tight. "But he never treated you any differently."

I scoff, but she ignores it.

"And things were good for years until old habits started to creep back in."

Neither of us says anything.

"If you want his name… I'm not sure where he is now or if he'd be open to—"

"I don't." I shake my head. What difference does it make to me now? I thought maybe I needed to know, but now that she's here and willing to tell me, I realize I don't.

She nods and looks toward the house. "I'm sorry for all this. How it's turned out… I wanted to protect you."

"From him?" I ask.

"And her, but maybe that's not my place."

My jaw tightens. "It's not."

Her fingers twist in her lap. "Your father is going to lose tomorrow."

"I heard."

"I suppose you don't care, and I can't really blame you." She stands. "He's all the family I have."

She looks so sad, as if she's out of options. Too late to start over and figure out a life she loves.

"Holden rarely comes home. I tried with you, but—" Again her gaze floats to the house. "I just can't, Brooks. I know you love her, but—regardless, I do hope you're happy."

"I am." I give her a curt nod.

"Good."

Another bout of awkward silence takes over.

"I should get going before your father wonders where I am. Holden is leaving today if you want—"

"I don't."

"Okay. Well, please know, I do love you. I always have. Even if it hasn't felt that way at times."

My heart pricks for a second that she's saying goodbye. This is her weird way of giving up on any kind of relationship with me.

"Bye, Mom."

"Bye, son. I'll let you know where we end up."

I say nothing because I'm not even sure I want to know. She walks back down the strip of land to her car. As soon as she's beside it, Lottie comes out of the house with a pair of shorts on. My mom stops outside her car, and I watch them talk briefly before my mom gets in her car and drives away.

Lottie walks back to join me in the barn. "You okay?"

"Yeah. What did you say to her?"

She shrugs. "I just told her that I love her son, and I'll give him a good life."

"And how was she with that?"

"She smiled, and said she knew that you loved me very much and hopes we have a happy long life together."

I like the fact Lottie seems at peace with it.

"Come here."

She walks toward me, and I swarm her in a hug, thankful we can move forward. The past is finally behind us, and we can start our lives—together.

Chapter Fifty

LOTTIE

Brooks and I have fallen into a routine. I've pretty much moved in with him, but every morning, he still comes into The Harvest Depot for a morning coffee.

I do my pottery in my shed, and I've started selling it at the store, plus online. Mostly, I throw whatever I have inspiration to create up for sale. Maybe one day I'll make it into more of a business, but I'm pretty in love with my life right now.

As if my body knows he's coming, right before we open, it buzzes with excitement until I hear the door chime ring.

Brooks comes in looking all sexy in his sheriff uniform. Although I just saw him an hour ago and had him early this morning, I want him again. I'll take whatever he offers.

"Hey," he says, casual and carefree, strolling across the room to me.

I prepare his coffee, writing a name for him on the cup, but he doesn't immediately look at it, tugging me into him as if he needs me as badly as I need him. "I think we should both just quit our jobs. What do you say? Spending all day naked in bed sounds really good to me."

I hug him tightly, and we stay in an embrace for I have no idea how long.

My parents come into the store.

"Of course they're here and all over each other," my mom says.

"You're lucky I like you," my dad adds.

We break apart, but Brooks still tucks me in at his side.

"What's up?" I ask.

"Saylor, you good to watch the store for a bit?" my mom calls.

"Sure thing," she says from the back.

"You have a little bit of time, right?" Mom asks Brooks.

He presses a button on his radio and gives them some code.

"Perfect, come on."

Mom and Dad walk out the back door of the store. Brooks picks up his coffee, and we follow, sharing a look because we don't know what's going on. My parents get into the front seats of their UTV, and we file into the back.

"You're not taking us up to Daisy Hill, are you?" I ask. "Brooks isn't ready for a talk."

Brooks looks at me and puts his coffee in the holder between us. I'm not sure he's even looked to see what I wrote on his cup yet. It would be weird not to get a reaction if he has.

"If you're lucky, you never get taken up to Daisy Hill," my dad says over his shoulder.

"Why are you acting as if it's a bad thing, Lottie? It got you out of your own way." Mom sips her coffee that she must have brought from home.

Brooks's fingers graze along my neck, and when I look at him, he's staring at me, a crooked grin on his face. I'll never get enough of the way he looks at me.

"Are you going to tell us where we're going?" I ask. "Brooks has to work."

"I'm all right." His fingers roam under my hair, along my neck, in a light massage.

"Stop rushing. We've been looking forward to this," Dad says.

"Now, I'm scared." I widen my eyes at Brooks.

Neither of my parents say anything as we pass other buildings on the property—all of our houses, their house, and The Getaway Lodge—until we're on the back part of the property on open land. Dad stops the UTV, and I glance at Brooks in confusion. He shrugs, and we both get out.

"Nice of you to tear us away from work to bring us to a field," I say, bending down and picking up a dandelion. "Look, babe, a field of dandelions."

"Okay, smartass, I'm rethinking this now." Dad looks at Mom, but she laughs.

"No, you aren't."

He nods, agreeing with her.

"So, we know you have Brooks's house, and he's got the barn where he fixes up those trucks," Mom says.

"Which reminds me, when do I turn in my father-in-law card where you gift me one?" Dad laughs, but I wouldn't be surprised if he actually wants one of Brooks's trucks. Brooks could probably quit his job as sheriff and do it full-time if he wanted.

"That's for another time." Mom walks around for a beat, gazing over the land and the lake. "This is yours." She turns around and opens her arms. "To do with as you wish."

My heart skips a beat, and I have to swallow back my emotions.

"Your dad and I would like you to build a house here. We'd like you to live by us because, you know, we like to be overbearing and suffocate our children."

We all laugh.

"It's your decision though. I'm sure your brother and sister would love to split this property so they can have a larger lot if you don't want it."

I glance at Brooks, and he surveys the land. I'd love to build a house here and live close to my family and cousins, but I love Brooks's house too. I love how secluded it is. That definitely has its perks.

Just the other night, he took me in the barn, on his workbench, with the door wide open. No one could hear us except for Mack, who saunters away every time we're having sex. This would be different. We'd have closer neighbors.

"You don't have to decide right now," my dad says. "Think on it."

My mom and dad step back and pretend to be discussing something about the vegetation or the trees, clearly giving us our space.

"What do you think?" I ask.

"I know you always thought I wanted to live here, that it was the reason I married you." He raises his eyebrows. I playfully shove him. "Honestly, I like the idea. I know you love your family, and it would be close for your work. You could stay in bed with me longer." His gaze grows a little heated.

"But there are some negatives."

"I think the positive outweighs the negatives. We can keep my house. I'd still have to go out there to fix the trucks anyway."

"Unless we built something here. Maybe a garage."

"True."

"I think I want to," I say.

"Me too." He chuckles.

I'm so happy we agree.

He puts his coffee on the ground and puts his hand in his

pocket. I read the name on the cup that he's yet to acknowledge.

"You haven't sipped your coffee yet?" I ask.

"I'm waiting for it to cool."

"I think it's cool by now." My tone holds a little bite to it, but I finally wrote something sweet and loving, and he hasn't even noticed.

"Fine. I'll take a sip."

He bends at the waist, and I look at the land again, picturing what we might build here. I'll be near to Sadie too. If Brooks and I ever decide to adopt or do surrogacy, our kids can play together all the time. They'd grow up here just like I did with my cousins. It's a life I want with Brooks, but I don't want to force him into anything.

"Lottie," he says with a little annoyance, causing me to look over at him.

He's on one knee, holding a ring.

I gasp. "What are you doing?"

"What does it look like I'm doing?"

"I thought you were taking a sip of your coffee."

He blows out a breath. "I've been carrying this ring around with me for weeks, unsure when to propose. Wanting it to be perfect. I know we're surrounded by weeds and not flowers, but this is where we'll build our life together, so it's the perfect place for me to ask you again to be my wife."

"I'm already your wife."

"Just say yes, please?"

"Look at the coffee cup," I say.

He blows out a breath and glances at the cup. "LOML? Lottie, I'm looking for a yes."

I fall down to my knees and sit back on my ankles. "It means love of my life, silly."

"So that's a yes?" He's smiling now.

"Yes." I hold out my left hand, moving my ring finger up and down.

"I know which finger."

"Just helping you out." I wink at him. He slides it on, and the sun sparkles on the diamond. "It's beautiful. I would have been happy with our silver bands though, just so you know."

"I wouldn't be."

We kiss, and my mom and dad come over to congratulate us. My mom admires the ring, and my dad tries to sell Brooks on him taking our last name again. After we tell my parents what we've decided, Dad and Mom leave us the UTV to get back. They hold hands as they walk back toward their house.

As we sit on the land where our new house will someday sit, I lean my head in Brooks's lap.

"Would you have wanted something more planned out and romantic for a proposal?" he asks.

"No, this was perfect. I feel a kinship with the weeds."

"Babe, you're a rose, vibrant with beauty."

"Nah, I'm happy to be a weed."

He makes a humming noise. "I feel like I'm missing something."

I wrap my hand around his neck and bring his mouth down to mine. "Good thing we have the rest of our lives for you to try to figure it out."

I laugh, and he comes down the rest of the way. "I can't wait." And he seals it with a kiss.

Epilogue

LOTTIE

Brooks and I don't waste any time starting our life together. We hire an architect to draw up plans for our house and plan our reception straight away.

It's been the most exciting time of my life. The happiest time.

Brooks's dad lost the election, which means Willowbrook has a new mayor for the first time in a long time. His parents immediately moved closer to Omaha, buying a house in some other town he has a friend in. We're not sure what will happen with them, but I can't lie—I breathe a little easier knowing I'm not going to run into them. Holden is back in Texas and never reached out to Brooks before he left. My husband doesn't seem upset, but I worry at some point the loss of his family will crash down on him.

We've decided to forgo renting The Knotted Barn like my family expected and opted to hold a big party on our new land before we break ground this Monday. We're married already, and I don't want a fancy affair. I just want Brooks and our life. Mack too, but that goes without saying.

A trellis is set up right where our front door will be. It's decorated with flowers and a sign that says, *Welcome—The Watsons*, much to my dad's dismay. He might never stop fighting for Brooks to be an Owens. Let's be honest, he kind of is anyway.

There are picnic tables draped with green runners spread around, and Jenson made a whole bar-b-que buffet for people to make a plate and find a seat. Alcohol and drinks are in barrels spread around the grounds while plants are the centerpieces with candles in giant fluted glass. Brooks and my cousins hung twinkle lights over everything.

But my favorite part is the flower garden.

It pays off that Bennett is a landscape architect because he's already decided which flowers will be in our garden and where every tree will be planted. He may be a tad anal about it, but it will be beautiful once we're all settled. For the party though, he's set up a bunch of raised gardens set away from where the construction will be. Each guest can plant a flower and put a stake with their name in it and a note to wish us well.

"Six inches," he says to Jude.

"I won't plant it at all if you keep watching over me like I'm a child using a knife for the first time." Jude glances at Ben, and they both roll their eyes.

"I know you think I just play with dirt all day, but there's actually a reason I put things where I do."

"Is here fine?" Jude asks, sticking his small shovel in the dirt.

"Yes, but... oh, I'll just do it." Bennett takes the shovel from him.

Wren comes alongside me in the dress we bought for her. "Hi, Aunt Lottie." She's our flower girl even though there was no walking down the aisle. "Do you need anything?"

I look around the space. The guests are going to arrive soon. "Do you see Uncle Brooks anywhere?"

"I'll find him for you." She runs toward Romy and Poppy, asking if they've seen Brooks.

He was just here, and now I have no idea where he's gone.

The workers from The Perfect Petal come in with more flowers, and I follow them to one of the raised gardens.

"Oh, not there!" Bennett leaves my cousins to do what they want with one garden, rushing over to the new flowers being put out.

"Hey, it's okay, I'm not picky," I tell him, but he blows out a breath.

"If we don't plant them right now, you'll lose some. I told you to just have them pick it out, and I would plant each one. Or someone from The Perfect Petal could handle it."

I laugh and touch his arm. "That's no fun. I want it to be their way of planting something for our future. Every time I look at this garden, I'll remember this day."

I glance at Bennett when he doesn't respond, and realize his gaze is fixed on a dark-haired woman moving the flowers to the tables for our guests to pick out.

"Delaney?" he says.

The woman looks up and draws back immediately when she spots my brother. Her eyes search the area but stop again on my brother. "Hi, Bennett."

"Heard you were looking for me? I hope it's because you want to go behind a tree," Brooks comes to my side and whispers in my ear. When I don't respond, I feel him look over my shoulder. "Am I missing something?"

I put up my hand, too transfixed on my brother's face. Delaney Richards was Bennett's high school sweetheart, and I haven't seen her since she left town their senior year.

"What are you doing here?" Bennett snipes, sounding... annoyed... panicked?

"I work here. Poppy just hired me." Her eyes are wide, and she seems uncomfortable.

"Seriously, who is that?" Brooks asks, and I shush him again.

So, she's working at the ranch's flower shop. Interesting.

"Danson, Ben put it three inches too far left. He's not listening to your rules!" Emmett yells across the yard.

Bennett blinks and steps back. "Welcome back to Willowbrook."

He turns and leaves, and Delaney's gaze follows him until she sees me watching. She nods at Brooks and me. "Congratulations."

"Thank you," I say softly, thinking I should say more, but I haven't seen my brother ever be that rude to anyone. She leaves before I can. I turn to Brooks. "Where were you?"

"Just making sure the band has our song. Tell me you weren't worried."

I shake my head. "Never. You know I'd hunt you down and drag you back to my side."

"Go, Mack!" Wren says and throws a tennis ball that almost hits Mrs. Parker. Her shoulders sink in. "Sorry." She and Mack chase the ball.

"Wait, is that Delaney Richards?" Brooks asks with a nod to the nursery staff heading back to the trucks.

I look over my shoulder. "I think so."

I search Bennett out and see that he's back at the raised garden with my cousins, giving them hell about how they're doing things. But his attention is across the garden even as he tries to act as though he's not staring at Delaney.

Brooks locks his arms around me. "If I'm right, this is our kitchen."

"I'm not sure, I think it's the family room."

"I feel like you just like to disagree with me."

"Maybe."

He kisses me—probably to shut me up. Maybe that's why I always disagree with him. He always kisses me to shut me up.

Two hours into the party, after our guests have eaten and the sun is descending, leaving the twinkle light sparkling against the purple and pink sky, Brooks leads me to the makeshift dance floor.

"Mr. and Mrs. Watson will now have their first dance," the DJ announces.

Brooks takes my hand while everyone claps. Tears fill my eyes as Brooks secures his arms around me, pulling me into him.

I'm sure everyone thinks we're going to do a slow dance, but we opted for something a little different.

"I Dare You" by Rascal Flatts and The Jonas Brothers plays, and he holds my hand, stepping back from me then pulling me to him. When we were deciding, Brooks brought me this song and said he thought it spoke to us and our story. I only had to listen to one verse to know it was perfect.

He spins me, dips me, twirls me. I let him lead, and by the time the song is ending, my cheeks hurt from smiling so much.

Brooks whispers, "I dare you," at the end of the song, with that smirk I fell in love with before I really knew the man behind it.

"I love you," I say.

"I know."

I laugh, but he swallows the sound with a kiss.

I'll never get enough of this man.

The End

Also by Piper Rayne

The Trouble with #9

Faking it with #41

Tropical Hat Trick (Novella)

Sneaking around with #34

Second Shot with #76

Offside with #55

Chicago Grizzlies

On the Defense

Something like Hate

Something like Lust

Something like Love

Kingsmen Football Stars

False Start

You Had Your Chance, Lee Burrows

You Can't Kiss the Nanny, Brady Banks

Over My Brother's Dead Body, Chase Andrews

Modern Love

Charmed by the Bartender

Hooked by the Boxer

Mad about the Banker

Single Dads Club

Real Deal

Dirty Talker

Sexy Beast

Hollywood Hearts

Mister Mom

Animal Attraction

Domestic Bliss

Bedroom Games

Cold as Ice

On Thin Ice

Break the Ice

Chicago Law

Smitten with the Best Man

Tempted by my Ex-Husband

Seduced by my Ex's Divorce Attorney

Blue Collar Brothers

Flirting with Fire

Crushing on the Cop

Engaged to the EMT

White Collar Brothers

Sexy Filthy Boss

Dirty Flirty Enemy

Wild Steamy Hook-up

The Rooftop Crew

My Bestie's Ex

A Royal Mistake

The Rival Roomies

Our Star-Crossed Kiss

The Do-Over

A Co-Workers Crush

Holiday Romances

Single and Ready to Jingle

Claus and Effect

Merry Kissmas

Cockamamie Unicorn Ramblings

Brooks and Lottie. What can we say? Individually and together, they fell on the page instantly. But as we've always said before, turning great side characters into heroes and heroines can sometimes prove challenging.

In all truthfulness, during the first three books, we didn't know about Brooks or Lottie's past. We just knew we wanted them together and that they would get married in Vegas. Sure, we knew Brooks wanted Lottie—that was clear in the first three Plain Daisy books—but we weren't sure where Lottie stood on it all, even though she was making him coffee every morning.

It helped that we didn't write ourselves into a corner with any mention of their past in previous books. Yes, we know, for once we didn't. So, we were free to brainstorm and come up with all the reasons why they couldn't be together.

Let's start with Brooks's Brother, Holden. Originally, he wasn't going to be Brooks's brother, but just some guy back in the day who hurt her. We thought that maybe Brooks knew Holden was cheating on her. That he had some secret that he had kept from her.

We threw around so many things, I'm not sure we remember them all. The brother was going to return earlier in the book, his parents weren't going to be as bad as they were, his dad wasn't going to be the mayor, her miscarriage and inability to carry a baby weren't a part of our original plan. All this to say, this might be the first book that we threw so much into the brainstorming sessions, we should have kept notes.

But in the end, we think their story was perfect and couldn't have ended up better. Lottie had a tough shell, but we believe it was genuine. With Rayne's own journey through fertility treatments, we hope we reflected the heartbreak of possibly not being able to give yourself or the person you love what they want, no matter how understanding they are. It shapes you just any trial or heartbreak does to anyone.

On that note, these two were fun to write. Their banter and the way they opened up and allowed one another to see all of them was special and something to admire.

As always, we have a lot of people to thank for getting this book into your hands...

Nina and the entire Valentine PR team. The organization, the promotion, and the way you keep us on point with deadlines. We appreciate you SO much!

Cassie from Joy Editing for line edits, who still took our book days late. Which is becoming a habit we hope to break. Please know you have our heartfelt gratitude for always working with us.

Ellie from My Brother's Editor for line edits and proofing. We give you barely any time, but you always come through.

Olivia Weston, for being our second proofreader. You're an awesome addition to our team.

Whiskey Ginger for our illustrated cover, which spoke perfectly to Brooks and Lottie, bringing them to life.

All the bloggers who choose to read us with so many

options out there. We are appreciative and honored to be on your list of must-reads and love reading all your reviews, edits, and more.

All the Piper Rayne Unicorns who support us every day, all day. We'd be lost without you answering our polls and telling us what you love and hate. We strive to give you the best Piper Rayne experience each and every time. We can't say much else except that you're awesome!

You, dear reader, who has an abundance of books to choose from. Thank you for picking up one of ours. We do hope you enjoyed the story.

We're sure you know who's next. Bennett and Wren (because hello, they're a package deal). Bennett's story has been shifting and changing as we write it, so we can't tell you much without writing ourselves into a corner yet again. Haha

See you soon back on the ranch!

xo,
Piper & Rayne

About Piper & Rayne

Piper Rayne is a *USA Today* Bestselling Author duo who write "heartwarming humor with a side of sizzle" about families, whether that be blood or found. They both have e-readers full of one-clickable books, they're married to husbands who drive them to drink, and they're both chauffeurs to their kids. Most of all, they love hot heroes and quirky heroines who make them laugh, and they hope you do, too!

Printed in Dunstable, United Kingdom

66785469R00211